Provence Love Legacy

by

Kate Fitzroy

1   *'a strange feeling of the unknown that hung in the air'*

Monday began like any other Monday. Michelle arrived early for work and opened up her design studio before her best friend and colleague arrived. She switched on her computer, then the coffee machine and looked round with satisfaction. Her design sheets were neatly pinned on the wall and selected colour charts and fabric swatches laid out in rows. Michelle looked across at the chaos on Kelly's large desk and sighed. She knew there was absolutely no point in worrying about it. Over the last three years of working together in their interior design business, the two girls had somehow turned their very different skills into a magic recipe for success. Just as the aroma of coffee began to spread across the studio, the door opened and Kelly burst in dropping bags and keys onto her desk.

'Oh, my sweet Lord, Monday mornings. Will I ever get used to them coming straight after the weekend? It's just not reasonable.'

Michelle could think of no possible answer so just poured a coffee and quietly laid it on Kelly's desk.

'Morning Kelly, good weekend?'

Weekend?' Kelly grabbed the hot coffee, sipped it and gave a huge sigh of pleasure. 'I can hardly remember it so it must have been good. This coffee is the best, thanks Mich, you're a life saver! Now where did we leave that re-fit art deco job in Pimlico?'

And so another week began. But this Monday was not to be like any other Monday in the whole of

Michelle's twenty-eight years of life. This Monday was to be a life-changing day but there was no sign of it that morning. The telephone rang non-stop as usual, the two designers worked hard, each in their own way. Michelle meticulously drawing and working on plans, every detail carefully noted. Kelly frantically answered phone calls whilst still writing emails, handling difficult customers with her easy charm and turning potential disaster into laughter. Certainly they were as unalike in character as they were in looks. Michelle, petite, dark haired with large, dark brown eyes, had a delicate pale beauty, beside Kelly's striking golden blonde, voluptuous 50's film star look. Both girls played the retro role to the full and when one favourite customer had referred to them as Audrey Hepburn and Marilyn Monroe, they had laughed but been delighted. Despite so many differences, they shared everything that was important to them. Their mothers had met at nursing college and remained firm friends, even though their lives had taken different directions. Kelly's mother had married soon after leaving college and rapidly had four babies, Kelly being the eldest. Michelle's mother was unmarried when she became pregnant. Michelle knew nothing of her real father and considered her stepfather as the only father she had ever needed. He was a doctor and a good, kind man who loved Michelle as his own and only child. Michelle and Kelly had gone through school together as close as twin sisters and with the same rivalry that had seriously improved their academic work. If Michelle had an A star for English lit., then next year it would be Kelly. So it had continued through art college together, until finally they had taken the big step of setting up their own business partnership.

   They always worked through lunch, eating the thin sandwiches that Michelle brought in each day and swigging from bottles of sparkling water. Both were diet conscious and too busy to think about real food until the evening. This day was no different in that respect, but now it was 5 o'clock and the phone calls were slowing up. They began the routine check back through their workload and began to think about leaving. It was then that this Monday became unlike any other. The door to the studio opened and a young man peered cautiously in at them.

'Excuse me, I am looking for Michelle Phelps?' Michelle and Kelly looked at each other and there was a moment of hesitation. The man had a strong French accent, a quiet voice and was well dressed. The style that so many French men thought was typically English but looked so chic and continental. Their studio was in a quiet mews in Chelsea and normally clients came by appointment only, but this man was definitely not one of their existing customers. Michelle broke into the silence.

'I am Michelle Phelps, can I help you?' The man advanced and held out his hand. Kelly rose to her feet and stood close to Michelle as though to protect her. Michelle shook the man's hand, saying, 'And you are?'

'My name is Leon Batiste, *enchanté*, Mademoiselle Phelps.'

Michelle shook his slim, cool hand and then answered coldly, as coldly as only a beautiful woman can speak. 'Please state your business, you have no appointment and we are both in the middle of some important work.'

'Yes, please excuse me... this intrusion... but I have been looking for you for some time. I am a private investigator working for a French lawyer in Aix-en-Provence.'

'Then I think you may have the wrong Michelle Phelps.' Michelle continued in her most dismissive tone, 'I can think of no reason why you should be looking for me.'

'I realise this is an unusual situation but it is a matter of inheritance and you, or someone of your name and age, has been identified in the matter. It is of some importance, I assure you.' The man shifted uneasily on his feet and looked toward Kelly for friendlier help.

'My friend, Michelle, has absolutely no connection with Aix-en-Provence or any other part of France, so maybe you should leave now?' Kelly spoke firmly and walked to the door, opened it and stood aside, waiting for the man to leave.

'I quite understand your hesitation but, *s'il vous plaît,* I must leave you this letter and my card. I shall call again tomorrow.'

The young man carefully laid a large, brown envelope and a small, white card onto Michelle's drawing board. His voice was polite, quiet but very determined.'

'*Au revoir, Mesdemoiselles, à demain.* Until tomorrow!' And, with a little bow, he left as quickly and quietly as he had arrived.

Silence filled the large studio as Michelle and Kelly stood side by side, looking at the drawing board, the brown envelope and the small white card.

Kelly spoke first and angrily, her cheeks flushed pink. She snatched up the card and read aloud, 'Leon Batiste, Détective Privé, 10 rue des Cordeliers, 13100 Aix en Provence. So, does this Leon think we don't even understand *à demain*... and has to add 'until tomorrow?' Her voice imitated the young detective's heavy French accent. 'Who does he think we are? Conceited frog!'

'More to the point, who on earth does he think I am?' replied Michelle.

Kelly gave a sudden wicked smile,'And come to think of it frogs can turn into princes, can't they? I wish I'd given him a kiss to try that out. He was hot, wow, so hot!' She laughed and threw the card back on the drawing board.

'Kelly, for goodness sake! Get a grip, this is not a fairy tale. I'll just open the letter and find out that I am not the Michelle he is looking for and then I'll phone him and that will be that.' As she spoke she picked up the envelope and held it for a long moment before ripping it open.

Kelly waited impatiently while Michelle slowly read the letter. 'Well, what does it say, Michelle? I am dying here of suspense.'

'It's all in French.' Michelle said slowly.

'*Mon dieu,* maybe I spoke too soon, bring back our A level days... can't you understand anything?'

Michelle silently passed the letter to Kelly who snatched it and began to read avidly. Michelle picked up the small, white card and examined it closely and then passed that to Kelly too, saying, 'Do you fancy a short break in Aix-en-Provence, Kelly?'

Kelly nodded slowly, for once she was quiet and thoughtful.

'I think I do.' She answered slowly. 'Yes, I think I do!'

The two friends looked at each other and then Kelly broke the silence and the strange mood saying,

'And all because of a frog and a French letter!'

They were both glad to laugh away the strange feeling of the unknown that hung in the air.

2 *'I need a large cappuccino'*

The plane circled slowly over Marseilles airport, swinging low over the deep, blue Mediterranean. Michelle rested her forehead on the port-hole window and looked down at the huge bay and the hills rising steeply behind. Daylight was fading and lights began to twinkle in a myriad of street patterns. She caught a glimpse of her own reflection in the glass and realised she was frowning. She turned to Kelly,

'Well, I guess we shall soon know what all this is about. It seems crazy, some sort of wild goose chase, but I had to come and I am so glad you came with me.'

'Oh, you know me, always ready for a crazy weekend away and maybe the goose will be golden. I am sure it must have something to do with your real father.'

Over the last twenty-four hours the two friends had gone through every possible scenario to explain the carefully guarded words of the French lawyer's letter. All they really knew was that Michelle was invited to attend a meeting with the lawyer to discover if or if not she was entitled to an inheritance.

'But surely my mother would have told me if my real father had been French... all she would ever say was that she met him through her nursing work. Ans that there was no way she was going to marry him... or something like that. She hated talking about it and, in a peculiar way, so did I.   My whole life I have just loved my stepfather... and never even thought of him as that... he was just my Dad.'

'I know, I know... and he is just the perfect Dad, too. You definitely don't need another one!' Kelly spoke in a comforting way, sensing her friend's anxiety. Then she added wickedly, 'Unless, of course, your real Dad turns out to be loaded or the President of France or something. What is so annoying is that our hot detective wouldn't say a word more. Not a word.'

'Well, he did arrange our flights and there is a hotel booked... all paid in advance... and a car waiting to meet us. Anyway, he might not know any more.'

'I spose so, yeh, he is really cute! I think I might need the services of a private investigation in the very near future.'

'Kelly, you promised me you would behave. Just forget the guy. This is a business trip.'

'Exactly!' Kelly replied with a grin, 'And you know what that can lead to!'

The cabin lights dimmed and the plane began its steep descent to land, so the conversation ended there.

The next morning, at precisely eleven o'clock, Michelle was sitting nervously in the dark and formal office of the French lawyer, Maître Xavier.

'Thank you for coming over for this meeting.' The lawyer spoke seriously, in a low voice, and looked at Michelle over the top of his gold-rimmed glasses. 'It is a matter of some importance and my bureau has been searching for a Michelle Phelps for over six months now.' He continued quietly, in perfect English and with hardly a trace of an accent. In the slight pause Michelle spoke quickly.

'I am sure there must be more than one Michelle Phelps in the world and I think you must have the wrong one. Please tell me what all this is about.'

'Indeed, although the name Phelps is quite unusual there are others. However it appears from our research that you are the only surviving relative of our deceased client, le Marquis Michel de Rosefont.'

'Deceased?'

'Indeed, le Marquis de Rosefont died eight months ago and apart from a hand-written letter there was no formal will and testament.'

'May I see the letter?' Michelle asked, and then added, almost to herself, 'And he was called Michel?' She shook her head in disbelief.

'At this moment it would not be appropriate to show you the letter, it is in the form of a secret letter, witnessed and left with me as his notaire. It was only to be opened and read after his death. This having been done we must now have final and definite proof that you are indeed the Michelle that we are looking for ... Marquis de Rosefont's only surviving relative, his daughter.'

Michelle drew in her breath sharply. It was, of course, what she had been thinking ever since that Monday, but to hear the words break into the silence of the gloomy office made her head spin. The dark oak-panelled walls, the bookcases of leather bound books, the tall shuttered window casting shafts of bright light across the rich rug on the floor... the room whirled madly around her and she gripped the arm of her chair. The lawyer was still talking in his sombre, calm voice.

'... and the evidence found showed the marriage of your mother to a Dr. Phelps, her recent demise and then, finally, led to you in London. My private investigator has been very thorough in this matter. Now we need a final proof in the form of a simple DNA paternity test to compare with that of your alleged father.'

Michelle struggled to concentrate as the room slowed down from its wild circling. 'DNA paternity test, I see. That would be the final proof.' She repeated his words like a robot, her voice dry and high-pitched. Then at last her brain began to work again. 'Supposing I refuse, supposing I have no interest in following this line of enquiry... none at all?'

The lawyer looked up sharply, his quiet manner suddenly disrupted by her words.'I... err... *alors, c'est*... err... Mademoiselle Phelps that would be most unprecedented and unfortunate. I assure you we have gone to great lengths to find you and it is in your own interest to proceed. The DNA test is simply a painless mouth swab... no discomfort and performed in seconds... *je vous assure*...' He spoke hastily now, his slow, perfect English breaking down into rapid French, his solemn composure lost.

Michelle rose and held out her hand in a formal gesture of leaving. 'I need to think about this for a few hours. I'll return this afternoon... would 15.00 be convenient?' She spoke decisively, in control again at last.

'*Mais oui, mademoiselle, entendu*... er... yes, of course, this afternoon at three. *À bientôt*.' He stood and shook her hand, then ushered her from the room, now attentive and concerned.

'*Au revoir.*' Michelle replied, smiling to herself, thinking that she seemed to be an important client.

Kelly was waiting in a nearby café and looked up excitedly as Michelle entered and sat at the table beside her.

'Well? Tell all!' Kelly sat forward in her seat as she spoke.

'I need a large cappuccino and, apparently, a DNA test.' Michelle was about to explain further when Kelly suddenly gripped her wrist.

'Look over there at the table in the window, the guy that just came in... it's our hot frog-prince detective, Leon Batiste!'

Michelle shook her hand free from Kelly's excited grip and looked over her shoulder. Her hair fell half over her face, but even so she immediately made eye contact with the young man and he raised a hand in greeting and half rose from his chair.

'He's seen us, he's looking over this way!' Kelly's voice rose in excitement and without another thought she beckoned to the young man and pointed to the empty seat beside them.

'What are you doing?' muttered Michelle, 'Why did you ask him over?'

'Do you really need to ask that?' Kelly laughed and was already standing up to greet the dark-haired young Frenchman before Michelle could reply.

'*Enchanté*, mesdemoiselles! What a pleasure to meet you again.' His voice was silky smooth but there was a genuine ring to it and his wide smile was relaxed and confident.

'*Enchantée*, me too!' Kelly replied giggling, moving a chair to invite him to sit between them.

'There is no need to ask what you are doing in Aix... you have a meeting with Maitre Xavier, I assume.' Leon Batiste looked toward Michelle as he spoke but Kelly continued the conversation.

'*Dejà fait!* Michelle has just emerged and is about to tell me all about the mysterious affair.' Leon held up his hand quickly, his dark eyes flashing from one girl to another as he said,

'Please, *s'il vous plait*, this is Mademoiselle Phelps' very private concern. I was just the messenger, I won't intrude.'

The way he spoke gave Michelle confidence in him and she suddenly smiled and relaxed.

'Really, there is very little to tell... I am going to have a DNA test later this afternoon or tomorrow morning to prove my identity and then I shall know more. If I am indeed the Michelle Phelps that you were sent to find, then I may have inherited something from my French biological father.' Michelle raised her hands in the air as if to finish the matter but Kelly leant across the table excitedly.

'Oh Holy Moly, you mean you had a French father... I mean, he's died right? Or... or you wouldn't be inheriting. It's astonishing.'

Michelle blushed fiercely and looked down at the table. 'Well, nothing is certain yet, is it?'

'This is completely none of my business, *bien sur*,' Leon spoke calmly and quietly, as though sensing Michelle's discomfort, then added 'but you are a visitor in my beautiful city and maybe it would be a good idea to relax for a few hours? I could be your tour guide?'

Michelle smiled at him gratefully and nodded. 'Thank you, *merci beaucoup*, yes I think that would be a great idea...what do you think Kelly?'

Now it was Kelly's turn to look uncomfortable as she replied.

'Are you sure you want me to come too?'

'But of course!' Leon answered immediately. 'All three of us... but first... how about lunch?'

Kelly quickly resumed her usual bounce. 'That would be fantastic. I am simply ravenous. I've done nothing but drink strong coffee all morning, waiting here for Michelle. What do you think Michelle?'

'Well, I must go back to Maitre Xavier at three o'clock and now it's just gone noon...'

'Three hours is just the right amount of time for lunch in Provence, I am sure I have read that somewhere?' Kelly was now in the full flow of her usual energy. She jumped up and signalled for the bill, gathering her bag and jacket over her arm.

Michelle and Leon looked across the table at each other and smiled. It was as though they were old friends, acknowledging the crazy zest of Kelly, their mutual friend.

Then Leon stood up and politely held Michelle's chair as she too rose. 'I know a wonderful little bistro just round the corner. I eat there often... but maybe you would prefer something grander?' Leon spoke hesitantly, standing aside for Michelle to move away from the table first. Michelle looked back over her shoulder as they joined Kelly at the cash desk.

'No, no, a small bistro would be just right. Thank you.'

Kelly joined in the conversation. 'Did you say small bistro? Let's go! Sounds perfect to me and anyway Michelle, you're not a millionairess yet.'

Both the girls turned to look at Leon Batiste, but his face remained calm and inscrutable. If he did know anything of Michelle's supposed inheritance then he was giving nothing away. Nothing at all.

3 'the deep blue Provençal sky'

Suddenly it was Monday again. Just a week had gone by but Michelle's life was changed forever. The first shock had come when the DNA test showed a positive comparison to the man she now had to regard as her father, Michel de Rosefont. The second bolt from the blue struck when once again she was sitting in the shadowy, book-lined study of the lawyer, Maitre Xavier.

'So now, now it begins, Mademoiselle Phelps or, as I should say, Marquise de Rosefont?' Michelle grasped the arms of her chair again, determined not to let the room begin its mad spinning.

'Marquise?' she repeated, forcing her voice to remain in a low key.

'Why yes, Michel de Rosefont was the Marquis de Rosefont of La Bastide de Rosefont. The title and the Bastide and all his worldly belongings and responsibilities are undoubtedly yours and yours alone. The French laws of inheritance have not changed since the time of Napoleon. These laws were made to protect the rights of children, legitimate or illegitimate.'

'So are you saying that my mother was never married to this Michel de Rosefont?' Michelle asked, her voice barely disguising the contempt she held for this father she had never known.

'Married, *mais non!*' The lawyer looked at her over his narrow glasses with a supercilious smirk.

Michelle looked back at him. Was he looking at her or down at her? Her confidence and strength flooded back. 'Maître Xavier, I understand I should address you as Maître, although in England it would be like calling you Master, a very old-fashioned term once used to address small boys or minor prep school teachers. However, Maître Xavier...' Michelle paused, allowing time for her insult to sink into his bald head, '… however, I imagine you are employed, being paid in fact, to find me and read me the will. So please do so as quickly as possible. I have a business in London, and it awaits my return.'

Michelle looked out of the window and up at the deep blue Provençal sky and thought for a moment of her good friend, Kelly, who had rushed back to London to keep their work running smoothly.

Maître Xavier cleared his throat and nodded curtly. 'First you should read the letter that was found in your father's study and replaces a will in the event that he died intestate. I have also prepared a translation in English.'

Michelle reached out for the letters and began to read. The pompous Maitre Xavier was right, now it had begun. Then and there between the book-lined walls of his study, it began. Michelle Phelps, interior designer from London, began her journey in Aix-en-Provence to discover the truth about her new identity as the Marquise de Rosefont.

An hour later she was sitting in a café, basking in the golden Provençal sun-shine and sipping a fresh orange juice. Michelle looked up at the trees shading the small square, bright oranges hung between the dark green leaves, outlined against the intense blue sky. She suddenly felt so far from London and yet perfectly at home. Was this her imagination running wild or did she really have southern French blood running in her veins? Yet again she felt her world spinning out of control. She grabbed her mobile and quickly pressed Kelly's number.

'Hi Kelly, I'm just out of old Xavier's office... how are things with you? Did you get my text? The signal's not good. Can you hear me, Kelly?' Michelle spoke anxiously into her mobile, gabbling the latest news of her inheritance.

'Yes, yes, fine, I can hear you, I just can't believe you! Your father was a Marquis...which sounds like some huge wedding tent to me... and now you are the Marquise de Rosefont... I mean, is it some sort of weird joke or what?'

'It gets worse... I've inherited a Bastide near somewhere called Mimet in the Bouches de Rhone, south of Aix-en-Provence, I think... well, really I have no idea where it is!'

'Mich, this is mad... what on earth...?'

'Listen Kelly, the line is breaking up. I'll call you back when I get a better signal. But I'm going to hire a car ... by the way, your hot detective has been ever so kind and helpful.'

'I bet he has!' Kelly interrupted with a laugh.

'No, listen Kelly, for goodness sake, listen up! Leon has booked me into a different hotel, it's called, Provençal Royale, it's central and...'

'And is the kind and helpful Leon booked in too?' Kelly interrupted again.

'Are you going to listen or not? Leon has family near Aix and is staying with them. The important thing is that I want you to meet me at the hotel. There are Marseille flights or, I had a quick look online, the Eurostar train may be better... can you arrange work to get away for a few days? I really need...'

At that point the phone signal finally failed, leaving Michelle looking helplessly at her phone and the empty signal bar. She sighed and slipped the phone back into her bag and drew out an envelope. She gave a bigger sigh as she began to read the letter inside. Then she turned to the second page and read the English translation.

La Bastide de Rosefont, Mimet Janvier 12

To whom it may concern,
This letter is my last, dying attempt to revisit my past. My poor wife died ten years ago after a long and exhausting illness. We were married when very young, an arrangement that suited our neighbouring families more that it suited us. We had learned to live separate but amicable lives. When she first became ill, she was nursed by a young English woman named Anne Saxby. At the time I was working very hard, replanting vines and improving the cellars and the wine production. Hard work is no excuse for what happened. I fell deeply in love with the young and beautiful, Anne, and betrayed my sick wife. I know Anne loved me too but we both found it difficult to live with the guilt of our affair. One morning I awoke to find that Anne had disappeared without a trace. Another nurse from the agency was at my wife's bedside. I searched for months without success. I waited, hoping for a letter or a phone call or any sign that she would return. I never heard from her again. I resumed my working life and now, as it draws to an end, I am writing this letter to say that all my worldly goods and chattels I leave to the love of my life, Anne Saxby. I promised her that I would love her forever and it has been so. Finally, a last word to my beloved Anne - if this letter should find you then read again the book we both loved so much, and, here is another promise, you will find something of great interest.
Michel de Rosefont

Michelle folded the letter carefully and replaced it in the envelope. She looked again at the original letter in French and peered at the signature. Michel de Rosefont, the handwriting was in thick, black ink and well-formed, but there was a noticeable tremor in the letters. It looked the signature of a decisive but elderly man. Michelle folded the thick paper of the letter and placed it beside the translation in the envelope and then back into her bag. Something she had done many, many times over the last twenty-four hours. Michelle pressed her hand to her forehead. Above all the bewildering new information she was trying to absorb, there was her conscience nagging her to call her stepfather, the man who had married her mother. The kind, gentle man that she had always loved as her real father. She resolutely pulled her phone from her bag and pressed his number. Still no signal. Michelle gave an audible sigh of relief and closed her eyes, imagining her father faraway on a cruise ship, in blissful ignorance of the bombshell that had exploded in the life of the girl he truly thought of as his daughter. Had it been a great love affair, between this Michel de Rosefont and her mother? Had they really suffered from guilt as their affair took place whilst Michel's invalid wife lay in bed, her mother's patient? Why had her mother never told her the truth about her real father? Why...why... why? The questions rose up in Michelle's mind one after another. Questions that she could never ask as her mother had died only last year after losing a battle with cancer. Her father had given up his practice in Harley Street to nurse her himself. Now he was semi-retired but working occasionally as a ship's doctor. Michelle saw him whenever he was in England and understood only too well his need to absorb himself in work, to help him blot out his grief. Had he known the truth about her mother's French love affair? Had he known the identity of Michelle's biological father? More questions continued to crowd Michelle's mind. It was no good. Sitting in the glorious sunshine would not bring any solutions. She took a deep breath and then waved to the waiter. Time to pay her bill and face the future, whatever it might bring. First things first, she needed to hire a car. At least she could face the unknown on a set of wheels. Leon had given her the address of a car hire company and arranged to meet her there. All this time she had spent worrying and now she would be late. She waved again to the waiter and quickly paid her bill. Just as she was leaving the café, emerging from the shade and into the bright sunlight, she saw Leon on the other side of the square.

'Leon, wait!' Michelle called out and ran across the square. 'So lucky to see you! I was just going to try and find the car hire company. I thought I was late.'

'*Bonjour, Michelle. Comment ça va*? Late? *Mais non*, you are in Provence now, not London.' Leon laughed and shook Michelle's hand. 'Relax, we have plenty of time.'

Suddenly, Michelle felt the strain of the last few hours melt away, and said, 'I was sitting in the shade in the café over there. Would you like a coffee, or a drink perhaps, if you're really not too busy. It's so kind of you to help me out like this.'

'My pleasure, *absolument!* Ah, you have already discovered the Grand Café Orange, it is one of the best in Aix. Why yes, a coffee would be great.' He ushered her back across the square, somehow managing to guide her with his arm extended around her but not touching. And had he really given a little bow as he said '*absolument*'?

Michelle smiled, remembering Kelly's description of him as the hot frog prince. He certainly had princely manners and yes, he was hot... but Michelle had no wish to kiss him. Maybe she could leave that to Kelly?

4 'a typical French shrug'

Michelle had tried to phone Kelly, on and off, all afternoon without success. Between calls, she had enjoyed relaxing in the luxurious hotel room. First a long, hot perfumed bath, then blow-drying her hair, manicuring her nails, ordering a baguette by room service, reading the Paris Match... that had quickly sent her to sleep. This time she fell into a dreamless sleep and awoke refreshed. What had awoken her? Her phone! She fumbled to find it on the bedside table but missed the call. It was Kelly's number but there was no message. Michelle looked at the time and realised she had slept for over two hours and now it was nearly six in the evening. She had arranged to meet Leon in the hotel bar at six. Michelle jumped up and dressed hurriedly, pulling on her favourite pale, pink shift dress and grabbing a darker pink pashmina. She glanced in the long mirror beside the door and ran back to brush her hair again. Better, it was now sleek and smooth. Shoes, comfortable pumps or staggering heels? Heels. She quickly pushed her small feet into her very best cream Manolas and gained several inches in height. Looking again at her reflection in the mirror she saw a slight but confident young woman, immaculately groomed and dressed for an evening out. She nodded to herself with approval, grabbed her bag and left the room.
Arriving in the bar, just ten minutes late, she looked around the groups of people sitting at the tables and standing at the bar. There was Leon talking animatedly to... yes, Kelly! Michelle almost ran across the bar, her high heels tapping on the wood floor.

'Kelly, I don't believe it! How did you manage it?'

'You know me... always ready for some fun!' Kelly looked meaningfully at Michelle and raised her blonde eyebrows and widened her eyes, 'Just as the taxi dropped me at the hotel entrance, I bumped into Leon... so here we are! Now, what are you drinking? I am being very à la Française and drinking Pernod... it is actually rather disgusting and reminds me of aniseed balls, sorry, Leon!'

Leon looked from one girl to the other and raised his shoulders in a typical French shrug. 'You have completely lost me, mesdemoiselles, my English is not sufficiently...' He shrugged again more emphatically and threw back his head, laughing. Suddenly, seeing him relaxed in their company for the first time, both girls were struck by his Gallic good looks and charm.

'Your English is really good and so much better than our French.' Kelly patted him on the shoulder and let her hand rest lightly on him for a long moment. 'While you are with us I promise to teach you all the bad English I know... and Mich will take the matter very seriously, in a typical Mich way, and teach you stuff like subjunctives and idioms.'

'*Ah, mon dieu,* the English idioms.' Leon pulled a long, sad face and raised his elegant hands in the air. 'I have a whole book, it is called 'Learn an Idiom a Day'' He fell back into his chair and slapped his knees, *'C'est impossible!'*

Both girls responded in unison, laughing. 'Impossible!' Mimicking his accent perfectly.

Leon looked at them, his long, dark eyebrows drawn together in puzzlement.

'I'm sorry,' said Michelle, 'that comes straight from our school days. We had a very strict French teacher and every time she said *'c'est'* to us it sounded like 'say' so we began to repeat her. Like, she would say *'c'est la vie'* and we would chime in together with *'la vie'*! It was really very childish.' Michelle ended with a small smile.

'Childish and great fun... it livened up the whole class and she was such an old battle-axe!' Kelly added.

'Battle-axe?' Leon repeated.

Kelly smiled her best impudent smile and leaned over the table toward Leon, revealing more cleavage than was strictly necessary.

'An old battle-axe is an idiomatic name for a bossy old woman.' Then in her best imitation of Marilyn Monroe she cooed, 'Oh Leon, I could teach you so much, but I would be very strict too.'

'Behave yourself, Kelly!' Michelle interrupted, turning to Leon with an easy smile, she said. 'My good friend Kelly was a very clever but badly behaved school-girl and really she hasn't changed much since.'

Leon was still leaning back in his chair as he looked from one girl to another. His dark eyes were alight with humour as he spoke.

'I look forward to my English lessons very much, *mesdemoiselles*.'

Kelly leant back again in her chair saying, 'Enough, *suffis*, of this *mesdemoiselles* thingy, my name is Kelly Atkinson and this is Michelle, also answering to Mich. That is your first lesson!'

Once again Leon looked from one girl to another but his face was now serious as he replied. 'So, now I shall call you Kelly and I may call you Michelle... but tell me, is it still Michelle Phelps? Or Michelle de Rosefont?'

'It seems I am both at the moment, it is rather confusing, but at least the Michelle part is safe.' She smiled at him and then at Kelly.

'Thank you so much for making this all much easier for me, Leon. And you, Kelly, thanks for coming over so quickly, I don't know how you managed it but I am really glad you did.'

'*Pas de problème*, when a Marquise commands... who am I, a mere commoner, to disobey? Especially if the Marquise in question is somehow or other my best friend Michelle? You have a lot of explaining to do and I suffered the most god-awful plastic bucket seat air flight to get here so... now, I need to wash, eat and then listen to the whole fairy story.'

Leon clapped his hands together, saying, 'I understand only the part where you say 'eat' and that is my concern. I know a little...'

Both girls interrupted Leon, again in unison. 'Bistro round the corner from here?'

They all laughed and Leon raised his hands in submission and the evening began.

5 'it was a brilliant night out'

The next morning, Michelle sat eating a late breakfast, waiting for Kelly to join her. She sipped the strong, dark coffee and nibbled a croissant. It had been a very late night. After a great dinner in the bistro, Leon had suggested a nearby nightclub. It was a large cellar, thronging with young people dancing to loud music vibrating around the vaulted stone walls. Leon proved to be as wild a dancer as Kelly. Michelle had enjoyed dancing alongside, moving to the strong rhythm and forgetting the web of mystery that lay ahead of her.

Now the day had dawned and they were to travel out of Aix-en-Provence and south to find La Bastide de Rosefont.

Michelle replaced her coffee cup carefully in the saucer as she felt her hand tremble in anticipation. Was it excitement or fear? Before she had left his office, Me Xavier had solemnly, and before a formal witness, presented Michelle with the ancient deeds of La Bastide de Rosefont. The heavy, linen bound documents, tied with a strong cord now lay on the chair beside her and, alongside, a soft leather pouch of very large keys. Since receiving them she hadn't dared to let them out of her sight. She rested her hand a moment on the bag of keys and then ran her fingers over the outside of the old linen file. Somehow it was tangible proof that the Bastide existed and all that had happened was not a strange dream. Before she had time to think any more, Kelly joined her at the table, reaching silently for the coffee pot. Michelle watched and waited in amusement as her friend went through her usual morning after the night before ritual.

'I am never drinking alcohol again, Michelle! Never, do you hear? Just remind me next time I order a drink, and as for that evil Pernod... urghh!'
Michelle remained silent and passed the silver basket of hot croissants across the table.

'I couldn't possibly eat a thing. Are you joking me? Michelle, I'm seriously suffering here.' Kelly swept her long, blonde hair back then held her hand to her forehead as she continued. 'Actually the croissants do smell really good, maybe just one, or half one... might do me good?'

'Try one and see.' Michelle said in a mocking, sweet voice. 'I'm sure you will feel better if you could eat a little something. Better hurry, Leon will be outside the hotel at eleven, remember!'

'Well, actually I don't remember a thing except it was a brilliant night out, wasn't it? Leon is a great dancer, don't you think?" Suddenly she looked across the table at Michelle, her face already back to its usual liveliness. 'I mean, he is really, really cute, don't you think?"
Michelle turned her head to one side, pretending to reflect. 'Yes, he really is very, very cute! And so good to be with...'

Kelly interrupted. 'Come on Mich, you know what I'm saying here. Is he your frog prince or mine?'

Michelle still pretended to think and then laughed out loud.

'Definitely yours! I resign from the race, in fact I don't think I was ever in the running!'

'Are you sure, really sure?' Kelly's voice squeaked with excitement. 'I know we've been in this situ before now, but somehow... well, Leon seems sort of special. But I'm sure he is much more interested in you!'

'Don't be... when you left Aix last week, Leon talked about you all the time, asking if you were coming back, if you had anyone in London...'

'Did he, did he really? Oh Mich, I am so, so happy.'

'Good, but don't you think you had better get your bag down into the foyer... it's gone eleven already.'

'Oh my god, and I look a wreck...' Kelly rushed from the room, showing no sign of a hangover. Michelle sat a moment longer at the table and then, clutching the deeds and bag of keys close to her, she went to collect her hold-all and settle the bill. Leon was already waiting at the desk and chatting to the receptionist. He certainly was charming. Everything a Frenchman should be, elegant in a relaxed way, confident yet slightly shy. Yes, he was perfect but Michelle knew he was not for her. She didn't know why but she knew it completely. She smiled to herself as she thought about Kelly's excitement. She was glad, not just for Kelly but for herself too. It would certainly make the few days ahead run smoother if Kelly was absorbed in flirting with Leon. Kelly bored was a very tiring business and Michelle had plenty to do. She shouldered her bag resolutely and walked across the hall. Today she wore her faithful flat loafers. Shoes made for walking and coping with any rough ground that might come her way.

Leon turned to greet her, '*Bonjour Michelle, comment ça va?* You look wonderful! No ill effects from last night?'

'No, thanks, I feel great... how are you?'

'I'm fine. So, are you looking forward to your adventure today?' He took her hold-all from her and then eyed the large file and bag of keys that Michelle held fast under her arm. 'If that is what I am thinking then you should have it more securely, perhaps?' He spoke rapidly to the receptionist and in a moment the girl handed a hotel laundry bag over the desk. Leon passed it to Michelle as though sensing her reluctance to let go of her valuable belongings.

Michelle took it gratefully and slipped the file and bag of keys into the large white linen bag, emblazoned with the hotel's name.

'Thanks, good idea! Yes, I am very excited.' Michelle nodded and smiled at Leon, thinking suddenly that it was excitement she felt now and the fear had dissolved away to nothing.

Leon smiled back, catching her mood, 'Now then, my friend from the car hire company has brought it round to the front of the hotel... not so good parking there, encore! Perhaps better we wait for Kelly in the car?'

Leon accompanied her outside and they emerged from the hotel into brilliant sunlight. It had rained overnight and the whole world seemed washed clean. Michelle took in a deep breath of fresh air after the stifling air-conditioning of the hotel. She looked across the cobbled square, edged with tall leafy plane trees. A fountain sparkled and shone in the sun as though setting the scene especially for her. Leon was holding the driver's seat open for her when she joined him at the small rental car.

'Why don't you drive, Leon, you know the way and it will give me time to get used to the idea of driving on the right. Do you mind if I sit in the back? Kelly always feels carsick if she doesn't sit in the front.'

'*Mais oui.*' Leon quickly opened the back door and held it open until Michelle was inside. Then, he looked back at the hotel entrance and tapped his hand on the car roof as he said, 'Where is Kelly, we can't park here much longer or we will get a ticket.'

Michelle settled in the back and smiled to herself. Leon Batiste might find his impeccable manners and charm frequently stretched to breaking point whilst waiting for Kelly... even in his relaxed Provençal life style. But at that moment there was a piercing whistle, a two-fingered wolf whistle that any

London builder would have been proud of. Kelly was waving from the top of the hotel steps, wearing skin-tight, canary yellow jeans, a frothy white lacy shirt and struggling with three bags.

'*Voilà*, there she is!' Leon's voice showed his pleasure at the sight of Kelly. He jumped from the car and dodged the traffic to cross the square. Michelle watched with amusement as Kelly launched herself at Leon and gave him two enthusiastic kisses. Then Leon extricated himself and grappled with all three bags, somehow managing to escort Kelly back to the car.

'Hi, Mich, don't you want to sit in the front?' Kelly asked. Michelle answered quickly,

'You know you are always sick as a parrot in the back. Just jump in and let's get going before we get a parking fine.'

'But I don't get sick...' Kelly began and then caught Michelle's warning frown.

'A parrot?' Leon asked, his black eyebrows drawing together into a dark line, 'what is this about a parrot?'

'Don't worry, *mon ami!* I may travel with too much luggage but never a parrot. Just call it your idiom of the day.' Kelly settled herself contentedly into the front seat and Leon shook his head in bewilderment as they drove slowly away into the busy traffic.

'By the way, Mich,' continued Kelly, 'on the subject of luggage, have you any, absolutely any idea, how much I was charged by that bucket seat airline for being overweight?'

'But you are not fat, you are just perfect!' Leon interrupted, yet again completely misunderstanding.

'Why thank you kind sir... I shall just enjoy the compliment and let's forget the English lesson. By the way, you are very handsome when you frown, did you know that?' Kelly rested her hand lightly on

Leon's shoulder and he turned to her in time to receive full benefit of one of her most dazzling smiles. The car swerved briefly and there was loud hooting from behind them. Michelle closed her eyes and counted to ten. Perhaps she should have sat in the front after all?

The journey from then on was without mishap. Almost before they had left the suburbs of Aix, Kelly fell asleep, her blonde head resting comfortably on Leon's shoulder. Michelle remained quiet, looking out of the window at the new scenery. Once they left the auto-route, the road began to weave its way steeply uphill. Huge red rocks were scattered along the roadside as though by some giant hand. Now and then, they passed fields of lavender, the rows of purple flowers shimmering in the heat. The cloudless sky was a deep azure blue. Michelle opened the car window, tired of more air-conditioning, and breathed in the fresh air, laden with the perfume of lavender, thyme and rosemary. She began to relax, enjoying the peace of the rugged countryside. Her hand rested on the hotel laundry bag and her thoughts wandered back once again to her father, Dr Robert Phelps, the man whom she had always loved as her real father. She knew she should try to call him? Just as she was about to try his number, Leon broke the silence.

'We are now about ten minutes away from Mimet. Do you want to stop for a coffee or anything before we actually arrive?'

Michelle's heart thumped, and she hesitated, not knowing how to answer. Then Kelly awoke and made the decision for her.

'Did I hear we are nearly there? Oh my Lord, this is so, so, so exciting. How can you even think about a coffee stop?'

Michelle nodded in agreement and said quietly. 'Yes, of course, we should go straight to the Bastide, if you don't mind?'

'Not at all, I think it is best, too. We made good time, under half an hour from Aix. I don't know the village very well but the last sign said seven kilometres, and then of course we have to find the Bastide.' He passed a map to Kelly. 'You see I have marked it with a small circle in the square G7.'

'Very efficient.' Kelly nodded in approval and studied the map closely, then passed it back to Michelle.

Michelle looked, in her turn, at the small ink circle marked on the map.'La Bastide de Rosefont, it's marked by name.' Michelle said in surprise. 'I can't think why I hadn't thought to look at a map.' Her voice petered out into silence as she began once again to be engulfed by the surreal, new events in her life.

'Well, you have hardly had time to think. It is my job to find people and places.' Leon said kindly, 'I can't imagine how you must feel. *C'est bizarre!*'

'Bizarre!' both girls said in unison.

Leon laughed aloud as he said, 'Ah yes, the battle-hammer!'

'Battle-axe!' once again their voices sounded as one. They were all laughing when suddenly the roadside sign showed, Mimet.

'*Oh mon dieu!*' Kelly gave a small shriek of excitement, 'We've arrived at the village already, this is it, Mich! Now, please look out for a fairytale castle. I'll look on the right and you look left!'

Leon slowed the car as they drove through the sleepy village. The houses were shuttered against the strong sunshine and the streets were deserted.

'It's very quiet.' said Michelle in a small voice. 'Where is everyone?'

'Well, at noon, everyone will be eating. *C'est midi!*'

'*Midi!*' The girls repeated automatically, but they were too preoccupied to laugh at the silly joke.

'Look, what a beautiful stone bridge... oh, look Michelle, look down, it's fantastic!'

The car rolled slowly over the narrow ancient bridge. Michelle looked down into the deep, shady ravine to the thin line of a sparkling river between the rocks. Then, suddenly, she looked across the steep bank and saw a red-roofed turret outlined against the blue sky, half-hidden by a tall dark forest. Before she could speak, Kelly was almost screaming. 'There, there on the left. I've followed the map, once we are over the bridge there should be a small lane leading to your Bastide , Michelle. Oh my god, I can't believe I just said that... your Bastide !'

Leon drove on a few hundred metres and then swung the car sharply to the left, following a narrow drive. All three were now silent as the car bumped along the unmade road, swerving round potholes and brushing against brambles and overgrown tree branches. Then, suddenly, the lane opened out into a large circular drive and they had arrived. They all gasped aloud. The Bastide towered above them, four turrets symmetrically framing a large courtyard. The car drew to an abrupt halt. Michelle opened the car door and slowly got out, clasping the hotel laundry bag closely, and just stood, looking up at the pale rose-tinted stone walls, the many shuttered windows, the dark red terracotta pan-tiled roofs. The sun shone down, dazzling and bright. Michelle leant back against the car, feeling the warm metal through her thin dress. Was this real, was this truly her Bastide, was this where her mother had loved her real father? Then she felt the reassuring presence of Kelly beside her. Kelly in bright, yellow jeans. Kelly putting a friendly arm around her. This was all strangely, scarily, beautifully real.

'Shall I pinch you or what? Is anyone allowed to pinch a Marquise?' Kelly squeezed Michelle tight. 'Take a deep breath, Mich, this is it! And may I ask why you are clinging on like grim death to a bag of hotel laundry?'

Michelle felt a surge of laughter and excitement bubbling up inside her. She reached into the bag and pulled out the leather pouch and held it up in the bright sunlight.'The keys, the keys to the castle!' She ran across the gravel and up the steep, stone steps to the huge, front door. Kelly was again standing close beside her as Michelle carefully opened the bag and drew out a long, beaded chain with several large, ancient keys attached.

'Try the largest one first.' Kelly squeaked excitedly.

Leon joined them on the top step and said quietly. 'But I think the door is open.'

Michelle stretched out her hand and gently pushed the heavy oak door. It creaked and then swung wide open. Michelle turned to Kelly and Leon.'It's open!'

'We can see that!' said Kelly impatiently. 'Michelle, the next thing to do is quite simple, you just go in!' She gave Michelle a gentle push forward. Michelle took a deep breath. Kelly was right. It was simple but it took every ounce of her courage to take the few steps through the shadowy doorway. Once inside they all three stood for a moment. Kelly and Leon on each side of Michelle as though protecting her, sensing her fear. They were stand on the threshold of a vast and lofty hall. In the darkness it was just possible to make out a wide, stone staircase.

'Shall I try and open some shutters to let the light in?' Leon's voice echoed around the emptiness.

'Thank you, good idea.' Michelle stood rooted to the spot. Kelly took her arm, saying,

'Looks like one of our biggest interior dec projects yet, Mich.'

Michelle smiled gratefully, glad to be reminded of exactly who she really was in this world. Michelle Phelps, successful interior designer from Chelsea. Then, after a loud banging noise of wood and hinges, a shaft of light spread across the hall. Both girls gasped at the glimpse of black and white squared marble floor reaching to the magnificent double staircase. More and more light flooded in as Leon moved across the front of the hall, opening one shutter after another. They saw now they were standing under a huge chandelier. Despite the dust and cobwebs, the strong sunlight sparkled on each crystal drop. Michelle was about to speak when the deafening noise of a motor broke into the silence.

'Whatever is that?' Kelly dropped her arm from around Michelle and ran back to the front door and looked out.

'Oh my god, it's a Viking god on a dragon!'

Michelle and Leon exchanged a quick glance of amusement and then joined Kelly at the doorway. Outside a huge, red tractor chugged to a halt. Deafening noise and fumes filled the air and they all three watched as the fork-lift arm slowly lowered to the ground. Then the engine noise died and all was silent again. The tractor cab door opened and a tall, young man wearing a headset jumped down and stood legs wide apart, on the gravel looking up at them. Michelle took in a deep breath, for once Kelly had not exaggerated... he was a Viking god. And he looked prepared for war. He pushed his headphones to the top of his head, his dark, blonde hair curling around the black leather. His brows were drawn into a furious line and his tanned face showed a flush of anger on each high cheekbone. Then, crossing his bronzed muscled arms in front of him, he finally spoke.

'*Qu'est ce que vous faîtes ici?*' His voice was low but angry. For one mad moment Michelle felt surprised that he spoke in French and not some ancient Nordic language. Pulling herself together she answered in English.

'And what are you doing here?' She returned his question, stepping forward to the top of the steps and looking down at him with as haughty an expression as she could manage.

'Ah, English! So you are house-hunting and think you can buy any empty property you find. You think you can just walk in as though you own the place?' His voice was now scornful, his English perfect and with a trace of an American accent. Michelle clutched the hotel laundry bag close to her but held out the long chain of keys and shook them angrily at the young man.

'Actually, I already own the place, I am the new owner of La Bastide de Rosefont and I believe you are trespassing!'

The young man dropped his arms to his sides, his handsome face registering shock. Then, suddenly, his face lit up and he smiled. Such a smile. Michelle's outstretched hand also fell to her side and she stood, helpless, completely under the spell of that smile. Then he was walking toward her, mounting the steps two by two, until he stood very near, towering over her, holding out his hand in greeting.

'My sincere apologies, I had no idea... excuse me, my hand is dirty. I have been working in the vineyards and it is hot work. I came past earlier today to let some air in the place.' He turned his hand over and held out his wrist for her to shake. Michelle closed her hand lightly round his wrist and at the contact with his skin she felt an electric shock through her whole body. Something in the way his light, blue eyes darkened at her touch made her wonder if he felt the same. Why am I feeling so helpless, why do I want to throw my arms around him, why are my knees trembling, my skin shivering? The questions flashed through Michelle's mind one after the other. Then one final question burnt out all the others... is this love at first sight? But he was still talking.

'So, the new owner has been found? You are the *nouvelle châtelaine*? You have the keys to prove it, I see! And the washing?' He looked down at her with some amusement and Michelle realised she was still clutching the chain of keys and the laundry bag. Before she could think of an answer Leon stepped forward, holding out his hand toward the Viking. He looked small and slender beside the other young man, but also confident and determined.

'Leon Batiste, pleased to meet you... and you are?' Leon looked questioningly at the other man, with a slight air of defiance.

'My name is Sven Gilbert.' The young man shook Leon's hand and then turned back toward Michelle adding, 'Well I must continue with my work. I am sure we will meet again soon. *Au revoir!*' And with a giant leap down all the steps he was quickly back in his tractor, his headphone clamped on to his dark blonde curls, in place of a horned helmet, and roaring away down the drive.

'Oh my god, he is a Viking, did you hear that, Mich? Sven... I mean who gets called that unless you are Scandinavian?' Kelly looked down the drive as she spoke, watching the tractor disappear in a cloud of dust. 'Maybe he was a vision?'

'He looked real enough to me.' Leon said in a grumpy voice. 'What is all this about Viking god? I do not understand. Once again is my English. Is an idiom like the battle-axe?'

Kelly slipped her arm through Leon's in a friendly way and smiled at him. 'Don't worry about it, my sweet Leon. This time it's not your English, nor an idiom.

You see it's... well, sort of a girl thing? Don't you agree, Mich?'

'I'm not sure what I am agreeing to, but yes, I guess so...' Michelle's voice tailed away as she listened to the last sound of the tractor engine dying into silence. It seemed as though the sun had gone behind a cloud and she looked up to the blue sky. Not a cloud in sight. She sighed aloud and turned to Leon and Kelly who were standing with their arms still linked.

'As if I didn't have enough to cope with in this new life of mine without a Viking farmer-god appearing and disappearing out of the blue.'

6 'Leon's tanned face was serious'

Three long days later, Michelle began to believe she had discovered all there was of the huge Bastide that now miraculously belonged to her. She was becoming accustomed to the majestic presence of the chalky white Mont Ste. Victoire as the backdrop to every view. The waterfall on the turn of a river that ran at the bottom of the vineyards had been the biggest surprise of all. The summer months had dried the river to a slow stream and the water cascaded gently over the rock. Leon had told her that at the end of the winter, when the snow melted in the high mountains, it would be a fierce rush of icy water. Kelly and Leon were still staying with her and they were all camping out in the vast dusty bedrooms on the first floor. Leon and Kelly were now so obviously an item that it was almost embarrassing to be with them. Michelle had decided to give them some time alone together and gone for a diplomatic afternoon walk. Just three days, but some sort of routine had already developed. They spent the mornings exploring the Bastide, room by room, then went out to lunch in the village restaurant, then back to the Bastide for an idle few hours before beginning again on their tour of discovery. Leon took the role of archivist, neatly noting and taking a photographic inventory of the contents of each room. Kelly rushed around enthusiastically, imagining changes to the décor. By the evening they were all exhausted and dusty. Leon had persuaded the old boiler in one of the cellars to fire up and they luxuriated in long baths before eating a bread and cheese supper on the shady terrace. On one such an evening, as the sun was sinking behind the outline of the western turret, Michelle raised her glass.

'I just don't know how to thank you both for helping me the last few days. I simply could not have done it without you.'

Kelly clinked her glass against Michelle's and laughed, 'For goodness sake, Mich, I wouldn't have missed it for the world. It has been extraordinary... bizarre... surreal... I just don't have words for it... and that's really not like me, is it?'

Leon clinked his glass against Michelle's and then Kelly's, the rays from the setting sun sparkling to gold in the rose-tinted wine. 'I agree totally. An amazing experience altogether. Now, that we have listed what is involved... what is the next ... how do you say... the next path?'

Michelle took a sip of wine before she replied. 'The next step, I think, has to be financial. I suppose I need another appointment with the pompous Maitre Xavier.'

'Good idea!' agreed Kelly, 'Back to Aix and find out the bottom line. And talking of finance, I need to go back to London and see if we still have a business running. Before all this happened we gave a quote to that film director for a location work-over. I don't want to risk losing that if it comes up.'

'*Aussi moi...* I have to go to my office... and I need to invoice old Maitre Xavier. I think I can say that I have successfully found the right Michelle, Michelle de Rosefont, heir to the whole estate of the late Michel de Rosefont.'

'Do you think that's why your mother called you Michelle, I mean, it must be really, in memory of her love, I spose.' Kelly said thoughtfully. 'It's really so romantic.'

'I spose so,' agreed Michelle, 'but I do so wish she had told me more, you know, talked about it before she died.'

Leon's tanned face was serious as he looked at Michelle and said quietly, 'Perhaps it was because of your stepfather, the man you have always known as your real father. Perhaps your mother did not want to hurt him in any way. *Peut-être*... I do not know, but I think from a man's view.' He ended, sounding uncertain that he had said more than he should.

'Thank you, Leon, I think that's very possible, *c'est possible!*'

'*Possible!*' Leon and Kelly spoke as one voice, laughing together. Michelle looked at them both fondly, it really did seem as though Kelly had found not just romantic love but real friendship, too.

'I'll go and get the tray of food, you two stay here in the romantic setting sun... really the scene is too Mills and Boon to be true!' Michelle laughed, stood up and stretched adding 'No need to dress for dinner, *mes amis*, it's only bread and cheese and a bottle of good red wine... again!'

Michelle walked slowly across the terrace, her bare feet feeling the warmth of the sun-soaked flagstones. She looked up at the Bastide, her Bastide, unbelievably hers. Now, the last rays of the sun glinted in each window and, in the kind evening light, it didn't seem so impossible to imagine it alive with people, music, children's laughter, dogs barking, horses clattering to the stables. Michelle dreamed on as she went through the large doors into the grand salon. Then suddenly she stopped and listened. Was that the sound of a car drawing to a halt on the gravel on the other side of the building?

She quickened her pace and went across the main hall and peered through a small window that looked over the entrance.

'Oh good Lord!' Michelle muttered to herself, 'The Viking returns in full splendour!' She quickly ducked out of sight as Sven emerged from a silver, blue Maserati, looked up at the Bastide, then made his way toward the entrance doors. Michelle looked down miserably at her old t-shirt and torn jeans. She ran her fingers through her hair, still wet from the bath ... she had been wrong about not needing to dress up for dinner. Before she could even think about looking in a mirror, there was a loud knock on the door. Michelle counted to ten and then took a deep breath before opening it.

'*Bonsoir Mademoiselle*, I was passing by and wondered how you were settling down at the Bastide. I hope you will excuse me arriving without invitation.' Michelle stood rooted to the spot. He really was the most amazingly good-looking man she had ever seen... and that included film stars. Brad Pitt didn't come close. The deep breath she had taken seemed now to have stuck in her throat. She swallowed nervously and attempted a smile. Then she realised he was holding out his hand toward her. Was this a dream, a fantasy... was he going to lead her away to a magic land? Then she heard Kelly's voice calling to her and she came down to earth and hastily shook his hand. The handshake was firm and cool, his large hand enclosed hers for a long moment. He bowed slightly to look down at Michelle, then... surely not... was he going to kiss her hand? Michelle felt a nervous desire to giggle hysterically. The whole scene was just too ridiculous. There she stood, at the entrance of her very own Bastide, holding the hand of a Viking god as the sun set behind him. Kelly's voice, louder and nearer, brought her back to reality.

'Please, do come in!' Michelle smiled up at him, regaining her confidence. 'We have just finished our working day of discovery and enjoying the last of the sun on the south terrace. Won't you join us?'

'That would be very nice indeed, thank you.' He smiled back and nodded, his blonde hair falling forward over his tanned forehead in just the way it should.

'Follow me.' Michelle turned on her heel and led the way, suddenly conscious of the large tear in the back of her jeans. Nothing to be done about that and here was Kelly coming toward her.

'Kelly!' Michelle attempted to sound casual but her voice was annoyingly squeaky. She cleared her throat and tried again. 'Kelly, we have a visitor, our neighbour, Sven Gilbert.'

Kelly stepped forward and once again hands were shaken. Kelly, with her usual confidence and glamour, looked the perfect match to Sven's tall, blonde look. Michelle felt a sudden and unusual pang of jealousy. She spoke quickly, 'Shall we go back to the terrace? Leon will be wondering where we are.'

Kelly glanced first at Michelle and then at Sven. 'Yes, it's still lovely outside. We were calling you, Mich, as we've just opened another bottle of rosé. How nice to have a visitor.' Kelly turned around to go back the way she had come and Michelle followed a few steps behind and then looked over her shoulder at Sven. Yes, his eyes were riveted to the backside of her ripped jeans.

Leon stood up as they came through the doors onto the terrace. He, too, held out his hand for the formal French handshake. He looked dark and slim beside the towering, muscled Sven. They settled in the rickety iron chairs around the table and Leon poured the wine. There was a moment of awkward silence and then Michelle raised her glass.

'Welcome to La Bastide de Rosefont! *Santé!*' They all sipped the chilled wine and there was another short silence before Sven spoke.

'Ah, you are drinking our local wine. There is nothing better after a day working.'

'I totally agree,' Kelly laughed, 'and however much I drink I never get a hang-over... it's amazing.'

'Not so surprising.' Sven answered seriously. 'Our wines are made organically, absolutely no added chemicals. I imagine you bought this at the local Spar shop... they always buy my simple *vin ordinaire*. It is made in true respect of the environment, working with the lunar cycles. It is biodynamic!'

'Wow! And I thought I was just drinking a bottle of great plonk. You lost me somewhere in theory but in practice I think we all need to test it out... let's have another glass of this bionic stuff!' Kelly grabbed the bottle and refilled the four glasses. They all laughed and the atmosphere became a little more relaxed.

'You must excuse me, mesdemoiselles et monsieur, wine is my passion and I can talk about it for hours.' Sven looked at them in turn, giving them each the benefit of his perfect smile. 'But tell me how you are spending your first days here.'

Michelle took a deep breath, then said, 'Oh, we just haven't stopped. Leon... I am so sorry, I should have introduced you properly. This is my new friend Leon Batiste and my business partner and great friend Kelly Atkinson.'

Sven answered with a nod to Kelly and then to Leon. Michelle gave a sigh of relief, she couldn't have faced another round of handshakes... or worse, the risk of hands being kissed. She glanced down at Sven's shoes, large, shiny as conkers and surely handmade. Wasn't there some theory about judging a man by his shoes? But Sven was talking again.

'It must have been a remarkable week. I understand you knew nothing of your inheritance until recently.'

'That's right!' Michelle replied, 'It certainly has been a whirlwind. The last few days we have been working methodically through every room in the Bastide and Leon has been making an inventory.'

'Good idea.' Sven nodded seriously, his blonde hair falling forward again over his brow. 'It's important to know everything before you put the Bastide on the market.'

Michelle gave a shocked intake of breath before she replied. 'Oh, that's never going to happen. I have no intention of selling La Bastide de Rosefont. Not at all, never, *jamais!*'

She emphasised the last word and looked defiantly at Sven and then to Kelly and Leon. It was only at that moment that she realised her decision was made. La Bastide de Rosefont belonged to her now and that was how it would remain.

7   'a dark suit with a white shirt'

Michelle emerged from the shadowy gloom of Maitre Xavier's office and into the bright Provençal sunshine. She walked in the shade of the tree-lined boulevard, determined to enjoy the day. She remembered the small bistro that Leon had directed them to, but decided against trying to find it. But, it was lunchtime and no reason she could think of to miss eating Provençal cuisine. She stopped outside a corner brasserie to look at the menu. A waiter stood beside a stall of oysters and smiled in welcome.

'*Mademoiselle, entrez, entrez!* You like oysters perhaps, or the best steak in France?'

'Why not?' she replied, smiling as she walked into the large and busy brasserie. It was difficult to be alone after the good company of Kelly and Leon, but she was still determined to enjoy herself. There seemed to be a number of things she needed to be determined about. The notaire, Maitre Xavier, had read a long list of potential problems when she had told him she had decided to keep the Bastide .

'But, Mademoiselle... *excusez-moi*... Marquise de Rosefont... do you understand the huge responsibility... the difficulty of maintaining La Bastide de Rosefont? If you sell then I think I can find you a serious buyer. You will receive a very good price and you can return to your former life in London. *N'est ce pas?*'

Michelle sat at a small table in the window of the brasserie and smiled to herself as she remembered his words. All true, of course, and probably well-intentioned. He had continued to outline her financial situation. There was some rental income from the vineyards and cornfields, let out to no other than Sven Gilbert's family. But even Michelle could see that it was scarcely enough to live on, let alone repair and maintain the crumbling Bastide . She reflected, too, on what the notaire had called 'her former life.' Certainly she had enjoyed every minute of building up her own business. She and Kelly had worked so hard over the last three years. Michelle sighed as she thought of Kelly working alone in London, juggling to keep all the balls in the air. She pulled out her phone and rang their work number.

Kelly answered almost immediately. '*Bonjour* Marquise... how's it going?' Kelly's voice was as upbeat as ever.

'Oh, fine here. I am just worried about you having to cope all alone.'

'Well, you can stop worrying as I have a temp helping me with all the boring things... all the things you used to do... like tidying files and drawings, making decent coffee, usual stuff. And guess what... I was going to call you later... I have secured the contract with that film studio. They wanted to sign yesterday. It's outside of our normal work. The remit is to find the perfect location and then furnish, create the scene etc. They're going to give me a detailed remit on Thursday. The money sounds unbelievable. I think it's a good direction to go in.'

'Fantastic, I guess it's something we can do... I mean, it's way out of our normal comfort zone but...'

'When have we ever stayed safe, dear Marquise? You can talk, anyway, taking on a huge Bastide and land.' Kelly laughed and Michelle smiled at her phone. Kelly was irrepressible as ever and took everything in her high-heeled stride.

'Can you get back to France this weekend, Kelly?' asked Michelle.

'Try to stop me. I am missing my sweet Leon... and you too, of course, but not in the same way! I've already booked the high speed train and Leon is meeting me at Aix station. I'll speak to you before then, but the other phone is ringing non-stop. Must go, love you!'

Michelle sat in silence a moment and then, taking a deep breath, she called her father's number. How could she begin? Just how much did he know about her mother's past? But most of all... how to tell him that she had inherited from her real father? Michelle suddenly realised she was listening to voicemail and being asked to leave a message. Her father's voice was calm and quiet, the voice she had loved so much all her life. The phone beeped and Michelle tried to leave some sort of message.

'Everything is fine, Dad, just wanted to catch up with you. Call me when you have time off. Hope you're enjoying some cruise time.' The message ended abruptly. She impatiently threw her phone back in her bag. One thing was certain, she was not going to attempt to explain the sudden change in her life over the phone. Somehow, she would have to get him to come to France and then she could explain everything face to face. Michelle sighed and mentally added it to the million and one things already on her to-do list.

The waiter brought her a large menu. Michelle looked at it without enthusiasm. She really didn't feel hungry. The waiter hovered discreetly and then rushed off to serve another table. Michelle looked around the busy restaurant, full of people talking and laughing. She was alone in Aix-en-Provence with only her thoughts for company but she should make the most of some quiet time to think and plan. She was about to make her excuse to the waiter and leave when she saw a tall figure entering and walking straight toward her. Sven Gilbert. He was immaculately dressed in a dark suit with a white shirt, open at the neck and showing the perfect amount of tanned neck. His broad shoulders seemed to block out the light from the window as he weaved his way between the tables. This time there was no handshake but a fleeting kiss on each cheek. Michelle breathed in his aroma... was it just good soap...not strong enough to be *eau de toilette* or aftershave... just a very good, very clean smell.

'Incredible to meet you here! This is my favourite lunch time brasserie. How are you, Michelle? You are looking wonderful!'

'Of all the restaurants...' Michelle laughed, glad to have company. 'I came here quite by chance. I have been to see Maitre Xavier, just round the corner.'

'Ah yes, I know the notaire, I have used him for some matters in the past. May I join you for lunch or have you finished?'

'No, no I haven't even ordered yet. Please do join me... we can eat together.' Michelle's words petered out as she imagined some other things they could do together. Sven moved to hold her chair as she sat down again. Then he rested his hands gently on her shoulders. Michelle had a mad desire to throw her head back and lean against him. His attraction was magnetic. The moment passed and Sven took the seat opposite her. To cover her confusion, Michelle offered him the menu, trying to ignore that his knee was resting lightly against hers.

'Oh, I don't need the menu... they know me here.' He raised his arm and a waiter appeared from nowhere. '*Bonjour, Philippe, comme d'habitude pour moi... et pour Mademoiselle?* ' Sven looked enquiringly across at Michelle. 'What will you have? Or will you risk having the same as me?'

'I am always happy to take a risk.' She smiled, then added, 'But I never eat oysters, I'm sorry.'

'Neither do I, that's a coincidence!' Sven returned her smile and then giving the menu back to the waiter, he added.

'*Aussi, l'eau de robinet...* Michelle will you drink wine...or beer like the English?'

'Good heavens, no! I hardly ever drink at lunchtime... I should prefer water, just plain tap water please.'

'*Entendu!* Another coincidence then... I, too, only drink tap water at lunch ... we are obviously made to eat together!'

Michelle smiled feebly as her mind took in the idea of being made to do anything together... or everything. She quickly switched her thoughts off and, opening up her serviette, she determined to change the subject.

8 'a derelict Château in the wilds of Provence'

'You do realise he was probably stalking you, Mich!' Kelly was sitting on one of the ancient sofas in the small drawing room at the Bastide . She lolled back, leaning against Leon and sipped her wine.

'Don't be ridiculous, Kelly, as if a hulk like Sven would bother to stalk me. It was just sheer coincidence.' Michelle stood up and walked across to the glowing fire. The summer weather had come to an abrupt halt and rain lashed against the long windows.

'I think any red-blooded hulk would be happy to follow you, Michelle.' Leon said and was rewarded with a playful slap from Kelly.

'That's quite enough of the French gallantry, *mon amour,* but I still think it was a hell of a coincidence. Then all this chat-up about sharing the same taste for tap water... honestly, I've heard some good lines but that...'

The three friends were back together at the Bastide , chatting about the week past. In just a few days apart they had so much to tell each other. Kelly was bursting with her news. She placed her wine glass down on a small table and said, 'Listen up, I have far more interesting news than Mich's so-called chance meeting with the Viking god. I... all on my own, have secured the best contract we have ever had at the design studio.' She paused for effect and took another glug of wine before continuing.

'The film company I told you about... they seem really keen now and... you are NOT going to believe this... well, OK, you can have three guesses...what location do you think they are looking for...?'

'A derelict farm in Tuscany?' Michelle guessed, 'Scottish highland manse?'

'My turn,' interrupted Leon, 'it must be Paris... a grand apartment in the Marais?'

'No, no et non, *mes amis*,' Kelly gave a wicked smile, 'and don't forget we are employed to create the entire décor ... they are looking for a derelict Château in the wilds of Provence!'

Leon and Michelle both gasped and looked at Kelly in amazement.

'Never!' said Michelle, turning her back to the fire and sitting down promptly on the sofa next to Kelly. 'You are a little miracle worker, Kelly. How did you manage it?'

'Well, to be quite honest, it was mostly luck... and my not-inconsiderable charm of course... not to mention having to give a full explanation of how a Bastide was actually a Château.'

'Well, I can vouch for your charm, that's for sure.' Leon put his arm around Kelly and hugged her. 'These sort of contracts bring in *les gros dollars, n'est ce pas*?'

'Absolutely, big bucks from an American film company. I have a draft contract with me. The bottom line is more money than we made in the whole of our last year. Our design studio will make our bit and then... then there will be huge rental fees for Marquise Mich. I've already told them that La Bastide de Rosefont is simply ideal!'

'What sort of film is it then... historical romp? French revolution or what?' Michelle asked.

'Well, actually it's... well, it's more of a vampire epic!'

'Vampires?' Michelle's repeated in surprise

'Hmm... and zombies from what I can understand... what do you think, Mich?'

'I think I have the best friends in the world and that we ought to go out to the nearest best restaurant and celebrate! Vampires and Zombies at La Bastide de Rosefont... bring it on!'

They raised their glasses, laughing and happy in the firelight. Then Kelly added. 'And that's not all I have been up to... tomorrow I have a big surprise for you Mich!'

'Kelly you know I can't stand not knowing... tell me now, please, please... what on earth have you been up to?' Kelly smiled at Leon and they both nodded mysteriously. 'So Leon knows... so unfair, tell me, tell me.' Michelle was mad with excitement.

'No, Mich, you will just have to wait. You can torture me, refuse to give me food and drink but we are not going to tell you.'

Leon stood up and pulled Kelly to her feet. 'Come on you two crazy girls. Talking of eating I know a decent little bistro...' Before he could finish both girls had headed for the door still laughing.

'You always do know a little bistro, Leon. That's one of the many things I love about you.' Kelly said, looking over her shoulder at him with a brilliant smile.

9 *'raindrops studding his blonde hair like diamonds'*

'That was a fantastic dinner last night... and the crème brulé... the best I have ever eaten.' Kelly was sitting at the breakfast table, sipping coffee, and looking out at the rain-soaked gardens.

'Yes, great meal,' agreed Michelle, 'Even though you wouldn't tell me your secret... surely you can tell me now?'

'Really Mich you just don't get the whole idea about secret surprises, do you? If I told you now then obviously it would not be a surprise when it happens.' Kelly sighed and then suddenly jumped up from her seat. 'Mich, you are no longer to be in suspense... your surprise is arriving right now!'

Michelle ran to the window, rubbing at the glass to try to see the car that was coming to a halt outside on the gravel.

'It's just Leon... did he go to get croissants... or...oh my sweet Lord... it's Dad. Leon has brought Dad here! Oh my God, Kelly, you have arranged this. Fantastic, thank you, thank you.'

Michelle ran from the room and across the dark hall to the main front door. She quickly unlatched the heavy doors and flung them open. She ran down the steps, heedless of the rain, and into the open arms of the man she loved as her father.

An hour later, when the first excited explanations had been made over endless pots of coffee, Leon and Kelly decided to go to the village for food and wine supplies.

Dr. Robert Phelps, Michelle's stepfather, was a tall man, with iron grey hair and a dark tan. He stood up and stretched. 'I'm so glad you have such a good friend in Kelly. When I received your voicemail, I tried to call your mobile but there was no signal so I rang your office number. Kelly gave me a short account of all that had happened.'

Michelle was silent for a minute. Typical Kelly not to think about discretion or tact. But then, Michelle was so relieved not to have to tell her father everything from the beginning. Maybe it really was easier coming from a third party.

'The thing is Dad, I really had no idea how much you knew about... well, everything. I mean Mum's work here and the... well, the affair with Michel de Rosefont.' Michelle spoke quietly, looking up at her father with a small frown and Dr. Phelps rested his hand gently on Michelle's shoulder.

'Your dear mother and I had no secrets, Michelle. I knew everything. We both decided there was no need for you to know. You were a tiny, three-year old cherub when your Mum and I married. In every possible way that mattered, you were our dearly beloved daughter. I think if your mother had lived longer there would have come a time when she would have told you about your birth father. But I am sorry this has all come as such a shock to you now. Maybe we should have told you when you came of age? Somehow it never seemed important.'

'Oh no, you and Mum always did everything for me, for the best, I mean. After the initial shock it has really been an adventure. I was just so anxious that you would... I don't know... sort of be upset or something.'

'Do you mean jealous of your birth father? How could I be? That would be foolish indeed. I had the best life possible with your mother and gained the best daughter in the world. I am the lucky one and the past is the past.'

'That's such a relief, Dad. I'm so glad everything is out in the open at last. I wish Mum could have been here.' Michelle's eyes filled with tears.

'Come along now. We've been sitting at this breakfast table quite long enough. Why don't you give me a guided tour of this great Bastide that's landed in your lap?' Dr Phelps patted Michelle's shoulder and she jumped up and gave him a big hug.

'You're right, Dad, as usual... follow me!'

From that moment on the weekend passed happily, but, as is so often the way, much too quickly. Michelle and her father spent hours together exploring every room of the Bastide and walking the fields and vineyards. The weather was appalling but it just didn't seem to matter. They had so much to talk about and even more to decide. Late Sunday afternoon found them back by the fireside in the small drawing room as wind and rain battered the long windows. Kelly and Leon were sitting close together on the old velvet sofa.

'*Alors*, now you have explored nearly every centimetre of La Bastide de Rosefont, what do you think of it, Dr. Phelps?' Leon asked as he passed a delicate china cup of tea.

'*Merci*, Leon, I'm afraid that's almost the extent of my knowledge of your language. But before we go any further, please call me Robert. I know I am old enough to be father to you all but there's no need to make me feel it.'

They all laughed and Michelle said, 'Maybe I should call you Robert, too.' 'No, no, cheeky girl... I'm your Dad whatever history tells us!'

'OK, Dad, suits me. Now shall we tell Kelly and Leon some of the ideas we have come up with... Dad.'

'Well, they are mostly all your ideas, my dear, but I shall count myself lucky if I can be included in any way at all. Go ahead, you explain.'

'Well, Dad and I are thinking we could turn the Bastide into a very luxurious, sort of boutique hotel, dedicated to the art of Provence.'

'Yes, but with a slight difference,' added Robert Phelps, 'I have spent the last few years as doctor aboard luxury liners, cruise ships that offer art tours... you know the sort of thing. Art for the rich!'

'Hmm, sounds a very possible plot to me.' Kelly said thoughtfully. 'How about the set up costs... I mean it would be a vast outlay.'

'Well, your film company will help out there.' Michelle said, looking at Kelly and smiling, 'Thanks to you we have a start and we have to take advantage of that.'

'OK, I absolutely agree. I shall take the early train back to London tomorrow and get another meeting with the producer set up. We need to dot the I's and cross the T's with our solicitor first and then sign up as soon as possible.'

'Maybe I could travel with you?' said Robert.

'Of course,' agreed Kelly, 'that would be great, Dr.... I mean Robert!'

'I'll take you to the station first thing,' Leon said, 'and then I have some work to finish off in Aix... just to keep the dog from my door.'

They all looked at him in puzzlement and then Michelle laughed, saying,

'Wolf from the door, Leon, wolf not dog. Have you been studying that idiom book again?'

Leon smiled and gave a typical Gallic shrug, 'I shall never understand your English... but one thing I am sure of... we make plans but there may be wolves and dogs at the door of the Bastide . These plans need un sac d'argent... and there is a French idiom you may not know '*avoir les dents longues*' and it means something like to have the big ambitions.' They all nodded in agreement, staring into the fire, each thinking their own thoughts when the peaceful silence was broken by the distant sound of the clanging front doorbell. Michelle stood up and stretched. 'Who can that be?' she said, secretly hoping it might be Sven.

Leon extricated himself from Kelly's arms and jumped up. 'I'll come with you.'

Michelle was glad of his company as they left the warmth of the firelight and crossed the dark hallway. Leon pulled open the large door and there stood Sven, raindrops studding his blonde hair like diamonds. Michelle gave a small gasp, as once again she was struck by the hulking beauty of the man. But he was speaking,

'I am sorry to intrude on a Sunday but I noticed there is a tree fallen across the end of your drive.'

'Oh no, thanks for telling us... come in, please come in out of the rain.' Michelle tried to make her voice sound casual but every fibre of her body seemed to react to this man. His presence literally took her breath away and her voice was reedy thin as she continued. 'We're just having tea, won't you join us?'

Sven took a step towards her but stayed in the porch.'Thank you, but no, really I am dripping wet, as you can see.' He raised his hand and brushed his wet hair back from his forehead.

'Let me take your coat,' Leon said, 'We are just sitting by the fire and there is nothing at La Bastide de Rosefont that can be spoiled by a few drops of water.'

Michelle smiled, grateful to Leon, and pushed away the thought that she wouldn't mind if Sven took all his clothes off there and then. She straightened her shoulders, flicked her hair back behind her ears and cleared her throat before saying, 'Yes, please do join us, you can meet my father.' The word fell in the air between them all and she added quickly. 'Meet the man who has always been my real father.'

An hour later, introductions had been made, Kelly and Leon were back in their favourite position on the sofa and Sven and Robert Phelps were in deep discussion.

'So your wines really are organic, Sven? I am most impressed. I am sure it is the way forward. With the huge rise in petrol and diesel, the wine we drink in England has to be worth it. There is a strong interest in organically grown food and now it seems to me, in wine.'

'Exactly! Wine has to be worth its weight in transport costs. Quality is everything. *Biodynamie* is more than wine-making, it is a way of farming. It reflects the terroir, the tradition of working with lunar cycles.' Sven spoke enthusiastically, his face serious in the light of the fire.

'I can tell it means a lot to you.' Robert replied. 'It is important to have a real meaning in your work. But this weather... is it bad for your grapes?'

'Well, at the moment the grapes are just having a good wash. Cleaning off the earthy dust of the summer. All will be well as long as the swollen grapes don't get struck by hail.'

'Hail! Here in Provence?' Michelle joined the conversation.

'Oh you will find winter here can be very harsh. Two years ago we had a hail-storm just before harvest. The hailstones split the skin of the grapes and then the wine is literally watered down. It was a disastrous harvest. This wind today is nothing to how it can blow from the East. But, I have been talking too long and I only came here to warn you about your tree.' Sven stood up to leave. They all rose and stood a moment looking at the fire. Then Sven continued. 'If you like I can drag the tree to the side of the drive, my tractor is just nearby.'

They all looked at Michelle for a decision and suddenly she was aware of all the problems that could beset La Bastide de Rosefont.

'I should be very grateful, can I come with you to help?' she said.

Sven looked down at her, smiling as he would at a child. His light, blue eyes were mocking.

'No, there is no need. I shall just sling a chain around it and drag it a few metres. If I were you I would leave sawing it into logs until a bright autumn day. Don't worry, the sun will soon return. It is never as hot after the first strong rainfall like this, but there will be many wonderful, sunny autumn days yet. And we don't often get much snow.'

Michelle nodded, taking in the weather forecast, but still mesmerised by his light, blue eyes.

10   'brushing silkily against her skin'

Sven rested his hands on her shoulders and looked down at her, his eyes the colour of a Nordic sky. Michelle looked up at him, longing for him to kiss her. Not the brushing peck on each cheek but really, really kiss her, long and hard. She put her head back and looked at him and suddenly he was kissing her, holding her head in his strong hands. Then he was kissing her neck and she arched her back, pressing her body against him, aching with desire. His hands moved down her back and then encircled her waist. His head nestled, now, between her breasts and then he was opening the buttons of her blouse, slowly at first and then impatiently. She felt his hair, still wet from the rain, brushing silkily against her skin. She ran her fingers through his hair and pressed his face close against her. She became slowly aware of a tapping noise on the window.

Then she awoke.

Michelle sat up in bed, breathless and hot. Such a dream! Never had she had such a dream. The sheets were twisted around her and although the room was not warm she felt her body was on fire. She pushed her tousled hair back and held her forehead. The dream was still so real. Michelle smiled in the dark of the bedroom... how ridiculous she was becoming. One thing that was real was the tapping noise on the window. She threw back the covers and walked over to the window. The wind was whipping the branches of a tree against the rain-dappled glass. She cleared a small circle in the misted window pane and looked out. So this was sunny Provence? Trees falling, torrential rain and possibly hail and snow to look forward to in the winter. Michelle shivered, all the warmth of her body gone as she stood in the draught of the window. She pulled on her dressing gown and decided to go down to the kitchen and make a hot drink. She needed something to calm herself after that dream.

She was surprised to see the kitchen lights on as she approached down the long corridor from the hallway. Surprised and then pleased to see her father sitting at the kitchen table with a mug of hot chocolate. He looked up at her, smiling, 'Now, what makes you get up in the middle of the night? A nightmare?'

Michelle almost blushed as she answered casually, 'No, not really a nightmare... just a disturbing dream. I awoke suddenly and just couldn't get back to sleep. Then I began to think about all the things that need to be done at the Bastide. It's fairly daunting.'

'Exactly, that's why I couldn't get to sleep. I was worried about what you are taking on, Michelle. You have a perfectly happy and successful life in London. You could sell up here and be a very wealthy young woman, I should think.'

'That's true, I know, Dad. But this would be such an adventure. My work in London is great, I mean I do enjoy it but... I don't know... I am not sure how I could go back to it all now. Everything has changed. Even my identity.'

'Well, if you want my advice as your Dad, and as a medical man... you are really in a state of shock. Even good fortune can be traumatising. Maybe you should hold off making any big irreversible decisions for a while.'

'I suppose that would be the sensible way to go forward,' Michelle answered doubtfully, 'but somehow I just know I could never sell out without trying everything in my power to hold on to the Bastide. I've never experienced this feeling of ownership before. I mean I enjoyed buying my little studio flat in

Chelsea... and giving it a complete makeover... but somehow, it was always in my mind that I would sell it and upgrade one day. La Bastide de Rosefont is so vastly different... not just the sheer size of it but somehow the history and feeling it gives me. No, however mad it seems, Dad, I think I am here for the long term.'

'You're probably right, my dear, you always have known what you wanted to do, made your own decisions. It will certainly be an adventure and I'll do anything I can to help you, you know that.'

'I do, Dad, you've always been there for me.' Michelle gave a radiant smile, 'I do have a few ideas that you might well be able to help with.'

'Good, that's my girl. Now drink this hot chocolate and tell me all your wild plans.'

'Thanks, Dad, you always have made the best hot chocolate in the whole wide world.' Michelle sipped the frothy, hot chocolate and then spoke again. 'Well, I thought that first we should concentrate on Kelly's project. Renting out the Bastide and making it work for its own survival. The money earned from the film company should all go to repairs, starting from the roof down. If we can make the old place almost respectable then we can move on to having groups of guests coming for art history weekends ... this is where you can help. The people that organise your art cruises... could you get some contacts... ask around.'

'That could be easy, actually,' Dr Phelps nodded slowly, as though he was thinking it through. 'The travel company that recruit me as ship's doctor is run by a charming woman. She seems to think everything I do is wonderful, quite my fan, in fact.' He smiled at Michelle, 'Can't imagine why!'
Michelle looked across the large kitchen table and smiled back. She could suddenly quite easily imagine

why. Her father was a handsome man, with distinguished dark, grey hair and a tall athletic figure.

'Oh, I am sure I can think of a reason.' Michelle laughed. 'So you can chat her up then?'

'Michelle, what are you thinking? But yes, I think I may well be able to arrange some bookings. The names on her clientele list would be ideal targets. She's a good business woman and I am sure she will see the potential profit to be made. You need to have a proper business profile and projected plan of some sort. You would need someone very professional to take that on.'

'I know, but don't forget, Dad, I am not just your little girl, I am a business woman too. Also I need to have a good talk with Kelly and Leon. I am hoping they may want to join in the mad adventure.'

'I think it would be wonderful if they did. Although that would mean even more risk involved. You would be taking them away from their own successful work. And you talk of them as a pair, but are you sure of that?'

'Well, I have never seen Kelly as settled and happy as she seems to be with Leon. Yes, actually Dad, I think it may be the real thing.'

'And what about you, my dear girl? Anyone in your sights, romance-wise?'

'No, no... no-one. I'm just a very busy, working career woman. No time for romance!' Michelle stood up quickly and rinsed the mugs at the sink, her mind filling again with her dream.

11 *'the vineyards sloping downhill to the river'*

The next morning the wind and rain had disappeared, leaving the world outside shining bright. Michelle slept late after her disturbed night. As she came down the large staircase she saw Kelly and Dr. Phelps ready to leave. Kelly looked up at Michelle.

'Wow, Mich, as long as we have been friends I've never known you be up later than me. You must be learning aristocratic ways. I'd have brought you breakfast in bed if I had known.'

Michelle laughed and joined them in the hall. 'I slept badly, sorry to miss breakfast with you though.'

'Well, you certainly have a lot that could keep you awake. And that was quite a storm. With the hunk Sven going on about hard Provençal winters, enough to give you a nightmare. Did you dream about the roof blowing away?'

'Something like that, hmm...' Michelle answered, feeling a blush spread across her cheeks as she remembered why she had really woken in the night. Not long ago she might well have had a laugh about it with Kelly, but somehow things had changed. Kelly had Leon now, to talk and be close to, and Michelle, well, she smiled to herself... yes, she had her Bastide. Her father was talking and Michelle brought herself back from her thoughts.

'Leon has gone to bring his car round. He's taking Kelly and me to the station. Will you be all right on your own here? We have plenty of time if you want to come with us... you could catch up with things in London and come back here after a few days break. Maybe a good thing to stand back awhile?'

'No, Dad, I shall be fine. I have the hired car and I have a thousand things I need to do. Really, I shall be fine.'

'That sounds like the car now,' Kelly said, 'we'd better get going if we are to catch the ten o'clock TGV. I want to be back in London as soon as possible and set up a meeting with the film company. I'll call you as soon as I have any news, Mich.'
The two girls hugged and then walked to the front door arm in arm.

'Thanks, Kelly, I shall never be able to repay you for this one. If you do get that contract, I may even be able to stop the roof blowing off. Anyway, will you come back again Friday evening. There's so much we need to talk through.'

'Try and stop me.' Kelly laughed. 'I just don't know how I'm going to get through the week without my sweet Leon.' She pulled Michelle closer and whispered in her ear. 'Have you guessed already, Mich, this is the real thing. I am definitely in love, seriously... *c'est l'amour*!'

'*L'amour!*' Michelle repeated, giving Kelly a big squeeze as they opened the door to see Leon, standing holding his car door open, looking up at them. Kelly sighed dramatically, 'Isn't he just the sweetest, cutest man on earth?'

Michelle saw Leon's face light up as he heard Kelly. It certainly seemed like a two-way love affair.

Dr Phelps was standing behind Michelle and watching over her shoulder. 'I think you're right, Michelle. Kelly may well have found her soul mate. She seems so much more relaxed and calm.'

Just as he spoke, Kelly leaped the last steps down to the drive and, with a wild whoop, launched herself at Leon, encircling him with her arms and wrapping her legs round his waist.

'Oh yes, she's really calmed down, Dad.'

They laughed together and then made their farewells. Michelle watched until the car pulled out of sight at the bend in the drive. Silence surrounded her, broken only by birdsong and cicadas. The air was fresh after the torrential rain and the sky an impossible deep blue. Michelle took a deep breath and then turned back to look up at the Bastide, her Bastide. Sunlight lit the pale, stone façade and glinted on the windows. She nodded to herself and put her hands on her hips. Yes, the paintwork was peeling, some window panes were cracked, a few roof tiles had slipped but the building stood firm and proud, an ageing beauty, but a beauty nonetheless. Michelle went slowly back up the entrance steps. Today was the day to start planning and working. There was a small room on the first floor, at least, small by comparison with the other rooms. Set centrally to the rear of the Bastide, the long windows had a commanding view over the gardens at the rear, across the vineyards sloping downhill to the river and to the distant Mont Ste. Victoire. Michelle decided that this is where she would set up their working studio. It seemed that it had already been used as an office. Had her birth father sat at this desk and looked out this very window? Had he always been lonely and sad after her mother disappeared? Michelle sat for a moment trying to imagine his daily life. She opened the top drawer of the desk and flicked through the dusty files. Nothing personal or even hand-written. She opened all the drawers, one by one and found nothing but yellowing paperwork. The room was so sunny and light that it defied nostalgia. Michelle sat back in the large, leather chair and looked out of the window again. Then, suddenly, she sat up straight... there was Sven striding across the lawn, followed by a large dog. She stood up and he must have noticed the movement, as he looked up and waved. Michelle waved back, her heart racing, and ran out of the room and downstairs. Why did this man have such an effect on her? Michelle slowed down and took a deep breath, trying to pull herself together. She reached the rear door of the kitchen just as he knocked. She paused for a brief moment then opened the door. There he stood, as handsome, no, more handsome than ever. Words failed her and she simply stood aside to let him in.

'Bonjour Michelle, how are you this beautiful morning?' Sven smiled down at her, perfectly at ease. Michelle hesitated. Was he going to kiss her on both cheeks? She braced herself but the moment passed and he carried on talking.

'Do you mind?' he asked.

Michelle couldn't think of anything she would mind but then realised that he was indicating the very large brown and white speckled dog, waiting obediently on the doorstep.

'*Bonjour, Sven.*' She managed a reply, but why did this man make her voice squeak. She cleared her throat and continued, 'No, of course not... I love dogs.' The dog looked up at her and walked in as though it had understood every word. Michelle laughed, relieved to have something to focus on other than the rippling muscles of Sven's tanned arms. She stroked the dog gently and it leant against her, silky and soft. 'She's a beauty, I've never seen a dog like her.'

'She's a Braque Français Gascogne, not a common breed even in France, but I doubt there are any in England. We breed them for hunting. Usually they are magnificent gun-dogs but not this one...' He leant down and gave the dog a peremptory pat on the back, adding, 'Eh, Coco, you're worse than useless, aren't you?' Sven stood up again to his full height. 'One useless dog in a litter of four.'

'What do you mean, useless?' Michelle continued to stroke the dog as it wiggled in delight.

'She's gun shy. First time I took her out training she was terrified at my first gunshot. Now she runs a mile at the sight of a gun. Can't even cope with fireworks. Not going to breed from her in case it's a genetic fault. Useless!'

'I'll have her!' The words flew out of Michelle's mouth before she had time to think.

'Really? Are you sure?' Sven looked at her in surprise, his blonde eyebrows arched over his light blue eyes. 'If you like, you could keep her for a week or so on trial? She's not even a year old yet but she is house-trained... in fact, that's another problem I have with her... she always wants to come indoors. Our other dogs all stay out in kennels, of course.' While they talked the dog was looking from one to the other as though following every word anxiously.

'As long as she is happy to stay with me, I am sure it will be fine. Anyway, come on in, do you want a coffee?' At her words, the dog galloped across the flagstone floor and sat under the kitchen table.

'I don't think there will be any problem. I am sure she will be very happy to stay.' Sven laughed, 'And, of course, if you need to go to England any time, you can always drop her off at our place.'

'Well, that would be great... I'd love to give it a try. She will be company.'

'Are you here on your own now?' Sven asked, frowning.

'Well, only until Friday when they will all troop back again. I have so much to do it will give me a chance to plan and think things through.'

'You must know in your heart that it's ridiculous not selling and going back to London, surely that's what you will end up doing anyway?'

Michelle felt herself slightly antagonised at his cool assumption that she would not be able to cope. She poured the coffee and answered lightly.

'Ah well, we'll see. I am not going to make any long term decisions for a while.' She passed Sven a cup of coffee and sat down opposite him. If only he wasn't such a perfect example of manhood it would be easier to be dismissive. He was looking straight at her now and he really was irresistible.

'What are you doing this evening, Michelle?' Sven asked.

Michelle's heart thumped and she took a sip of coffee before answering.'Oh, nothing really, probably going through paperwork and accounts that I have found on a desk upstairs. Michel de Rosefont's office it seems.'

'You really don't think of him as your father, do you? Yet you look very like him.'
Michelle looked up in surprise, nearly dropping her coffee. 'I do?' she replied.

'Oh yes, wait until you meet my mother, she'll say the same. In fact, that is what I was going to ask you. Would you come to our place this evening and meet my mother?'

Well, it wasn't the romantic evening she had in mind... meet his mother. Oh dear, was he a mummy's boy? Michelle summoned up as much enthusiasm as she could to reply. 'That would be lovely, thank you.'

'Shall I pick you up... about seven?'

Certainly tempting, Michelle thought to herself but no, she had better hang on to a remnant of her self-sufficiency. 'No, I'll drive round, I have the hire car... and I've noticed your gateway and the Château Gilbert sign. I could almost walk it.'

'Is that a rental car outside? You must take it back, we have your father's car stored in a barn at our place.'

Michelle's eyes widened, 'His car? Oh, well, thanks, err, yes that would be sensible, I guess. Is it running then?'

'Yes, yes, I've kept it in perfect order. It must be about six months now. I run it round the estate once a week and we have a good mechanic who looks after our cars and tractors. In fact, he used to work here. How about if I collect you and then you could drive it back after dinner?'

'That sounds perfect, thank you so much.'

And so it was arranged and, Michelle had to admit to herself that it was a perfect plan. Not quite as perfect as an invitation to some candle-lit dinner in a chic and intimate little restaurant in Aix... but, well, it would be good to go out and meet the neighbours. At least, she supposed so anyway. She looked under the table at the sleeping dog and smiled. And she did have a beautiful dog. The morning wasn't a complete write-off.

12   'Coco loped behind, barking'

How could it possibly be so difficult to decide what to wear? Michelle looked at the pile of clothes thrown onto her bed. Nothing seemed right. It was ridiculous. How many times had she dressed up for much more important occasions in London... rushed home from work, showered and slipped into a dress and rushed out again. Endless times. Michelle sighed heavily and Coco, the dog sighed too. Michelle smiled and went over to pat the dog. Hmm, well, she just didn't seem to be the sort of dog that would be happy in an outside kennel. Right now she was stretched out full length on a Turkish rug right in front of the long mirror, taking full interest in Michelle's attempts to find the perfect thing to wear to the Gilbert's. Now, it was 6.30 and a decision simply had to be made. Michelle ruffled through the selection of clothes on the bed and pulled out the first dress she had tried on. It really did have to be the midnight blue, simple silk shift dress that she had bought in a sale at Massimo Gutti. She tried it on again and looked at her reflection. It suited her Audrey Hepburn style... not too retro but classic style. OK, so now shoes, she looked longingly at her black patent heels, at least four inches added to her height and, well, Sven was so very tall. She still hesitated, standing in stockinged feet, after all it maybe called a château but then it was also a farm, well, a wine farm she supposed. Questions and answers flicked through her mind and, looking in the mirror again, she had the sudden thought that her father and possibly her mother had also seen their reflections here. The glass was dark and pitted with age and when she screwed up her eyes she could imagine... but she stopped herself. Time was running out and it was no use putting it off any longer. She pulled out her black, patent flat pumps and slipped them on. Dressy, but practical. Then she pulled on a dark, navy cashmere cardigan which gave the dress a more casual look. Without looking in the mirror again she ran out of the room and down the stairs as the front door bell clanged. Coco loped behind barking and skidding to a halt on the marble floor of the hall.

Michelle pulled open the door and was surprised to find a short, stocky man standing there. Coco pushed past Michelle and made a great fuss of the man.

'*Bonsoir Mademoiselle Michelle? Je me presente, Jean-Paul Crozier,*' he gave a little bow, then looked at her closely before bending down to stroke Coco. 'I am chauffeur to the Gilbert. *Eh bien, Coco, calmez-vous, calmez-vous*!'

Michelle tried not to show her surprise and even disappointment not to find Sven on her doorstep. '*Bonsoir, merci...*' With nothing more she could possibly think of to say in English or French, she nodded briskly and walked to the car. Jean-Paul hurried in front of her and opened the rear door. Coco jumped in quickly, obviously more accustomed than Michelle to riding in a chauffeur driven vintage Bentley. The car springs creaked and complained as they made their way down the pot-holed driveway, then gained stately speed as they reached the tarmac road. Just a few minutes later they turned again through the impressive wrought iron gates to Château Gilbert. Here the driveway was smooth gravel, edged with tall cypress trees. Michelle made a mental note to get an estimate for repairing her own drive but, before she could begin to worry about it and a hundred other things that had arisen during the day, they arrived.

Château Gilbert was spectacular, no other word for it. Light shone from every window and the whole façade was softly floodlit. A sweeping stone staircase rose up to huge entrance doors, flanked by flaming torches. Jean-Paul turned the long car in a slow half circle and, with a final scrunch of gravel, pulled to a gentle halt. He sprang from the car and opened the door for Michelle. Coco jumped out first and galloped away to a gate leading to some barns. Michelle walked slowly up the stone staircase, enjoying the magic of the moment. Before she reached the doors, Sven emerged to meet her. Michelle almost giggled aloud to think that she had wondered if she would be over-dressed for a simple dinner at a nearby farm. Sven was wearing a crisp white shirt with gold cufflinks, immaculately tailored, dark navy trousers, his hair perfectly groomed ... hmm, Michelle thought to herself... very dressy casual... quite a look. He greeted her warmly with the obligatory fleeting kiss on each cheek and then escorted her across the hallway. Michelle took in the detail of the décor, Napoleonic splendour would be the best description, she decided, when reporting back to Kelly. Then, Sven was opening another double door and ushering her into a large, high-ceilinged salon. Here, the ivory painted walls were hung with tapestries and lit with candle sconces. They moved into the room and approached a small group of people standing, holding drinks, close to a baronial fireplace.

'May I introduce you, Michelle, first, my mother, Mme. Gilbert. *Maman* this is Michelle de Rosefont.' Michelle hesitated at the sound of her name being changed from Phelps and was about to correct him but the moment passed as a tall and beautiful woman moved to meet her, holding out her hand. They shook hands formally and Michelle was drawn into the group. Sven continued, 'And this is my sister, Gertrud and her husband, Pierre Lalande.' Once again hands were shaken in welcome. 'And finally, last but definitely not least, this is my fiancée, Melissa Brook.'

Michelle held out her hand and felt the young woman's long, slim hand in her own. Fiancée... Michelle struggled to look delighted. Sven moved to stand beside Melissa as though to demonstrate how magnificently they matched. Melissa was very tall, as dark as Sven was blond, and they leant slightly toward each other, both of them elegantly at ease. It was not even that they just looked like celebrities or super-models, they actually exuded wealth and power. Michelle mentally kicked herself for wearing pumps and then, raising her chin high, she pulled herself together and turned toward Mme. Gilbert.

'Thank you so much for inviting me this evening. It was very kind of you, *c'est très gentil de votre part.*' Michelle timidly added the words in French and Mme. Gilbert smiled graciously.
'Not at all, we are delighted to meet you. And you are so obviously the daughter of our dear friend, the late Michel de Rosefont. Astonishing... *l'enfant d'amour... fille comme père!*' Mme. Gilbert raised her hand and gently stroked Michelle's cheek as she continued. 'This must all be so confusing for you, my dear. It is even strange for us. I knew your father for twenty years or more. He was a good friend and neighbour, but always struggling not to show his sadness.'

Michelle dropped her head and looked down at the floor as tears formed in her eyes. This was all too much. One question burned in her mind but she did not have the courage to voice it. Had this woman known her mother when she worked as a nurse at La Bastide de Rosefont? The words could not be formed, so the question remained in her head. She struggled to say anything and silence seemed to fill the large room until the only noise was the crackling fire.

'Now, this just won't do, the poor girl has not even been offered a drink and here we all stand.' The voice that broke the silence was Melissa's and to

Michelle's surprise it came with a strong American drawl. 'For goodness sake, if ever there was a need for a glass of bubbly then this has to be it! Welcome to rural Provence, Michelle!'

They all laughed in relief at the broken silence and Sven poured Michelle a glass of champagne, saying,

'Indeed, it takes my Californian fiancée to bring us all back to order... not to mention letting out the secret that we are drinking champagne and not one of our own fine wines.'

Conversation became more general, slipping back and forth from French to English, and touching on wine and local news. Just as Michelle was thinking if she drank any more without eating she would fall over, Mme. Gilbert came over to her and took her arm.

'I have something for you in my study. Come with me for a moment.'

Michelle followed obediently. There was something in the serious, domineering manner of Mme. Gilbert that made her feel ridiculously childlike and nervous. They entered a smaller room, elegantly furnished and softly lit. Mme. Gilbert crossed to the desk and took a small key from her pocket and opened the top drawer. She took out a small, leather pouch and turned to Michelle, holding it out to her, saying, 'This is yours now, I have been looking after it since your father died.'

Michelle took the small, soft leather bag, realising it was identical to the bag she already had for the Bastide keys.

'Thank you,' Michelle said quietly. 'I think it is similar to the bag that the notaire gave me, more keys?'

'*Mais non, ma chère*, no, no... but that reminds me, I do have some keys for you.' She turned back to the desk drawer and picked up a bunch of keys. 'These are your father's car keys. I think Sven has

Michel's car ready for you but Jean-Paul will bring it round tomorrow.' She replaced the keys on the desk. 'Tonight you must enjoy dining with us and not worry... Jean-Paul will take you home later, *pas de problème!* But the bag is important, you must keep it safely... it is your family jewels.'

Michelle drew in her breath sharply, her head swimming from the champagne and now the shock of Mme. Gilbert's words. Family jewels. But surely not her family... her family was the comfortable life in Sussex with her mother, Anne, and her father, Dr. Robert Phelps. But Mme. Gilbert was still talking.

'You must make sure they are well insured, of course, but keep them safely as the insurance can never replace family history, and your family history is one of the longest in France.'
Michelle managed to mumble her thanks as she slipped the leather pouch into her handbag.

'*Maintenant*, we should go back to the others ... we all need to eat!'
Michelle quietly followed Mme. Gilbert out of the study and back to the party. It seemed that Mme. Gilbert was accustomed to giving orders and being obeyed and Michelle was in no state to do otherwise. There was something vaguely comforting about being told what to do... comforting but also slightly annoying. Why should this haughty woman assume that Michelle was actually part of the Rosefont family? Before Michelle could think any more on the matter, she realised Mme. Gilbert was giving another command, standing in the centre of the group she clapped her hands lightly as she spoke,

'*A table, mes enfants, à table*... come it is time to eat and if we don't begin soon the chef will probably give in his notice.'

She took Michelle's arm again and led her across the room and through another set of double doors into a long dining room. Michelle smiled in appreciation at the décor. She couldn't have done much better herself. Maybe the gilded ceiling was original? She looked up in admiration at the huge crystal chandelier that glowed in the centre... definitely antique Baccarat... the pale olive painted panelled walls, chalky soft matt finish... maybe original or very professionally hand-painted and distressed? She found herself nodding in approval and then realised the rest of the group were waiting for her to take her place at the long table. She was seated beside Mme. Gilbert, who was at the head, and with Sven on her right. The Viking god that she must now accept as off limits and happily engaged to a Californian beauty.

13   'if any girl had ever had a better friend'

'It's so good to hear your crazy London voice, Kelly! I just have so much to tell you... are you busy right now?' Michelle smiled and held her mobile a few inches from her ear as Kelly responded loudly and rudely... well, she had asked for that. Of course the studio was busy. The pace of London seemed a lifetime away as she sat sipping coffee in the morning sun on the terrace.

'And I suppose you are just playing the Marquise card and sipping coffee from a porcelain cup?'

'How did you guess... well, I won't keep you. I just wanted to report back that I had dinner at the Viking's castle last night. But never mind, if you are busy, of course...'

'You didn't! Dinner with the Viking... was it...err...romantic? Cut to the end, I'm too busy for all the erotic detail right now... what happened?'

'Well, dinner was wonderful... his family are very charming and his fiancée totally drop-dead beautiful.'

'His fiancée? Oh dear Lord, there goes the perfect Mills and Boon ending then... damn, I was sure you meant a candlelit supper *à deux*, and that you had made passionate love on a rug in front of a baronial fireplace... oh dear, so, what's she like?'

'Her name is Melissa, she is a six foot Californian golden-tanned beauty, heiress apparently to a vast wine empire... and, oh yes, she's even very nice. In fact, I liked her a lot and we have arranged to go riding later today.'

'Oh, you are so hopeless, Michelle. You're not supposed to like the competition.'

'Oh, I'm not even in the race. They are definitely made for each other. You know, they sort of look at each other when they're talking to anyone else. No, they are just a perfect match. The only thing is... I don't think Mme. Gilbert approves... or her daughter and son-in-law.'

'So what were they like and what made you think that?'

'Well, they're frightfully aristo although Mme. Gilbert said that La Bastide de Rosefont is two hundred years older than their place. My birth father is the old aristocracy and they are post Napoleon.'

'Oh right, really recently rich then, I've heard of nouveau riche but never expected to meet the real thing. But what made you think they didn't approve of Sven's engagement?'

'I don't know how to explain, really, they sort of ganged up and were frightfully snobby. Not exactly dissing the entire United States but as good as. All hidden under impeccable manners, of course.'

'Hmm, I wonder what that means? Probably just the usual French thing I suppose. I'll ask Leon what he thinks. He's not at all typically French. Oh, Mich, you have no idea how much I miss the guy when I'm back here. I just can't wait for Friday. But, in the meantime I have to warn you that the first visit from Seb Raven, the film location scout, will be some time next week.'

'Oh goodness, I had no idea it would be so soon.'

'We have to grab the chance... he's looking at a place in Belgium this week but I think I have him hooked on La Bastide de Rosefont. It has ticked all his boxes on paper. Trees close to the walls, over-run gardens, square turrets, derelict driveway...'

'OK, enough, Kelly. You're reminding me how much I have to do to the place. Last night was a strict lesson on how it should look. Honestly, Kelly, the

Gilbert's place is absolutely perfect. We couldn't have done it better ourselves.'

'Well, I don't think I have ever heard you say that before. But don't worry... with the amount of dosh the film company could throw at us, you should be able to start renovation works. Anyway, must go now... Leon's on the landline. *Au revoir, ma chère marquise*, toodlepip!'

And Kelly was gone. Michelle put down her mobile and sat a moment wondering if any girl had ever had a better friend.

14 'a glass of cold wine'

The Provençal sun had returned in such strength that at the end of the week Michelle was laying a table for dinner on the south terrace. She spread the antique embroidered cloth and began to lay the old silver knives and forks. She had spent the week carefully exploring all the cupboards and drawers in the Bastide. Such treasures she had found she had carefully cleaned and washed. Everything was old, well worn but beautiful. The sort of things that she and Kelly would have sourced in London antique markets and auctions for clients seeking the shabby Château look. Michelle looked across the lawns to the sun setting slowly behind Mont Ste.Victoire and smiled... well, she had the complete shabby Bastide. Coco, stretched at full length on the warm stone flags of the terrace, lazily raised her head.

'You're right, Coco, I think that's a car approaching. Let's go round and look.' The dog jumped up and lolloped ahead of her as they skirted the terrace walls and made their way to the front drive.

'Yes, it's Leon's car. Great, they're early. Now I shall have someone else to talk to apart from you, Coco!' Michelle patted the dog and they waited, side by side as the car drew up.

Kelly was first out of the car. 'Mich, you're standing there outlined against the sunset, ready for the film cameras to roll... but do tell me...who is your new squeeze?'

'This is Coco, yes, definitely my new love... isn't she gorgeous?' Mich rested her hand on the dog's head. Kelly was already squatting down on the terrace and stroking the dog. 'Oh, Mich, he's so, so beautiful! Is he really yours?'

'Well, yes, I have sort of adopted her from Sven. Apparently she's gun shy and no good as a hunting dog.'

'Perfect then.' Kelly said enthusiastically as she stood up. 'I think it's very clever to be shy of guns and I don't think we shall be hunting with or without him.'

Leon joined them and took over admiring the dog.'He's a she, actually, Kelly you know nothing... and a real classic beauty. Pure bred Braque Gascogne, a fabulous dog.' Leon nodded appreciatively. 'And, *peutêtre*... maybe a good guard dog, too.' They all looked down doubtfully at the large dog who had now rolled onto her back on the gravel as Leon tickled her chest.

'Hmm, maybe... I'm not sure. I haven't actually had any visitors to test her out. Well, actually I did have one visitor, Jean-Paul. He's the Gilberts' chauffeur or mechanic or something. Anyway he used to work for my... for Michel de Rosefont.' Michelle hesitated in confusion. She glanced at Kelly and knew that her friend would know she had been about to say 'my father'. It still seemed a strange disloyalty and the word stuck in her throat. She continued hurriedly, 'Anyway, he brought this old car round and apparently it's mine.'

'Old car, how old, Michelle?' Leon said excitedly. 'I love old cars. Where is it now, can we go and see it?'

'Boys and their toys, eh!' Kelly sighed dramatically. 'I swear Leon knows every old car on the road. Come on then, let's get it over with, let's go look and then perhaps we can have a glass of wine.'

The three friends strolled over to the huddle of old barns and stables. Michelle pulled open the large double doors of the first barn and they peered into the gloom, then Leon gave a low whistle of approval, *'Quelle bagnolle! C'est magnifique!'*

'*Magnifique!*' Both girls chorused, looking at each other and pulling faces of exaggerated despair.

'It's a beauty, Michelle, and in concours condition. A perfect Citroen DS ID 19 Break, probably 1961, yes, it must be. Look at the bodywork! Impeccable!' Leon prowled round the car, examining it closely and then stood back, 'Do you have the *carte grise*? What do you say in English... er, the paperwork of registration?'

'Oh yes, all the papers were in the glove box. I had to take them to the notaire and the insurance agent. I put all our names on the insurance so you can drive it too.'

'*Mon dieu!* Indeed, it would be amazing!' Leon opened the door and looked in the glove box and took out the wallet of papers and began to look through them. Kelly opened the passenger door and slipped into the front seat.

'Hmm, actually I do approve of the I creamy pink coachwork... and the seats are beautiful tan leather and so well-polished... I can actually smell lavender polish... and the walnut dashboard...fabulous! Yes, I have to agree with you, Leon, it is a wonderful old jalopy.'

'Jalopy, I know not this word, jalopy but wait a moment. This is interesting... well, amazing. The car was bought in 1961 by Michel de Rosefont. Imagine... all that time and one owner... *c'est formidable!*'

'Oh really, Leon, I'm getting tired of the say game. Why do the French say c'est over and over again? All I can say is that it may be lovely but it is also huge. You could get a double bed in the back! But how does it drive, Mich. It must be hell to park.'

'Well, I've only driven it to Aix a couple of times and then to the village and back. That caused a bit of a stir. I parked outside the Spar shop and when I was in the queue, several people came over to me and introduced themselves. It seems that my ... er... Michel was not very popular locally. From what I could understand, anyway. The guy behind the cash desk seemed thoroughly rude. He was muttering something about *'les anglais'* and *'étrangers',* but I couldn't understand really.'

Leon turned quickly from admiring the car and looked at Michelle, saying, *'Un paysan sans terre...* he thinks only of his own small world. You know, some of these small villages are cut off from the world around. They resent intrusion and do not think of the profits from tourism. If Picasso had not purchased his huge Château here on Mont Sainte Victoire the villages around would be even poor than they are.'

'That's interesting! I didn't know about Picasso's Château. We must visit it!' Michelle and Kelly exchanged glances.

'Definitely, it would be great for adding to our trips for art lovers staying at the Château.' Kelly's face was full of enthusiasm and Michelle added.

'Exactly what I was thinking.'

'You two girls always think the same!' Leon laughed, 'But I'm not sure the Château is open to the public all the time. Maybe for special events... I shall find out for you.'

'Thanks, Leon, there must be so much we have to research locally. But I hope it doesn't upset any of the locals. I mean we are intruding really.'

'Don't worry, that is a path I can smooth for you. You will need staff and there is a big need for employment so I am sure you will soon be more popular than your father... I mean... Michel de Rosefont.'

There was a moment's awkward silence, then Kelly jumped out of the car and slipped her arm through Michelle's, leading her away from the barn.

'Come on, Mich, let's go have a glass of cold wine. All this new family history is getting to me and goodness knows how it must be for you. I guess you will have to get used to calling this Marquis guy your father at some point.'

Michelle looked gratefully at Kelly, she always did understand and not only about their shared business interests.

'I know, it's just that it sort of seems wrong and disloyal to my Dad' Michelle said miserably.

'Well, cheer up, girl. You can just call him Michel or Marquis or Papa... or Father Christmas if you want... or anything else you can dream up. You know and I know that Dr Robert Phelps is absolutely your father and has been all your life.'

'That's true, Kelly, exactly.' Michelle nodded her head and brushed away a tear.

Kelly continued, 'Mind you, I wouldn't object to having two or three fathers if they all gave me a Bastide or a few vintage cars. Now, for God's sake, can we have that sun-downer?'

They all laughed and walked back to the Bastide and then made their way round to the south terrace where Michelle had left glasses and a bottle of rosé wine in an ice bucket. Leon uncorked the bottle and filled the glasses. The rosy tinted sky reflected the wine and the cicadas began their evening song.

'This is paradise, Mich, don't you think. Heaven on earth!' Kelly sipped the wine and closed her eyes in approciation, then added, 'But have you been lonely here on your own, Mich? Is it spooky?'

'Well, no, not really, in some strange way I feel quite at home here. I have been so busy that the week has flashed by. As I said, I went to Aix twice this week for business appointments and I have been round at the Gilberts' and riding with Melissa.'

'Riding with the Californian fiancée... sounds fun if only her fiancé didn't happen to be the man you fancied. Ah well, business appointments sounds more like the Michelle, I know. What have you been up to, Mich?'

'Actually Melissa is really nice and we had a good chat after our ride. I don't think she gets on very well with Mme. Gilbert and she misses her own life in the States. She wants Sven to live over there when they are married. Anyway, the business appointments were all boring stuff really. I met the accountant who handles the Rosefont account, the insurance agency, then I went to old Xavier again for more paperwork and signing everything in triplicate, then the bank manager ... and he doesn't speak a word of English. I have so much to tell you and that's before I begin to tell you about the bag of jewels. Anyway, let's drink up and then eat, everything is ready.'

'Did you just say...bag of jewels?' Kelly's voice rose in excitement. 'Oh my sweet Lord, Mich, family heirlooms? Show me, show me!'

'Kelly, sit down and relax for a moment. As I said, let's drink the wine and then have a bite to eat. I have so much to tell you but we'll eat pizza and salad first. OK?'

'Ah, I see you are beginning to understand the Provençal slow way of living, Michelle. Felicitations!' Leon raised his glass to Michelle and they all sat quietly finishing the bottle of wine until the sun sank behind the bulk of Mont Ste.Victoire.

'I just can't believe how much you have done this week, Mich!'

It was an hour later, still warm enough to be outside and tiny bright stars were beginning to stud the dark sky. Leon lit all the candles in the large gilded candelabra that they had brought outside. Kelly spread her arms wide as she spoke.

'And we are certainly sitting more comfortably, these cushions are a vast improvement to the terrace chairs.'

'I bought them in a chain store in Aix...oh, you haven't seen our new office chairs yet. I found a small designer store and bought four sumptuous ivory leather office chairs... Danish, of course. It suddenly seemed important to have something bright and brand new amongst all these valuable antiques.' Michelle said.

'Antiques and now jewels!'

They all looked at the jewellery spread out on the white tablecloth, sparkling and glinting in the light shed from the candles.

'I think this is my favourite!' Kelly picked up a large pendant and held it up. The dark red stone glowed with fire as she turned it round. 'Do you think it's a ruby?'

'I love this ring' Michelle said, slipping it on her finger. 'The dark gold setting is so beautiful... it looks very old.' She took off the ring and began to replace all the jewellery into the leather pouch.

'Whatever are you going to do with them, Mich? You can't cart them around in your handbag all day and under your pillow every night... it's ridiculous. I mean they might be incredibly valuable.'

'I know, I'm having them valued on Monday at a jewellers in Aix... then I thought I could leave them at the bank...' Michelle looked from Kelly to Leon, then added doubtfully, 'or sell them, I suppose.'

'No, no you can't do that!' Kelly and Leon responded in one voice. Then Leon added.

'It would be a shame to sell jewels that have been in your family for years, possibly hundreds of years.'

'But that's the point, I really don't think the jewels are from my family... I mean, my family, my real family is the very ordinary Phelps one in London.'

'I can really get that, Mich, I mean, I know your family life... all your life. This Bastide stuff is way confusing... but on the other hand it is a huge adventure handed to you on a plate and you have never been the girl to turn down a challenge.'

'Thanks, Kelly, and you too, Leon. You do help keep things in perspective... at least a bit!'

'Always ready to bring you back to dull planet earth, my dear Marquise, but now, continue the fairytale...tell us more about the car...does it turn into a pumpkin at midnight?'

'Does it run as well as it looks?' Leon asked, 'Shall I take a look at it tomorrow?'

'Thanks, but *pas de problème* as the Gilberts keep saying. Apparently Sven has had it serviced and he has driven it round the block once a week.'

'By round the block, she means around her lands, Leon. That's not an idiom but more idiotic London girl talk.' Kelly sighed in mock despair as she continued, 'And talking of lands... have you found out how much of France you own yet? It's just the sort of thing a girl should know!'

'Well, yes, actually... apparently being a Marquis or Marquise is something to do with owning lands on the edge of a county which is also why this is a fortified Bastide and not a Château. Mme. Gilbert said that their family was less important than the Rosefont family, although they have been gaining land... partly through marriages... for the last two centuries.'

'OK, sorry I asked!' Kelly interrupted, 'Cut to the chase... how much land have you inherited, Mich. It's a need to know thingy!'

'The notaire has checked the deeds of the lands to be two hundred hectares... I've looked it up... it's just under five hundred acres.' Michelle's words fell into a shocked silence as she continued. 'Apart from the vines and the forest... there are seven hundred and fifty olive trees.'

Leon gave a low whistle and Kelly drew in her breath sharply and then said, 'Oh my god, Mich, that must be a hell of a lot of wine and olive oil... what will you do? I mean, I like a drink and a good salad dressing as much as the next girl... but seriously, it will have to be managed... or farmed or something or other. You don't even like gardening.'

'Well, the lands are all leased out to the Gilberts and that provides the only income connected to La Bastide de Rosefont. Old Maitre Xavier kept shaking his head and looking worried about that... apparently Mme. Gilbert had been trying to persuade my father to sell out to them but he had always refused. I mean my birth father.' Michelle added the last few words hurriedly. This was the first time she had slipped into using the word 'father' for Michel de Rosefont. She caught Kelly's glance and knew again that her friend understood completely. Michelle looked up at the sky. The stars were now shining so brightly that the midnight blue sky was filled with light and the new moon hung over all, a pale glowing crescent. Everything was over-whelming and in the warm night air, Michelle shivered and pulled her cardigan around her shoulders. Then Kelly spoke again.

'Well, Mich, you've really done it this time. I mean you've dropped me in some crazy projects but this beats all. Anyway, just to let you know, I think it's all simply fantastic and I'm going to help you all the way.'

'*Moi aussi*, and me. If I can help in any way I would be happy.' Leon said quietly.

Michelle smiled at them both gratefully.

'What would I do without you two? You're right, Kelly, it is fantastic and it is a huge challenge. I guess

I am still trying to believe it all. I'm getting over the idea that I am some sort of impostor here and that it really does all belong to me. Somehow I will make it work. I do have some ideas... but first of all, tell me about this film scout, Kelly.'

'I thought you'd never ask! The deal is practically wrapped. Just waiting for a visit from Seb Raven next Wednesday as he gives the final okay. I showed him all the photos and film of the place... I pulled together a wonderful presentation, although I say so myself.'

'I didn't even know you had taken any photos or film footage.' Michelle said.

'Well, Leon took most of it. I just found the spookiest parts of the Bastide . You know, atmospheric cobwebs, dried up fountain and cracked window panes... oh yes, and he loved the tall trees in the circular forest on the north side. I'll show you later. He also let drop that the Belgium château that they have been considering doesn't really have room to park all their trucks and huge pantechnicons and stuff. You have masses of parking around the barns and even in front of the Bastide.'

'Pantechnicons... oh my god, will they be able to get up the drive?' Michelle said in alarm.

'You know it wouldn't cost the earth to throw some gravel along that.' Leon said thoughtfully. '*Je connais un mec*... I know a guy in Aix who made good my family's farm drive. It might be worth it?'

The three friends sat close over the table and, in the light of the new moon, they made plans for new life at La Bastide de Rosefont.

15 'every inch of her long tanned legs'

Michelle took a deep breath and relaxed her shoulders. Coco walked over and stood close, leaning against her.

'You're a natural poser, Coco.' Michelle rested her hand on the dog's head. 'And you're the perfect height. I can just stand here playing the part of the Marquise de Rosefont and not even bend over to rest my hand on your noble head.'

It was Wednesday morning and Kelly had called from Aix station to say that she was on her way with Seb Raven. The last few days had flown by at the speed of light and now, if a shabby Bastide could ever be said to be ready, then La Bastide de Rosefont was the one. It was a perfect September day, the sky bluer than was possible anywhere other than Provence. Michelle breathed in the pure air laden with the perfume of wild herbs and quietly wondered if now she could ever live anywhere else. Then she heard the sound of a car making its way slowly over the pot-holed drive. Michelle stood at the top of the steps and waited. A chauffeur-driven limousine rounded the final corner and drew up in front of the Bastide . Kelly jumped out as soon as the car stopped, she was wearing an immaculate close-fitting white dress, short enough to show every inch of her long tanned legs but with a demure high square neckline. Michelle smiled to herself... hmm, perfect choice. Then a short, thick-set man emerged from the far side of the car. He was casually dressed in typical American Ivy League style, chinos, a short-sleeved cotton shirt and loafers. He stood still a moment, then slowly looked around in silence for several minutes, and finally said,

'This is great, I mean it's just fantastic, Kelly, how on earth did you find it?' The man's voice was loud and with a strong American accent. He paced around the dilapidated fountain and then turned and saw Michelle standing with Coco.

'Oh, sorry, you have to excuse me, I just didn't see you there. I guess the setting just got to me.'

Michelle walked down the steps with Coco close at her heels. 'Not at all,' she said, her voice sounding more cool English than ever before. 'Welcome, *bienvenu à La Bastide de Rosefont*!' Now she sounded like Marie Antoinette. Michelle exchanged glances with Kelly and nearly burst out laughing. But, Kelly took up the same game, as she said formally,

'May I introduce you to Michelle, Marquise de Rosefont, Michelle this is Seb Raven, location manager for FGM films.'

'Pleased to meet you... Marquise. Thanks for inviting me. Why, you're English... that's kinda a surprise and a great relief... I don't speak a word of French!'

Michelle shook his outstretched hand and held Coco's collar with the other. The large dog was giving a very low growl.

'And this is Coco, who seems to think she should pretend to be a guard dog.' Michelle smiled as she spoke. Seb Raven leaned forward and patted the dog gently and stroked her ears.

'No worries, Coco, you're doing a grand job. But while you're still wagging that tail I guess I'm not too scared!'

They all laughed and the atmosphere became more relaxed as they walked up the steps and into the cool of the entrance hall.

'Oh my god, does this have the wow factor or not?' Seb's strong voice seemed to ricochet around the walls as he moved into the centre of the hall.

Michelle had arranged the long, louvred shutters to be half open, so that the strong sunlight fell in shafts of light across the black and white marble floor and over to the foot of stone staircase.

'I'm not going to pretend, ladies! This is amazing and, if it goes on ticking all my boxes and we can come to terms, then I think I can say that Vampire Revolution is going to be filmed right here.' He gave a resounding clap of his hands and then turned a full circle with his arms spread wide, as if to encompass the whole scene.

By the end of the day, both Kelly and Michelle were exhausted by Seb's endless enthusiasm. They stood side by side with Coco between them, once again at the top of the steps as, with fixed smiles on their faces, they waved farewell until he disappeared back down the drive in his chauffeur driven limo. The minute the car was out of sight, Kelly sat down on the top step.

'Phew, what have we started, Mich?' she said, stretching her back and looking up at Michelle.

'Well, it's simply amazing, really Kelly, and all down to you. But yes, he certainly knows how to work a day through. If only he'd call me Michelle and not Marquise... that's all your fault... I'm exhausted. Let's take a bottle of cold rosé out on the terrace.' She held out her hand and pulled Kelly to her feet. 'You can't sit there... you'll ruin your white dress and imagine what the neighbours will think!' They both laughed as they looked around them.

'Sure thing, Marquise!' Kelly drawled in a mock American accent. 'With only three hundred acres around us...' she stopped abruptly and dropped the accent. 'It's not just exhaustion from Seb's gushing enthusiasm... I think I'm in shock from the huge amount of money you screwed out of him. Do you realise you almost doubled his first offer?'

'Well, he kept agreeing so easily I just decided to go for it. I mean, he made no secret of the fact he wanted to film here. Come on, Kelly, let's drink a toast to vampires and zombies whilst we watch the sun set.'

Kelly stayed on the rest of the week and the two friends had plenty of time to talk, somehow falling back into their usual pattern of working together, even though they were in Provence and not in Chelsea.

'You know what, Mich? I have a big idea...'

They were sitting in the office that Michelle had taken over for their working studio. The large desk and leather armchair remained in a corner, but now there were four ultra-modern Danish office chairs placed at a long oak table right under the window. This was laid out with drawing boards, modern desk lights, four laptops, a printer and telephones. The girls were seated here and looking idly out the window to the sun-drenched vines.

'Funny, so do I, but I have been mulling it over and sort of delaying putting it to you. It's only an outline idea, of course.' Michelle tapped her pencil on the table and looked nervously at Kelly.

'Oh God, you sound so serious. When have you ever hesitated telling me anything? Well, it can't be about Sven, the man of your dreams.' Kelly laughed and didn't notice Michelle blushing.

'Definitely not the man of my dreams... just a dream man who happens to be my neighbour and happily engaged anyway.' Michelle answered quickly, trying not to recall the graphic detail of her erotic dream. 'Anyway, you go first, tell me your idea.'

'OK, if you're ready ... well, I think we should sell up the studio in Chelsea. There you are, I've said it!'

'I don't believe it! That's exactly what I was going to say, too. I just never thought you would even want to consider it.' Michelle looked at Kelly in surprise.

'Well, it's partly selfish, I guess. But you must have realised by now that I really am in deep with Leon. I mean, it's not a fling... it's the real thing... and we want to be together all the time.'

'Of course, of course... I quite get it... and allow me to be deeply jealous. No, seriously, Kelly, I can tell it's different... you've never been like this with anyone before.'

'Well, you can't say I haven't tested the market...but we're actually thinking of getting engaged.'

'Fantastic, I think he's a really great guy. Kind and sweet but no walkover...he keeps you in order.'

'I'm really glad you approve... it's important to me. But getting back to the business side of things. You know the temp I employed for the last few chaotic weeks? Well, you don't know her, of course, but anyway, she's mad keen on our work and her Daddy just happens to be mega-rich. To cut a long story short, I think he might buy us out and put his spoiled daughter straight into our hard-working shoes. I mean, she's quite good at the job and has all the right contacts with the Chelsea set... she might even have a slim chance of making it work. What do you think?'

'Wow, you have been busy. Well, I am a bit shocked. I mean, we have also worked our socks off in those hard-working shoes,' Michelle sighed as she thought of all the hours they had spent building up the client list. 'and its still in its infancy as a business... but now all this...' Michelle waved her hand around in the air above her head and then pointed out the window to the vineyards stretching away to the mountain.

'If I'm to make a go of it, I need every scrap of energy... to be honest I was hoping yours too. My idea was that you and Leon might throw in your lot with mine. We could set up a new company with the three of us as directors.'

'Fantastic, we could use the film company as our first client and go on from there. Leon and I will find a flat or something in Aix...' Before Kelly could finish, Michelle interrupted.

'I don't suppose you would consider a barn conversion here or an attic flat? I mean, this is a big place for a lonely spinster.'

'Wow, that sounds too good to be true. Let's wait until Leon gets here later and we'll talk it through. I'm having to get used to the idea of not making snap decisions for myself. Now we'd better get back to some of the queries that Seb Raven emailed this morning. What did you think of him, Mich?'

Michelle thought for a moment, doodling a drawing of Seb on the design pad in front of her.

'Well, he's certainly a workaholic... even worse than us, I should think. I mean, he just didn't stop all day. Even through lunch, he talked FGM film business non-stop. He didn't even come up for air. And talk, I've never known a man talk so much...'

'Did you like him then?' Kelly interrupted.

'Oh for god's sake, Kelly, I know where you're heading. No, I did not fancy him!'

Kelly laughed, 'Well, I just thought I'd ask. I can usually tell when you're interested in someone but you were so set in your charmingly polite Marquise role that I hardly recognised you all day... well, until it came to negotiating. Then I think he was quite surprised that the cool elegant Marquise could haggle like a street market stall-holder.'

Michelle laughed too, 'Well, as I said, he didn't put up much resistance to the price hike. But, oh my God, if only he wouldn't call me Marquise every two minutes!'

'I know, it was just too funny, and the way he drew out the word, Maqueeeese, rhyming with cheese. I think he just loved the foreign sound of it. And he was obviously smitten with you. Nodding and agreeing with every word that dropped from your aristocratic lips. Holy Moly, I don't know how I kept a straight face.'

'Stop, stop, and Kelly, just because you're in love you don't have to imagine every man that crosses my path is going to be my romantic hero. Anyway, it's not Sven and it's certainly not Seb. So calm down and let's get back to work. As if I would have time for romance anyway with all this going on.'

Kelly sighed, 'But it's just so wonderful being in love, Mich. I had no idea until I met Leon. Every time I think of him I just melt, It's not just romantic, it's sort of comforting too.'

'Well, that's sweet, Kelly and I am very happy for you but right now could you please concentrate on not melting and get back to the list of queries?'

'Yes, yes, I know, and there are some really big issues to think through. For starters, can we let them use the paddock for their vehicles and trailers, do we have a suitable area for helicopter landing, do we want to handle the catering for a crew of fifty, will we be able to extend the six month rental time if they over-run shooting? Do we Mich?'

The girls both burst out laughing as they knew the answers. Once again they would jump in the deep end and say yes, yes, yes and yes.

16   'the strap of her nightdress'

Michelle ran but her legs were heavy, as though she was running in deep water. Seb Raven was running after her, getting nearer. She dared not turn round but she could hear his heavy footsteps on the gravel. She ran round the fountain, trying to reach the steps to the Bastide before he could catch hold of her.

'*Marquise, Marquise*, wait, I just want to talk!' Still she tried to run faster, not believing his words. He wanted more than to talk to her, she knew. Fear clutched at her as she felt his hand reach out and catch the strap of her nightdress. The silk ribbon tore away from the lace bodice and she made a desperate attempt to escape his hand as it reached for her bare breast. She tried to scream but her voice had lost all power.

'*Marquise. Marquise.*' His voice was closer, loud in her ear, and she could feel his breath hot on her skin. Then Coco was there, galloping down the steps and barking, barking...
Michelle awoke. Hot and befuddled. Her dream still stronger than reality. Slowly her heartbeat calmed down and then she realised that Coco really was barking. She rose from the tangled sheets of her bed, pulled her long hair back and took a deep breath. Then, hastily pulling on her silk dressing gown, she went to the door and opened it cautiously. Coco had recently taken to sleeping outside her bedroom door on the landing. But Coco was not there and the barking seemed to come from the kitchen. Michelle ran quickly down the long staircase and into the hall. She grabbed a heavy candlestick from the entrance table and ran along the long stone-flagged corridor and into the kitchen. Coco turned quickly to look at

her but continued madly barking at the back door. Michelle approached the door, holding tight to the candlestick.

'Who's there?' her voice was still dry from her nightmare and she repeated louder, 'Who's there?'

'Michelle, it's me, Dad!'

Michelle laughed with relief and began to pull back the bolts on the heavy oak door. Calming Coco and holding her firmly by the collar, she undid the final lock with the key and opened the door. There, indeed, stood her father.

'Well, this is a fine sight! My daughter holding a hound in one hand and a candlestick in the other. Are you going for the Gothic look?' Coco had stopped barking and was now welcoming Dr Phelps by circling around excitedly. Michelle gave her father a big hug, nearly crying with the relief of the moment.

'Great Scott, this is a better welcome than I was expecting, but do you think you should put down that large candlestick before you do harm?'

Michelle laughed and with her arm still around her father, led him into the kitchen, Coco still bouncing in excited circles around them.

'Oh Dad, it's so great to see you... I thought you weren't coming until next weekend?'

'Well, I had the clever idea of jumping ship in Marseilles. There's another ship's doctor on board and two nurses so I really wasn't needed for the last stretch back to Southampton. But tell me... where did this beautiful dog come from?'

'This is Coco,' at the sound of her name Coco wagged her tail and looked up at Michelle with adoring eyes. 'I have adopted her from the Gilberts', my neighbours and tenants. Well, the Château next door.'

'What an excellent idea, she makes a good companion and an excellent guard dog. Although you did look terrified...'

Michelle hurriedly interrupted her father, 'Oh, that's just because I woke from a horrid nightmare.'

'Oh dear, you had a nightmare when I was last here. It's probably all the sudden changes in your life and your subconscious is trying to work them all out for you. Can you remember what it was all about? It may help to talk about it.'

'Oh, don't worry, Dad' Michelle went across to the stove to put the kettle on. She could certainly remember every vivid detail of the dream. 'It was just one of those dreams where you try to run but your legs won't work... sort of panic. But it's all ridiculous and anyway, you're here now.' She turned back to her father and gave a big smile. 'But you must be exhausted,Dad, it's just gone five o'clock. Have you had any sleep and how did you get here?'

'Well, I arranged a car with a driver from the port but I thought it would take much longer. Sorry to wake you.'

'Don't worry about that, I was glad to wake up. There is so much to do that I am usually up about six anyway. It's such a beautiful part of the day here.'

'I hadn't realised how close to the Mediterranean coast this place is. You know, Michelle, you have inherited an amazing property. I know it's greatly in need of renovation but if location is everything then it couldn't be better. Ah, the smell of fresh coffee, now that's just what the doctor ordered!'

Michelle carefully placed two large cups of frothy, milky coffee on a tray and said, quietly,

'I know Dad, location, location, location... but let's go out on the terrace, the sun is coming up now and I want you to see how beautiful the dawn is in Provence... and I have so much to tell you.'

17   'my degree was forensic psychology'

'I just can't believe it's called '*pissaladière*'... that's a ridiculous Frenchy name for what is almost a pizza. Mmm, it's so delicious though.' Kelly took a large bite out of the crisp slice of pastry and continued talking with her mouth full. 'Mmm, so yummy... much better than pizza.'

They were all sitting in the shade of the terrace enjoying a quick lunch. The morning had passed in a flurry of exchanged news. Kelly had related all the details of her contract with the film company, Michelle had updated on her week spent at the Bastide, Leon had told of his local research and comparison of hotels in the area and Dr Phelps, who was now happily ensconced as one of the team, brought good news about his cruise company being interested in including the Bastide in their art visits.

'But then I had no idea that La Bastide de Rosefont was so near the Mediterranean coast.' Dr Phelps sat back in his chair and laughed, 'That's how I ended up arriving at the ungodly hour of five a.m.! I thought the taxi would be at least a two hour run. Anyway, it's a great location. I have already spoken to the boss lady who runs the whole show. She's very excited. She's talking of including two nights in a Provençal Bastide, whenever the liner docks at Marseilles. The Provençal Bastide being, of course... your very own Bastide de Rosefont.'

Kelly clapped her hands excitedly. 'That could be perfect, Robert, if we rake in as much money as we can from the film company, then clear up the Vampire mess and renovate the old Bastide with the dosh. We should be able to make at least ten luxurious suites on the first floor alone.'

'Hold on, wait a moment' Michelle interrupted, 'This is getting out of hand. How can I expect you all to pitch in like this?'

'Because we want to.' Leon spoke quietly. 'Kelly and I have talked of nothing else.'

'So we set up a company and Bastide de Rosefont is managing director.' laughed Robert Phelps. 'You two girls know more about business than I do but I am happy to sell up my house in Sussex if it helps.'

'Dad you love that place, you and Mum have done so much to it... and the garden.'

'I know, sweetheart, it's true. It has been a wonderful home, but ever since your dear mother passed away... and you so busy in London, well, I have found it very difficult to be there alone. That's partly why I took on the cruise ship work... it gets me away from the dreadful loneliness of the place.'

Michelle looked at her father, suddenly realising how selfish she had been. Thinking always of how she missed her mother and not thinking how hard it was for her father. She reached out and took his hand.

'Maybe Bastide de Rosefont can be good for all of us. One of my ideas is that the whole top floor, all the attics should be turned into three apartments. One for Kelly and Leon, one for me and one for you, Dad. I had hoped you would be able to spend as much time as possible here but, of course, if you sold the house in Sussex you could make this your base.'

'I want to say something,' Leon spoke quietly again, looking down at his empty plate and seeming embarrassed, 'I feel I am not ...err... how do you say *amenant à la table*... bringing to the table... I have nothing to offer.'

'On the contrary, Leon,' Robert answered quickly and in a stern voice. 'You are the only one in this new team of four who knows anything about the local area, the Provençal traditions, even the language. How could we manage without you?'

'Dad's absolutely right, Leon, we all depend on you.' Michelle added. 'You are all very kind and I hope is true all you say... also I think my education... *mon lauréat en psychologie*... perhaps is useful?'

'You have a degree in psychology, do you? How did you move on to work as a detective?' Robert Phelps sat forward in his chair, his face alight with interest.

'Well, my degree was forensic psychology... and I have a natural inclination for finding the truth, I suppose. I began with a few cases of missing persons and then... somehow it became what I was doing... it was not exactly … err…*mon but de la vie*... my aim in life but... ' Leon faltered to a halt and Kelly sprang up suddenly from her chair and landed herself on Leon's lap and threw her arms around him, saying,

'And now you have met me... and I am your entire reason to live... even I know that in French... your raison d'être! Apart from which, if you weren't here, then I wouldn't be here and Michelle and her Dad would be up a creek without a paddle... to put it politely.'

Leon gave her a hug and said, 'I am guessing this creek paddle thing is another idiom... now I begin to know when I hear one even though I do not understand.'

They all laughed and returned to their planning... happily oblivious to the trouble that was lying in wait

18   'a stream of angry French'

It was Sunday morning, the sun shone out of a cloudless blue sky and they were all enjoying breakfast on the terrace when suddenly Coco sprang to her feet, barking loudly. She rushed from under the table, pulling the edge of the tablecloth and scattering cups, glasses and plates around her as she galloped round the house in the direction of the front door. Michelle ran after her, ignoring the broken crockery and spilt coffee and orange juice. Leon followed and caught up as she reached the front steps. Now, Coco was barking ferociously at a small battered grey 2cv van that was parked beside the derelict fountain. Michelle ran forward and held the dog's collar, pulling her away. The driver wound down his window and shouted a stream of angry French and threw a cigarette stub onto the gravel. Leon now stepped forward and spoke calmly, but the man in the van was spitting with rage. He spoke so fast and with such fury that Michelle could not understand a word. Leon was now replying angrily and pointing to the driveway. Suddenly, the driver wrenched the wheel and turned a tight circle, skidding in the loose gravel and then headed straight toward Michelle, where she stood by the steps, restraining Coco. As the van gathered speed she jumped onto the steps, pulling the dog with her. The driver gave a vicious turn to the wheel and the van mounted the first step, missing Michelle and Coco by inches. Michelle fell back and lay along the second step, clutching Coco as the van skidded away, spraying gravel. Leon ran over to her and helped her to her feet as the van disappeared down the driveway.

'*Ça va*, are you all right, Michelle?' Leon put his arm around her shoulders and then held the dog who was still straining to chase the van.

'Yes, yes, I think so, I've just grazed my elbow as I fell back.'

At that moment, Kelly and Doctor Phelps rounded the corner and ran over to them.

'What the hell's going on?' Kelly shrieked.

'Are you all right, Michelle? Let me look at your arm. Can you walk. Better go inside and wash that cut right away. Any other injuries?' Robert Phelps ran a professional eye over Michelle. 'You'll probably have a few bruises falling on the stone edge like that... whatever happened?'

They all moved slowly up the steps and into the cool of the hall. Michelle looked at Leon and said, 'That's the thing... I have no idea. I mean this madman drives up to the front door, shouts for five minutes and then tries to run me over... and poor Coco.' She stroked the dog's head and it attempted to lick her grazed arm.

'Well, I'm afraid it's an old wives' tale that dog lick is good for cuts.' Robert spoke kindly but firmly and steered Michelle towards the staircase, 'So let's go up to the bathroom... I have my medical bag upstairs and I'll put a dressing on that elbow.'

'Shall I come up with you, are you shaky Mich?' Kelly spoke quietly and took Michelle's hand, her usual happy face was quiet and concerned.

'No, I'm fine ... just a bit shaken and completely puzzled.' Michelle turned to look at Leon. 'I mean. What was he shouting?'

Before Leon could answer, Kelly spoke quickly. 'Your Dad's right, Mich. Go and have a wash and brush up and Leon and I will clear up the breakfast disaster and have a large pot of strong English tea waiting for you when you come down again. Go on, follow the doctor's orders.'

So, it was at a clean tablecloth and with cups of tea that they were soon listening to Leon's explanation.

'He is the man that runs the Spar grocery in the village.' Leon began.

'Of course, I didn't recognise him.' Michelle interrupted. 'I told you he seemed rude when I went in to buy some coffee. I couldn't understand him then and I certainly didn't get a word of what he was shouting at me just now.'

'You didn't forget to pay, did you, Mich? Seems a rather excessive response if so!' Kelly said and they all laughed.

'Well, it was probably a good thing you do not understand all he said... and I am not talking about idioms, you understand. He used some very bad language and a lot of Provençal dialect. But the point he wanted to make was serious, I suppose...although ridiculous...' Leon looked down at his tea cup and looked embarrassed.

'Leon, whatever do you mean?' Kelly reached out her hand and rested it on Leon's shoulder. 'It must be hard to be translator but you must tell us what he said. No good hiding anything.'

Leon looked up and then nodded, as though Kelly's words had given him strength to continue. 'Well, the man, apparently called Pascal Mazin, yes, this man from the Spar shop... *alors*... he says he is the illegitimate son of Michel de Rosefont and that you, Michelle have no right to be here and that Bastide de Rosefont belongs to him.'

There was a united gasp and intake of breath from Michelle, her father and Kelly and then a beat in the silent moment of time as they all tried to take in Leon's words.

Kelly was the first to speak. 'But Michelle had a DNA test... I mean the notaire said... did you tell him that, Leon?'

'No, I said nothing, except told him to leave.' Leon replied.

'Very wise, Leon. That was the best thing to do. In my experience, anyone that angry would not listen to logic. You acted very well.'

'Except then he tried to run over Michelle. It was horrendous, he swung the van round and drove straight at her.' Leon shuddered and put his head in his hands.

Michelle patted him on the back. 'You are more shocked than I am, Leon. I was safe on the second step... and poor Coco.' Michelle leaned down and stroked the dog's head, where she had resumed his usual place under the table. 'But can you explain anything else he said at all...apart from swearing?'

'Well, there was something about his poor dead mother... and that he had never been recognised as Michel de Rosefont's son. He kept saying *'trop, c'est trop'*... er... that enough is enough... and then there was a lot of swearing about foreigners, the English in particular, destroying the local life... oh yes, ruining his farm. Another thing I noticed was that he reeked of alcohol even though it was early morning. Certainly he has problems.' Leon ended, shaking his head as though in disbelief.

'I see. Well, that could account for the irrational behaviour if he was drunk at nine in the morning. Maybe he had been drinking all night.' Robert said.

'Even so!' Kelly interrupted, 'I can confess to having been up all night dancing and drinking...' she glanced hurriedly at Leon and gave a wide smile, ' in the distant past of my wild youth, of course, but I can't remember ever driving drunk, let alone driving straight at someone. He's insane.'

'But supposing it is true.' Michelle spoke quietly and, before anyone had time to reply, Coco stood up, not quite dislodging the tablecloth, and began to bark and wag her tail.

'Now what?' Michelle grabbed her collar as the dog was about to gallop off again.

Robert and Leon both stood up quickly. 'You stay here with Coco, we'll go and see who it is now.' Robert spoke firmly as Michelle began to stand.

'Good idea, guys. Off you go! I'll stay and watch Michelle doesn't try anything brave.' Kelly picked up the teapot and poured herself a cup. 'We shall do what the English do best and have another cup of tea.'

'You don't think it can be the mad Spar grocer back, do you?' Michelle half rose from her seat.

'Sit down, Marquise. Let the men do what they do best... go on, have another cup of tea and a chocky biscuit. Anyway, Coco is wagging her tail like mad so she seems to think it's OK.'

'True, but ...' Michelle still held tight to the dog's collar, 'But I'm not so sure Coco is too good at this guard dog stuff.'

'Well, she made a damn good job of barking and chasing off the Spar guy. Anyway, I hear voices approaching and they sound friendly.'

At that moment Robert came into view round the corner of the building, closely followed by Leon and Sven.

'Just a friendly neighbour visiting, girls, no cause for alarm.' Robert said as Coco slipped from Michelle's grasp and bounded over to Sven, barking excitedly.

'Hi, Coco, what a welcome! Am I interrupting you all at tea time?'

Michelle stood up and smiled, 'Of course not. We're delighted to see you. Please join us. Coco, enough, sit!' The dog slunk under the table with a big sigh and everyone took a chair and began to talk at once.

'We were just telling Sven about our unwelcome visitor this morning.' Robert said, 'He knows the guy apparently.'

'Oh yes, Pascal is well known in the village. Always a miserable devil and with a ridiculous chip on his shoulder.'

'Sorry, chip on his shoulder? What is this?' asked Leon with a worried frown.

'Don't worry, my love,' said Kelly, throwing her arm around Leon. 'Just another idiom... means he has a problem, sort of inferiority complex... well, I can't explain really.'

'*Il a une puce sur son epaule*, is probably a rough translation,' Sven said, 'But in a way it's more than that. He and his mother used to have a lavender farm some way from here. She had a dreadful drink problem and Pascal inherited it and the farm... she died a year or so ago and he has let the whole place go to rack and ruin. In the end he was so deep in debt that he had to sell. Anyway, a young couple, came along and paid a good price.'

'So why does he work at the Spar now... and why does that make him hate the English? Sounds like the buyers saved his skin to me.' Kelly said indignantly.

'True enough... but by the time he had paid off his debts and the huge mortgage on the farm he didn't have much left and what he did have he soon spent on gambling and booze. He won't keep the job at the Spar much longer... he's hopeless and always running out of the most basic stuff. I know him as we sell our *vin ordinaire* there... and he's a slow payer. Anyway, the young couple... well, actually the guy is a French potter, married to a beautiful girl who used to be a super-model in London... anyway, they renovated the farm and put in a swimming pool. In the summer months they run residential pottery courses. They're doing very well. I often go over there to take some cases of wine and have supper with them. Of course, Pascal thinks he could have done all that... in his dreams or in his cups.'

'OK, I sort of understand why he bears a grudge but why suddenly does he pick on Michelle?' Kelly asked, her voice rising in anger.

'Most of all, why does he think he is my half brother?' Michelle said in a quiet voice.

Sven looked at her, his light blue eyes serious and his face unsmiling.

'That is the most ridiculous thing I have ever heard. There is no way Michel would have gone with that woman. Impossible to imagine.' Sven thumped the table to emphasise his point.

'Well, it would have been at least twenty or thirty years ago. I mean Pascal is probably about my age... maybe older.'

'Definitely older!' Sven said quickly, 'He must be at least ten years older than you!'
Michelle felt his eyes still on her and began to blush. Before she could reply, Leon spoke,

'Well, I have been wanting to find a way to help you, Michelle, and now I think I can. Give me a few days and I will find out everything you need to know. Just leave it to me and forget all about it for a while.'

'Really, Leon, would you do that?' Michelle smiled with relief.

'*Pas de problème, chère Marquise!*' Leon gave a mock salute which was interrupted by Kelly giving him a big kiss and a hug, saying,

'That's my boy, Leon. How I love you!'

Everyone laughed and the atmosphere round the tea table relaxed. Michelle picked up the teapot and said, 'More tea anyone?' She was about to go into the kitchen door when Sven began to talk and what he said made her stop in her tracks.

'Actually I came round to tell you two things. First that we will begin harvesting tonight and that I hope we don't disturb you and secondly, that Melissa has broken our engagement.' His voice was calm and his face showed no emotion. There was a long silence and then Robert spoke.

'Sorry to hear that, Sven. That must be quite a shock for you.'

'Not really,' Sven continued in the same quiet voice. 'She couldn't put up with my mother any longer. She went back to the States the other day. In fact, she hitched a lift on the private aeroplane of that film guy you had round here.'

'Oh my goodness, Seb Raven? The film scout? How did they meet?' Michelle asked in dismay.

'Oh, he came round to see if we had any objections to the filming... of course we said it would be no problem. I mean, we can't hear or even see you from our place. Anyway, he stayed for a drink and talked to Melissa about his work in LA... I guess it made her feel homesick... and we had already had a big row that morning. She wanted me to tell Maman that I would go to live in California after we married. I couldn't agree to that... I mean... my life is among the vines here. Anyway, suddenly Seb was leaving and said he had a private jet at Aix airport and the next thing I knew was that Melissa said she'd like a lift. That was that!' Sven finished, his voice still measured and in control.

'Oh, cheer up, probably just a lover's tiff. And you're right, she suddenly felt homesick, I expect. She'll be back soon.' Kelly had come back to the table and spoke firmly, patting Sven on the shoulder.

'Oh, I don't think so. She left her engagement ring on the bedside table.' Sven shrugged and still appeared calm. *'C'est la vie!'*

Another awkward silence fell over them all and this time not one of them could think of anything to say at all.

19 *'standing taller than everybody there'*

Michelle smiled to herself as she went to bed. Her father had wished her 'sweet dreams' as they parted on the landing. Well, it was a good thing he didn't know about her latest wild dreams or were they nightmares? She lay in the dark thinking back over the day. How lucky she was to have Leon there to find out about the Spar guy. She threw back the light eiderdown and turned restlessly. It was hard to stop thinking about the van driving straight at her and Coco. She certainly did not want to dream about that or anything connected to it. Supposing she was not the sole owner of Bastide de Rosefont? How could she go forward with any of their plans? What would happen with the film location contract that Kelly had ready to go? She turned again in the bed and pulled the covers over herself again. She sighed and switched on the bedside light. A moth flew round the halo of light, batting its soft wings against the glass shade. Quickly she turned off the light again, unable to watch its inevitable death. The moon cast its light through the open curtains. She smiled ruefully. Such a romantic moonlight, a white, silvery light made for lovers. She thought at last about what she was avoiding thinking about. Sven's broken engagement. He had been strangely calm with his announcement. Did that mean he had not been deeply in love with the beautiful Melissa? How could he let her go back to California without a struggle? Why had he let his mother rule his life? Unanswered questions followed one after another. Impatient with herself, she jumped out of bed and went to the window. In the bright moonlight she was surprised to see several sets of headlights in between the rows of vines. Of course, the harvest. The grape harvest had begun. Sven had talked all afternoon with her father about the tradition of the Provençal vendange. She ran to the wardrobe and pulled out some old jeans and a T-shirt. This was something she could not miss.

Five minutes later she was running across the back lawn, followed by Coco, and down into the vineyard. Now she could hear voices and laughter. As she drew near she could easily make out Sven, standing taller than everybody there, his blonde hair almost silver in the moonlight. Then to her surprise she saw her father there too, standing with a large basket strapped to his back. Trust Dad to be in on the experience, Michelle thought to herself, then she called out.

'Hi, can I help, too?'

Sven turned quickly at the sound of her voice and walked toward her, Coco bounding ahead to greet him.

'Did we wake you?' he asked, as he removed his working gloves and held out his hand in greeting. '*Bonsoir*, Michelle.'

She took his hand, bracing herself for her usual electric shock reaction to his touch. Strangely it felt just comfortable to have her hand enclosed in his.

'*Bonsoir*, Sven. Can I help in any way?' she asked.

He looked doubtfully down at her as she stood in front of him. 'That's very kind of you but we have almost finished picking the grapes that are ripe enough. We are just about to take a break. Will you join us for a glass of wine? Your father has been a great worker, he learns fast!'

Robert Phelps walked across to them, still wearing the large basket strapped to his back. 'Did I hear you talking about me? I hope you are telling Michelle that I have been completely useless!' Robert laughed, trying to shrug off the leather straps that held the basket.

'Not at all, you have been great. Here let me help you off with that.' Sven lifted the basket and slung it over to a pile that were stacked near the tractor. 'It's hard work going up and down the lines collecting from the pickers. You have done more than your share.'

'Well, even at my best I was taking double the time of the others. But it has been a great learning curve!' Robert sat down gratefully on a bale of hay and Sven poured him a glass of wine from a large leather flask. 'Thank you, Sven, I can do with this! Cheers, *à votre santé*!'

Sven poured a glass for Michelle and another for himself, then sat beside Robert on the hay bale. Michelle sipped her wine and felt acutely aware of the nearest group of wine-pickers staring at her. She turned toward them and raised her glass high, saying,

'*Bravo! À la votre*!' There was an immediate and warm response as the harvesters all raised their glasses to her in return and then went back to chatting together.

'And bravo to you, Michelle. The locals will soon get to like you if you are open and friendly. They're good people.' Sven clinked his glass against Michelle's and smiled at her. A smile that could have sold a billion or so tubes of toothpaste.

'It just does not seem possible that the weather can turn as you say it will.' Robert said, looking up at the clear, star-filled sky.

'You'd better believe it. Now we are picking at night as the grapes are too hot in the day... the yield is better from the cool night-time grapes, but all the time we have to be ahead of the risk of frost or worse... hail. Here, at the foot of Mont Ste.Victoire, the extremes of weather are always ruling us.' As he finished talking he waved an arm toward the huge bulk of the mountain that gave an eternal backdrop to the vineyards.

Michelle looked at him as he continued to talk, thinking how his handsome face shone with enthusiasm. She could understand now why he could never leave to live in California. She looked up at the sky where the stars were so bright that there was little space for the sky between, then across to the looming darkness of the mountain... was this to be her life now? She knew in her heart that it was to be so... whether it was the Rosefont blood in her veins or just the sheer beauty of the place... it was where she wanted to be. She turned to her father and Sven who were still talking avidly about the harvest.

'So, will you be picking again tomorrow night, Sven?' Robert asked.

'Tomorrow all hours... we can't stop now with the weather about to turn.' Sven spoke positively. 'In fact, I am just about to organise a few hours off for this shift and bring in some fresh hands. You'll have to excuse me but I had better get back to it.' He stood up and nodded to them both, then walked over to the group of pickers and began to talk to them.

Michelle sat next to her father on the hay bale, suddenly feeling tired. 'I can't think how they keep going,' she said, 'I feel exhausted and I haven't done a thing.'

'Well, I am finished. I'd be no help to them now. I need a long, cool bath and a few hours sleep. In some ways I felt more trouble than I was worth. The pickers work so fast and they have great camaraderie... real teamwork. I was really more in the way and yet they were so kind as to put up with me. Yet another mad Englishman.' Robert laughed, rubbing the back of his neck.

'Come on then, Dad. Let's slink back to the Bastide and get some sleep. Tomorrow is another day.'

They walked back together, Coco trotting alongside, and just as they reached the terrace the moon went behind a cloud and complete darkness surrounded them.

'Well, looks like Sven may be right about the weather, there is a bank of cloud rolling in... and the wind is starting up.' Robert held open the kitchen door as Michelle walked ahead.

'Well, it still seems warm to me.' Michelle replied, yawning. 'I'm off to bed. *À demain*, Dad... let's see what tomorrow brings.' How was she to know then, tired and sleepy as she was, that tomorrow there would be more to worry about than the grape harvest?

20   *'help with the harvest'*

'No, no, no!' Kelly's voice rang out from the first floor office and reached the kitchen where Michelle and her father were eating a late breakfast. Michelle jumped up saying,

'Sounds like trouble in the office... probably Kelly's computer has crashed. I'll go and see, Dad, excuse me.' She grabbed her coffee and went quickly up the staircase, followed by Coco.

'What is it, Kelly? Is it your computer?' Michelle sat down by Kelly who was now strangely quiet and scanning through her emails.

She answered slowly, 'No, not the computer, the computer is fine. In fact my emails are coming in thick and fast... but you'd better read this one for yourself.' She turned the laptop toward Michelle who read the email in silence before saying,

'Well, I guess something may have hit the fan this time.' At that moment Dr Phelps came in to the office.

'You two girls are un-typically quiet… what's going on?' He, too, took a seat at the long work table that stretched along the wall under the window.

'Well,' said Michelle in a low voice, 'Our American friend, Seb Raven, has written to say that due to the high cost of renting Bastide de Rosefont, he may have to consider his original plan to film in Belgium.'

'Oh dear, oh dear.' Robert shook his head, 'So what will you do? Offer him a lower price rental?'

'Certainly not!' Both girls answered in unison.

Robert burst out laughing, 'You two girls were made from the same mould. I'd never make a business man... I'd buckle every time.'

Kelly gave a small smile and then said thoughtfully, 'It's not good news but I think it's a typical try-on. We have to stay firm.'

Michelle nodded in agreement. 'Yes, definitely... there's no way he wants to film in Belgium. He has already told Kelly that the location is too constricted.'

Kelly was nodding now, too. 'Yes, exactly. This is just a bid to get the price down. What do you think of this draft reply, Mich?'

Michelle read Kelly's email reply and smiled, 'Perfect, send!'

'Now what are the two of you up to?' Robert asked. 'What did you say?'

'Oh just he has to let us know soon as we are about to begin renovation work, so... if he wants it looking dilapidated ... well, that was the gist of it.' Kelly said.

Robert sighed and looked worried. 'That's a brave move. There's a lot of money involved here, girls.'

'Don't worry, Dad, we're good at this sort of thing. When he comes back we'll offer him something sugar-coated to puff up his ego.' Michelle said.

'Yeh, maybe a discount on any days they over-run ... or discount catering costs for more than fifty crew...something we can dream up to make him feel he's won.'

'And I thought it was Leon that had taken the degree in psychology.' Robert sighed.

'Hang on, another email just in from our own office in Chelsea... read this Mich!' Kelly swivelled the laptop back to Michelle again.

'Oh my, so she does definitely want it.' Michelle said thoughtfully, looking at Kelly.

'What, the film guy has replied already?' asked Robert.

'No, Dad, this email is from Jemima, the temp that Kelly has organised to hold the fort back in

Chelsea. Her father has written to formally make it clear that he would like to buy us out.'

'Phew, this is all too much for me.' Robert shook his head in bemusement. 'Anyway I can see people working in the vineyards out there, so I'm off. Give me the simple life of a peasant farmer.'

'Yeh, right... there speaks the cruise ship doctor from Harley Street. Off you go Dad, and don't worry.' Michelle laughed as Robert headed for the door.

Once they were alone together Michelle looked at Kelly and grimaced.'Brave talk as usual but fingers double-crossed, Kelly.'

'I know, I must say it was a bit of a shocker from Seb Raven and now this to think about from Jemima's rich Daddy. Not to mention waiting on my lovely Leon to get in touch about the mad Spar man. Ah well, *c'est la vie.*'

'Do I have to say it?' Michelle sighed.

'Nah, rather you didn't... let's go and make some fresh coffee and pretend we're not waiting for life to straighten out again.'

'Good idea.' Michelle closed the lid of the laptop firmly and looked out of the window at the view across the lawns to the vineyards. Today the familiar outline of Mont Ste. Victoire seemed extraordinarily clear. The sun was bright and the sky the deepest indigo blue. 'What a stunning day, I suppose we should help with the harvest, too. Sven is working night and day to get the grapes picked before the weather changes. He expects freezing weather and possibly hail on the way.'

'Well, two things immediately strike me, a) his name is Sven and therefore an archetypical Scandy expecting snow and ice and b) you can count me out from any harvesting... my law is do what you're good at... and I just know I would be useless at picking grapes, whereas we have plenty of work to do here.' Kelly ended firmly.

'That was a long b), I think you lost me somewhere, but I get where you're coming from... Sven certainly looked rather doubtful when I offered to help last night.'

'Last night...what's been going on? Holy Moly, the Viking god has only been off the engaged-to-someone-else list for twenty-four hours. Tell me all!'

'Nothing to tell, come on... coffee in the kitchen.' Michelle walked out of the office whistling as she went.

'Now what does that whistling mean?' Kelly asked, but there was no reply as Michelle was already heading downstairs.

By the end of the day nothing had been resolved. The two girls worked hard in the office, becoming accustomed to the distant drone of tractors plying back and forth between the vines. Occasionally a loud voice or laughter rang out and they would look up and see the groups of pickers reaching the top of the sloping vines, nearest to the Bastide. They were determined to finish their recent London projects and other humdrum jobs of invoicing and accounting... anything to keep their minds off their worries. By five o'clock they had caught up with most of the backlog of work and sent instructions to the temp, Jemima, for the week ahead.

'I suppose Jemima is hoping to hear from us about more than these every day emails.' Michelle said, breaking the silence.

'Well, she will just have to wait a while. It seems we are all playing a waiting game today. No news from Leon, nothing back from Seb Raven either... I hate the not knowing. So frustrating.' Kelly stretched and ruffled her blonde curls. 'Shall we call it a day?'

'Yes, I guess so. Dad is still out there... he must be exhausted! I think I'll walk down to the vines and find him... try and persuade him to stop now. Do you want to come, Kelly?'

'Tempting, it certainly is a beautiful evening, but I think I'll just have a quick shower and wait for Leon. He simply must be back soon although he hasn't phoned or texted all day. Goodness knows what he is up to. Anyway, you will probably just happen to bump into the newly eligible Viking god and I don't want to cramp your style.' Kelly laughed as she gave a final check to her inbox before closing down her laptop.

'Give over, Kelly. The poor guy is probably still hankering after the beautiful Melissa. Anyway, I think I'll take that fruit cake I made on Sunday. It might go down well with the pickers.'

'Good idea, and keep a large slice for Sven. Don't want him wasting away. Good job you made such a large cake and it is quite delicious. Leave me and Leon a slice each please.'

'Well, I made it because Dad loves it actually. The recipe was one my mother always used. Poor Dad, I am only just realising how lonely he has been since she died.'

'Well, I am sure he is lonely by choice. Can you imagine all the widows on board a luxury liner suddenly needing a doctor. He is film star stuff even though he's not so young any more.'

Michelle laughed. 'Yes, I see what you mean. That's something else I've only just realised... he is quite a looker in a vintage way! Oh well, if all goes well, we can design a great attic apartment for him here and he won't need to be lonely.'

'Hmm, as you said, if... why doesn't Leon let us know something.' Kelly looked at her phone in annoyance. 'I've sent three texts in the last hour and no reply. It's not like him.'

'What with that and waiting for Seb Raven to come back to us, it's all just too much. I'm going for a walk. Come on, Coco. See you later then. Don't worry Kelly, it's often impossible to get a signal round here... Leon is probably out of range somewhere.'

'Spose so, you're probably right. See you later then. I'm going to pinch all the hot water and have a deep bath. It seems to be getting colder suddenly.'

'True, I was hoping to go for a sunset walk but it is clouding over now. Still, I'm definitely off now.'

As Michelle reached the top of the vines, Coco bounded ahead and gave her usual ecstatic greeting to Sven. Once again he was sitting on a bale of hay next to her father. They seemed deep in conversation but, as the dog jumped up at them, they both looked up and saw Michelle. Robert's face lit up with delight and Sven turned on his usual wide, dental ad smile.

'What a nice surprise. We had just decided to take a break.' Robert said, greeting her with an affectionate kiss. Sven stood up and offered his hand to shake, as usual, polite and charming.

'I've brought you some cake, Dad, and enough to pass round if you think it's a good idea?' Michelle took the tea towel off the basket and showed the slices of cake to Sven.

'Fantastic, the harvesters will love it, I'm sure. Is it an English recipe?' Sven peered into the basket.

'Well, yes, I suppose so. It's a traditional fruit cake that my mother always made. Luckily I made a large one on Sunday.' Michelle said shyly, offering the basket to Sven.

'No, you should take it round yourself, I'll come with you.' Sven said.

'Well, I'm going to pinch a big slice now and then head back to the Bastide. I've had enough for one day and it suddenly seems the air is cold.' Robert said.

Sven looked up at the sky with a worried frown. 'You're quite right, it's what we've been dreading. I've known this before... there's a build up of heat and then the air suddenly chills... and just look at the clouds, swirling in all directions. Anyway, thanks Robert, you've been amazing today, really a great help.' Sven patted Robert's shoulder. 'I hope your shoulders are all right.'

'Oh, I'll be fine. That's one good thing about being a doctor, one knows how the body works and how to avoid strain. Nothing wrong with me that a good, hot bath won't cure. And thank you, Sven, I've learnt so much today about grapes and wine. I've always taken a layman's interest in wine but I've learnt more today than I could ever find in books if I read for a year. You're a clever young man! Now, I'm off for that hot bath!'

'I hope Kelly has left you some hot water, she just had the same idea as you. You'd better hurry!' Michelle laughed and waved as Robert walked stiffly back up the sloping vineyard toward the Bastide.

'Do you have trouble with the plumbing at Rosefont?' Sven asked.

'Oh, not really, it's just antiquated, I suppose. I hope to see about it soon.... If...' her voice tailed away.

'No more news about Pascal, I suppose? You know I can't believe he has any possible claim.' Sven looked seriously at Michelle.

'No, no news yet.' Michelle kept her voice light, 'I came out for a walk to try and forget him and everything for a while.'

'Of course, of course.' Sven said hurriedly, 'Anyway, as I was saying, if you need a good plumber I can give you the address of the man we use.' And so, discussing hot water systems, they walked on down the hill toward the group of pickers. Michelle tried not to smile as she imagined telling Kelly about her romantic walk between the vines with the handsome Sven... talking about plumbing.

The grape-pickers were delighted with the cake and all seemed to find it delicious. Glasses were filled and everyone seemed happy to greet Michelle and even drink her health. It was reassuring after the vitriolic abuse that Pascal Mazin had thrown at her. The general conversation seemed to be about the change in the weather and Sven translated to Michelle.

'The workers agree with me, there's bad weather on its way, feels like a storm blowing in as the wind is starting up from the East. Luckily we have picked nearly all this slope now and our vines on the other side of the river are more protected. Still, you will have to excuse me, we must press on, every moment counts now.'

'Can I help in any way?' Michelle asked hesitantly.

'Well, actually if you could drive over to Château Gilbert and try to find Jean-Paul... do you remember you met him, your father's...sorry, I mean Michel de Rosefont's chauffeur. If you could ask him to load up about twenty more hay bales and bring them over here as soon as possible. That would be a great help... if you don't mind.'

'Of course I will,' Michelle said hurriedly, beginning to walk uphill.

'My truck is in the lane just by the forest, if you don't mind driving it? It would be quicker than going back for your car.'

Michelle swung around and caught the keys that Sven threw to her and then ran toward the lane with Coco at her heels. Sven's truck was parked practically in a ditch. She climbed into the high-mounted driving seat and Coco jumped past her and into the back. Michelle sat for a moment inspecting the dashboard and then found her feet couldn't even reach the pedals. She managed to wrench the car seat forward and then fired up the engine and with a small lurch moved forward, out of the ditch and onto the lane. Well, she had wanted something to take her mind off her worries and here she was with Coco, driving a very large farm vehicle into the gathering dusk. Michelle smiled again, thinking here was another romantic moment to retell to Kelly.

By the time she reached the drive to Château Gilbert the day had darkened almost to night. Dusk had fallen fast and she hurriedly found the headlights and turned them full on as she turned into the farmyard at the rear of the Château. Luckily the first person she saw in the open barn was Jean-Paul. Grinding to a rather sudden halt, she switched off the engine and jumped down from the truck. As usual, Coco rushed ahead of her and was greeting Jean-Paul before she reached him. She hurriedly explained that Sven wanted the hay bales and Jean-Paul seemed to understand instantly. Calling to two other farm-workers to help, the truck was soon loaded to the gunnels.

'Do you wish me to drive you returning?' Jean-Paul asked in hesitant English.

'No, *c'est bon, merci... ca va!*' Michelle felt her few words of French already exhausted and so with a lot of smiles and handshakes she was once more back in the driving seat. As she drove slowly along the dark lane back toward the Rosefont vineyard she spoke to Coco for company.

'I just have to learn to speak French, Coco. It's all right for you but I really need to communicate round here. I think Leon will have to give lessons if... oh damn it, why are there so many ifs today, Coco?' In answer, the dog pushed her large head forward over the car seat, rested it heavily on Michelle's shoulder and gave a deep sigh.

The moment she arrived back in the lane and parked by the tractors, Sven and four or five workers ran to meet her. Sven raised his hand as though to thank her but immediately set to unloading the bales of hay. Michelle slipped out of the driving seat and watched as the men threw the large bales from the truck to the tractors. Sven worked at twice the speed of the others. He towered over them and his muscled torso worked like a machine as he tossed the bales across from one vehicle to another, making them look as light as empty cardboard boxes. Michelle stood back in admiration... surely he was a Viking god? As soon as the last bale was loaded, Sven jumped into the leading tractor and led the way down the vines. Michelle stayed still, holding Coco's collar and wondering what to do next. The procession of four tractors made its way slowly down the sloping vines, the glare from the headlights bobbing up and down as they passed over the rough land. She decided to follow them down and let Coco loose to race ahead. Grass grew between the rows of vines and she walked easily, although beginning to feel the cold wind go straight though her thin shirt. When she reached the bottom of the slope the workers had already unloaded the hay bales. Sven was striding around placing one at the end of each row. He turned toward Michelle and, even in the darkness, his smile shone white.

'That was a fantastic help, Michelle, thanks. Now stay close to me as we are going to set light to the hay.' Michelle's eyes widened in surprise but she was quite prepared to stay close to him.

'*Un, deux, trois!*' Sven's voice rang out in the night and at his command, each bale was set alight. Smoke rose into the air and curled away up the hill. Sven strode from one bale to the next and, as small flickers of flame appeared, he ordered water to be thrown. Soon the air was full of smoke but all snaking away from them up between the lines of vines. Sven came back and stood next to Michelle.

'This is an emergency measure.' His face was grim, 'It will bring the temperature up a few degrees when the rain starts.'

Michelle looked up at the starless sky and shivered.

'You're cold Michelle, I have a coat in the other truck back here. Quickly, come with me.' He put his arm around her and led her away from the smoke and down toward the bottom of the valley where several more cars were parked. Then it began to rain. Not ordinary rain but piercing icy drops that hurt the skin. They began to run with Coco racing ahead. Just as they neared the shelter of the cars, Michelle slipped and fell. She cried out in pain as her ankle twisted. In a moment, Sven had picked her up and was carrying her like a child and running towards the cars. Quickly he opened the passenger door of an old estate car and placed her gently onto the seat. Sven looked at her anxiously.

'Are you hurt?'

'No, I just twisted my ankle. I'll be fine.' Michelle spoke bravely but her ankle hurt and she was freezing cold. Sven was still standing outside the car, apparently oblivious to the freezing rain pouring over him.

'Let me look.' His large hands were surprisingly gentle as he felt her ankle. Michelle leaned back against the seat, wondering how she could or should resist running her fingers through his wet hair. Then he was reaching past her and pulling a blanket from the back seat. His body so close to hers that her breast touched his arm and she could feel the warmth from his body. He wrapped the blanket carefully around her and then gently stroked her wet hair away from her face. He looked at her, still frowning with concern. Michelle waited for his kiss and almost closed her eyes, but suddenly he pulled away from her, tucked the blanket more firmly around her and slammed the car door shut. Then he was in the driver's seat and starting up the engine.

'I think it may be just a slight sprain.' He said, as he drove slowly up the hill. 'The best thing is to get you back to your father and let him have a look at it.'

Michelle pulled the blanket close around her and sighed, here was another fine scenario for Kelly. Coco pushed her wet head forward and rested it again on Michelle's shoulder.

In fact, when they arrived back at the Bastide, there was no chance of chatting with Kelly. Sven insisted on carrying Michelle from the car and into the kitchen where Robert quickly took over.

'I'm afraid it's all my fault.' Sven spoke anxiously. 'We were caught in the downpour and running for shelter. The Provençal earth is normally so dry that the first drops of rain turn it to slippery mud. I should have warned Michelle.'

'Oh, don't worry, dear boy, just a sprain and believe me it's not the first time Michelle has fallen over. She was a madcap child.' Robert stood up from examining Michelle's ankle. Michelle felt irrational anger at the way the two men were treating her like a child but before she could interrupt, Robert was speaking again.

'What about you, Sven, you're wet through ... how about a hot toddy?'

Sven shook his head, his blonde curls shaking drops of water onto the floor. Michelle's anger turned to repressed laughter as she thought how like a great big dog he looked. There was something about Sven that she just didn't get. Was it his cool Scandinavian blood? Her thoughts were interrupted as she realised Sven was saying goodbye.

'Thank you both for your help today and I'd love to stay but I must get back to fire-watching. We'll be taking shifts all night.'

'Did you say fire-watching? What's up?' Robert asked, his face alight with interest.

'We're trying to raise the temperature above freezing at the bottom of the valley by lighting a series of damp fires. Do you want to come and see?'

'I certainly would! I've never heard of anything like it!' Robert was reaching for his waterproof coat on the back of the kitchen door as he added, 'You'll be OK, Michelle. Just keep your foot up for a while and...'

'Don't worry Dad, it hardly hurts at all now and it's not even swollen. Off you go!'
The two men looked at each other and exchanged what could only be thought of as looks of relief. Michelle sighed as the door closed behind them. She spoke to Coco who was lying in her usual place under the kitchen table.

'Do you know what, Coco. I don't think men ever really grow up.' Coco wagged her tail, thumping the flagstone floor in agreement. Suddenly, the kitchen door flung open and Kelly burst in.

'Holy Moly, Michelle, are you talking to yourself or the dog? Anyway, good news at last. I drove around until I finally got a signal... practically in Aix before I even got two bars of signal... it seems the wind has taken down the main antenna for this area. Anyway, as soon as I hit signs of civilisation there were six messages from Leon. I phoned him and although the line was dreadful we had a small but sweet chat. He's in Paris and has been trying to get in touch, of course. He'd heard about the bad weather hitting down here, so he was as worried as I was. Oh my god, this being in love stuff is exhausting.' She flung herself down in a chair at the table opposite to Michelle and continued, 'And what the hell have you been up to... why is your foot on a chair...have you hurt it? What's been going on?'

'I was afraid you'd ask that.' Michelle replied, closing her eyes with exhaustion. 'Do you think you could make a cup of tea and throw another log on the fire... then, if you really insist, I will attempt to tell you all about... well, nothing much really!'

21 'wearing a wedding ring'

The next day the sky was blue, the air still and the sun burning hot again. Michelle took her coffee out onto the terrace and looked down toward the vines. Today there was a shimmer of mist in the valley and the vast Mont Ste. Victoire rose up to the sky, shining with a whitish, luminous glow.

Her father joined her at the table, saying, 'Quite a view, isn't it, Michelle. One can quite see how Cezanne would have been obsessed with it... and then Picasso.'

'I know, Dad, I'm going to find out as much as I can about the painters round here... there is so much to research. I'm really looking forward to having time to go to some of the local galleries, too. Just in limbo at the moment though.'

'No news yet from Leon, then?' he asked, sitting beside her and sipping his coffee.

'Well, the phone lines are all down and even the mobiles are not getting a signal. Last night Kelly drove toward Aix and picked up a weak signal on the outskirts of the town. She spoke briefly with Leon but all she could make out was that he was in Paris, hoping to find out more... or something. Anyway, we still just have to wait, I guess.'

They sat for a moment in silence, both deep in their own thoughts. Coco jumped up and wagged her tail, looking up at the first floor windows. Michelle looked up and saw that Kelly was tapping on the window of the office and beckoning to them.

'Looks like Kelly does have more news.' Michelle hurriedly set down her coffee and ran indoors with Coco bouncing excitedly beside her. Throwing open the office door, Michelle spoke quickly, 'What is it, Kelly? News from Leon?'

'No, but it's news from Seb Raven... he's agreed our terms and wants to move his team over here the first week of November. How's that! High five!' Kelly slapped Michelle's hand enthusiastically, adding, 'He's emailing the contract later today.'

'Phew, that's great news, Kelly. Although there is one problem...'

'I think I know what you're going to say, Mich... supposing you don't own the Bastide after all?' Kelly replied slowly.

'Exactly!' Michelle spoke the one word quietly. At that moment Robert joined them.

'I heard most of that... congratulations girls, you are tough customers, all right. Anyway, I have a real gut feeling that Leon will find something out today and let us know... one way or the other? I suggest we take our minds off the waiting and go into Aix. Take in some galleries and have lunch. Also we should get good mobile signals in the town and we can keep in touch with Leon.'

'Sounds like a good plan to me.' said Kelly.

'Me too!' agreed Michelle.

And so it was that a few hours later they were sitting in the café that Michelle had found on her first day in Aix en Provence. The sun was shining brightly but the air was cooler. The café owner had taken down the large, orange parasols and the cobbles were washed clean with yesterday's rain.

'You were an extra long time in that last gallery, Mich. Anything to do with that truly beautiful man you were talking to?'

'Oh, he was telling me about Cezanne.' Michelle replied.

'Hmm, must have been his life story then. I thought you were never going to leave.'

'Well, we shall need to do a lot of research if we do set up art tours from the Bastide.'

'True enough,' agreed Kelly, 'I'm surprised you didn't ask him out to Rosefont... I'm sure he'd love to advise you further.'

'Oh do shut up, Kelly. I keep telling you... just because you are madly in love, it doesn't mean you have to find someone for me. I am perfectly happy and busy, thanks.'

'Yeh, right, moping around after the Viking god, giving the cold Marquise shoulder to poor Seb Raven... what are you like? Anyway, I thought the gallery guy looked cool.'

'Yes, he was cool, but he was also wearing a wedding ring. Now, can we talk about something else, do you think?' Michelle picked up the menu and began to study it.

Kelly and Robert exchanged glances and then Robert made an effort to change the subject.

'Well, Aix en Provence really is a delightful town... or is it a small city? And full of culture... you know it will make a perfect visit for art lovers from the cruise ships. Only half an hour or so from Marseilles where we always dock.'

'Do you think your boss lady will really plan Bastide de Rosefont into one of her schedules?' Michelle asked.

'Certain of it... she was very keen when I gave her a brief outline. There's an opera season in Aix as well... and everyone loves Provence. No doubt about that!'

'The only doubt then is that I actually do own the Bastide. I was tempted to go and see old Xavier but then I thought it best to leave it to Leon.'

'Well, Leon did say to give him a few days, Mich. I know he will do his best, but if he can't find anything out then perhaps you should go to see Xavier.' Kelly said, and they all nodded thoughtfully and began to look at the menu again, as the conversation petered out. They were just about to order when Kelly's mobile bleeped. She squeaked with delight and hurriedly answered it.

'It's a text from Leon. He must have heard us talking about him. He just says he'll be back in time for dinner tonight and will bring definite news one way or the other. What the hell does that mean?' Kelly looked at the phone in annoyance and snapped it shut. 'I'll phone him to find out what he's up to.' She pressed his number and then snapped the phone shut again. 'Now, he's on voicemail, damn. I hate this waiting around.'

'Well, the poor chap's obviously busy and doing his best. Anyway, tonight he says we shall know all.' Robert tried to speak calmly and added, 'Come on now, let's order and forget all about it until tonight.'

By seven o'clock Michelle, Kelly and even Robert had given up trying to forget all about it. They sat together in the kitchen, soup simmering on the stove, a large quiche ready to eat, salad already dressed. There was nothing more to occupy themselves with... everything was ready down to the last knife and fork laid on the table. Michelle stood by the tall dresser, rearranging china plates that did not need rearranging. Kelly was reading a magazine although it seemed she stayed on the same page. Even Robert was nervously tapping his pen on the table as he attempted a crossword, his usual calm manner broken. Suddenly, Coco wagged her tail and stood up, rushing over to the back door.

'It must be Leon, he's coming round to the back door.' Kelly rushed over and flung the door open and was just in time to stop herself from hugging a surprised Sven.

'Oh, so sorry, it's only you, Sven! Oh sorry again, that came out the wrong way. It's just I was expecting Leon!' Kelly scrambled to regain her composure as she stood back to let Sven into the kitchen.

'Sorry to disappoint you, Kelly. I just wanted to see how Michelle was today... her ankle?' He looked across at Michelle and then from behind his broad back, flourished a small bouquet of roses. 'For the invalid!'

Michelle took the roses and smelt their delicate perfume. 'Oh, thank you, they're simply perfect. I feel such a sham. My ankle is perfectly all right... in fact, we went in to Aix today and went round some galleries. My ankle is as good as new!'

'Well, I'm relieved to hear it. How about you, Dr Phelps... any aches and pains after all your hard work?'

'No, I feel capital! The exercise did me good. Have you managed to get any sleep yet?'
Sven laughed, 'Absolutely, I slept all afternoon. The hay fires saved the grapes from freezing and the storm has gone as quickly as it came. Apparently, just a few kilometres from here, there was a dreadful hail storm and acres of vines ruined. We were very lucky. Tomorrow we shall be picking the last runs of vines on the opposite slope to here. Then, it will be time to celebrate. We always have a *vendange* party and I was hoping you would all join us... Leon, too, of course, if he is around?'

As though hearing his name, Leon came into the kitchen. Kelly shrieked with delight and threw herself at him. 'We've been waiting and waiting and then you sneak in without us even hearing you, even Coco missed out!'

'*Bonsoir, tout le monde!*' Leon kissed Kelly on both cheeks and then spread his arms wide. 'I return with good news!' They all looked at him, waiting for him to continue. Leon walked over to Michelle and stood in front of her, gave a mock bow and then said in a serious voice. 'Marquise de Rosefont, I am delighted to report that you are the true, one and only owner of La Bastide de Rosefont!'

Everyone clapped and cheered as Leon looked from one to the other with a wide smile on his face. 'I shall tell you all about it but first I think I deserve a glass of wine and a great lot to eat!'

They all hurried to serve the soup and Michelle quickly laid another place for Sven who was hovering near the door.

'Please join us... it's only soup and quiche but there's plenty of both.' Michelle smiled at him as she placed the delicate roses on the table as a centrepiece.

'I'd love to but I must get back, *Maman* expects me, and I still have work to do. Thanks anyway... and we hope to see you all at Château Gilbert for the harvest celebration on Saturday night... about seven? I've asked some local friends I'd like you to meet... some English residents near here.'

'That would be great, thank you, we shall all look forward to it.' Michelle saw him to the door and then watched his large outline as he walked off into the night. Was he a born loner? Maybe a mummy's boy... there was something that she couldn't quite work out. But now was not the time to think of it... now, she wanted to hear everything that Leon had to say.

And he had just begun to talk. '*Alors*, I have made my research and finally I have the proof by DNA, definite proof in the DNA profile that Pascal Mazin is of no relation to the Marquis de Rosefont, none at all.' Leon clapped his hands together, then tore a chunk of bread and ate it hungrily.

'DNA, but how...' Michelle began to ask and Kelly spoke at the same time.

'But how on earth did you get him to agree to a DNA test?' she demanded, leaning across the table as Leon continued to eat his bread. 'For goodness sake stop eating and tell us all.'

'Let the poor man have his soup, we've waited this long and it seems as though the news is good.' Robert spoke, beginning to drink his soup. 'And the soup is excellent, Michelle. You could serve this to your film crew, I'm sure.'

Leon looked up quickly and put down his soup spoon,'So is it all agreed with Seb Raven, do you have the location contract?' he asked.

'It's ready to go, but we'll talk that after... after you have told us everything that you have been up to the last two days. Come on Leon!' Kelly spoke firmly.

'*Très bien*...' Leon put down his soup spoon and sat back in his chair, '*Très bien, mes enfants, c'etait un fois...*' Leon raised his hands in mock defeat as Kelly threw a piece of bread at him, 'Very well, in English, once upon a time... well, it is like a fairy story, non?'

'It will be more like a murder story if you don't just spill the beans.' Kelly stood up and went round the table to sit on Leon's lap.

'Spill the beans... you want a story about a giant-killer... or is one of your idioms, Kelly?'
Kelly put her hands around his neck, gave him a long kiss and then said fiercely,
'Talk!'

'Ok, ok, *je craque*, I give in.' Leon laughed and settled Kelly more comfortably on his lap.
'First, when I left here I went to the village. The Spar shop was closed and I went to the little bar opposite. No surprise to find Pascal Mazin there, drinking alone at a table, *ivre comme un seigneur*, I think you say 'drunk as a lord'? But aristocrat ... non! And I was determined to prove that. I tried to start up a conversation with him, I bought him a cognac but it was useless, he was so intoxicated that he spoke just the rubbish. There were two or three other men in the bar but I could get nothing out of them... nothing of any use. They all told the same story of how Pascal

lost his lavender farm to debt, but nothing new. Anyway, I already had in my pocket what I needed most? Can you guess?' Leon smiled wickedly as they all looked at him, waiting for him to continue.

'I swear, as much as I love you, Leon, I shall kill you if you don't get on with the story.' Kelly muttered darkly.

'If you kill me, you never hear the story... this is the basis of interrogation, *ma chère*! You don't even want to guess? Then I will have to tell you all. In my pocket, in a sealed polythene bag, I had a cigarette end. The very one that Pascal had thrown at me before he drove his van at Michelle. I picked it up from the gravel that afternoon!'

Kelly spoke first, 'Now that... that was downright brilliant. Maybe I won't kill you after all!' Kelly ruffled Leon's dark, silky hair affectionately, her eyes shining with admiration.

'*Merci, mademoiselle*, thank you for my reprieve. Anyway, I was driving to Aix, thinking I would stay at my aunt's and then take it to Xavier first thing in the morning. Then I thought again. Did I trust Xavier? Perhaps not... and anyway it is not legal to take DNA evidence without the permission of the person. I had thought to ask Pascal, to try and talk sense with him but he was completely, totally incapable. Also I could see long, legal problems ahead. So, I drove just to the station and took the train to Paris. There, I know a good laboratory, an old school friend of mine works there and she agreed to test the cigarette.'

'Hold on a moment, did you say 'she'... how good a friend is this she?' Kelly glared at Leon.

'She is a very good friend and I stayed the night at her place.'

'What?' Kelly jumped off Leon's lap and put her hands on her hips, about to explode with rage when Leon held up his hand.

'Stop, Kelly, before you begin. I stayed the night with her and her husband and their two children. In fact I slept on the bottom bunk in the children's bedroom and very uncomfortable it was, I assure you. And I tried to call you many times before I realised the lines were all down in a storm here.'
Everyone laughed and Kelly sat down at the table defeated as Leon continued, 'Anyway, it took longer than I thought as the laboratory is very busy and, of course, this was a private test that my friend had to make in between others... and, as I said not strictly legal. Finally, I picked up the full result just before the lab was closing. It proved without a doubt that there was no genetic link to the Rosefont family.'

'But how did you know the genetic pattern of the Rosefonts?' Robert asked.

'Well, fortunately I still had the dossier for the search that Maitre Xavier commissioned me to make. I had the original DNA of Michel de Rosefont and that of Michelle. It didn't take a genius to see there was no similarity at all with this Mazin.'

'But you are a genius, Leon. Don't you all think so?' Kelly turned to them all and raised her glass. 'This is to my darling genius Leon.'

They all drank his health happily but Leon continued, 'Wait, there is something you must all understand before you congratulate me. This whole thing is not truly legal.'

'You keep saying that but what do you mean?' Michelle asked

'Well, normally one has to ask permission err... how can I say in English...' Leon struggled to find the words and Robert butted in,

'I think, if it is the same as the law in the UK, if you want to test someone's DNA, as you say, you have to obtain their written permission.'

'*Exactement!*' Leon nodded in agreement, 'It is the same law in France. Remember, Michelle, Maitre

Xavier asked your permission to test your DNA... well, taking Pascal Mazin's cigarette is...well...' Again he came to a halt without finishing his sentence.

'But now we know that he is not the son of Michel, or the half brother of Michelle. Surely that is what really matters?' Kelly spoke defiantly. 'You have done so well, Leon.'

'I agree with Kelly.' Michelle spoke quietly but with confidence. 'Knowledge is power. All we need to do now is to call his bluff.'

'Bluff... what is bluff?' Leon asked.

Michelle continued. 'Just as we handled Seb Raven, earlier today. We shall stand firm.'

'I agree absolutely.' Kelly said, 'And I think I know where you are coming from, Mich. We simply tell the Spar man that he should go to see old Xavier. Then, as day follows night, Xavier will demand a DNA test and that will be that.' Kelly stood up and clapped her hands as though finishing the problem. 'Now, if everyone has had enough soup and excitement, I shall serve the quiche and salad and open another bottle of wine.'

'Absolutely!' agreed Michelle, beginning to clear away the soup plates. 'Now, we need to discuss the next big issue. The Seb Raven's contract will ask for a November start date. So, there's plenty more to talk about!'

'And then there's the minor issue of the offer made for our design studio in Chelsea, Mich. Slice of quiche anyone? It's been a busy day and it's not over yet!'

22 'Mont Ste.Victoire glowed pink in the autumn sunlight'

Michelle and Kelly were at work early the next morning, sitting side by side at their usual desk.

'Well, we're an hour later here than London but what's the time in LA?' Kelly asked.

Michelle flipped open her phone,

'It's an eight hour time difference, eight hours earlier so right now it's just gone midnight in LA.'

'Yeh, I thought it was something like that. I suppose if Seb is back in California he won't be sending the contract until at least late afternoon here.' Kelly looked gloomily at the email inbox, scrolling through a list of messages she didn't really want.

Michelle nodded in agreement.'It would certainly be good to get it in black and white. In the meantime we should concentrate on selling out our own business. If Jemima's father is serious we need to get some advice,'

'Yeh, exactly. I thought the same. Really we both need to get back to London and make appointments with our accountant and the bank manager... and probably a load of other things to do.'

'It's a leap into the unknown at the Bastide. Are you sure you're happy with the idea?' Michelle asked.

'What do you mean? Would I rather live in Provence with the man I love, throw myself into a whole new adventure work-wise... or, oh yes, slave away at a desk designing wonderful places for other people and living in a bed-sit studio in an overcrowded city... oh, and I forgot to mention the view from this desk... it's monumentally fantastic. No worries on my behalf, Mich.'

Michelle laughed and they both looked out of the window. The leaves were turning to a bright gold on the vines and Mont Ste. Victoire glowed pink in the autumn sunlight.

'It is such a view, isn't it. I sometimes look up and can't quite believe it.'

'I know, the mountain just sort of hangs there. You know when you're in a restaurant and there's someone famous there, too...like, you don't want to stare but they are just sort of irresistible and your eye keeps on...' Kelly suddenly gave out a small shriek,

'Email from Seb Raven, just in... my God, he's working late... and there's an attachment.'
Michelle stood up and looked over Kelly's shoulder as the file slowly opened.'This is it, Kelly, we have the contract. Shall we print out 2 copies and go through it slowly or do you just want to cc it to me?'

'I think print hard copies and then we can take it outside in the sunshine to read. You know what, Mich? We couldn't do that in posh, grimy Chelsea.'

It took over an hour to wade through the complicated contract from Seb Raven. Robert and Leon had pottered around, making coffee and leaving Michelle and Kelly to work. Finally the four pages had been read and re-read and Kelly spoke first. 'Quite a few points to check out, don't you think, Mich?'

'I agree, I was thinking we could forward it to our solicitor... I think she will know how to handle it or at least have a colleague that will specialise in this sort of contract. I mean, it's sort of a tenancy agreement, I suppose.'

'Exactly what I was beginning to think. I mean the day rental price is amazing but we need to be sure about any loopholes before we sign. I'll go up to the office and email her now.'

'Well, I'm coming up too. I think we should talk about the Jemima-Dad's offer and ask her about that at the same time.'

'True, I guess we need a day together in the office.' Kelly called over to Leon who was reading the newspaper. 'Sorry, my love, but I really have to work today. It's lovely out here but...'

'No problem, I was just waiting for you to finish reading that contract. Robert and I have the idea of going to the Spar for some shopping.'

Michelle and Kelly both looked up sharply.

'Do you mean to go and confront Pascal Mazin?' Michelle asked with a worried frown.

Robert looked up from where he was sitting in the shade at the end of the terrace. 'We do indeed, my dear. The sooner, the better.'

'But he might turn violent. Remember how he was the other day... totally out of his mind.'
At that moment, Coco jumped up and, wagging her tail and barking excitedly, made her usual dash for the front drive.

'I think maybe the cavalry have come to reinforce our small army.' Robert laughed and stood up to greet Sven as he came round the corner of the terrace with Coco circling around him.

'*Bonjour, tout le monde!*' Sven called out, raising his hand in greeting. 'Bonjour, Sven! We were just talking about you! Won't you have a coffee, there's a fresh pot just made.' Kelly said.

Sven looked puzzled as they all laughed. 'Talking about me? Good things, I hope?'

'Definitely good. In fact, we were going to ask you a favour.' Michelle smiled up at him.

'Anything. I should be delighted.'

'Well, we need you to go to the Spar with Robert and Leon.'

Sven, nodded but his handsome face showed his bewilderment.

'Sit down, Sven and we'll tell you all about it!' Kelly smiled and patted the chair between hers and Michelle's.

The week then flew by in the way that a week can when every minute of the day is full of work. By Friday evening nearly all the problems had been tackled and solved, even Pascal Mazin.

'I can't believe he just upped and left!' Kelly said, as she stared into a large saucepan of pasta. She twirled the strands of spaghetti with a long handled spoon. 'Have you ever thought, Mich, that life can be like a pan of boiling spaghetti?'

'Well, no, I can't really say I have.' Michelle laughed and continued to lay the table.

'I mean, this week has just flown by in a great swirl and we keep stirring and trying to keep everything from sticking together.'

'That's just about the funniest metaphor you have ever come up with, Kelly.So you're saying that life is a pan of pasta?'

'Exactly,' Kelly said happily, 'and now it's the exact moment to drain it, so get Robert and Leon to sit down.'

'Ok, the sauce is ready too. And don't even begin to tell me what that represents in our lives. Really Kelly, you're mad!'

'I know, isn't it great!' Kelly poured the large pan of pasta through a colander, steam rose around her as she continued, 'I'm too hungry to be philosophical right now, but I guess the sauce is what makes it all worth while.'

The first few moments of the meal passed in appreciative silence. Then Robert spoke first. 'Delicious, absolutely delicious.' He wound some spaghetti round his fork and raised it up as he asked 'And who is the chef I should be thanking?'

'Oh, a combined effort. I cooked the pasta... to perfect al dente and Michelle messed around making the sauce.' Kelly answered.

'Of course, I should have guessed. A typical combined triumph... just how you two girls have been working all week.'

'Oh, don't you start Dad. It's just a bowl of pasta, OK?' Michelle laughed and grated some extra cheese onto her bowl. 'Well, I thought we should eat simply tonight as tomorrow is the harvest party at the Gilberts.'

'That will make a good ending to a successful week.' Robert said. 'The contract is signed with the film company, negotiations have begun with selling your Chelsea company and what else... oh yes, the mad Spar man is sorted!'

'I was just saying to Mich earlier... I can't believe he just upped and left the village.' Kelly said.

'Well, it was the best thing he could do. I have not told you quite everything.' Leon flashed a wide smile and continued to eat his pasta.

'What do you mean?' Kelly asked, turning to Leon.

Leon made signs to show his mouth was too full to talk and Kelly punched his arm.

'Leon, you can't just say something like that and carry on filling your face with spaghetti.'

'Mmm, mmm, *ça va*, Kelly. Now I tell you! While I was waiting for the DNA profile I spent some time checking police records. Et voilà, just five years ago, Pascal Mazin was in prison for... how do you say... *la réception des marchandises*.'

'Receiving goods, it sounds like to me. So how did he get his job at the Spar? I should have thought a record like that...well...' Robert said thoughtfully.

'Well, he was in prison in Marseilles and it seems his mother told everyone he was working in Tunisia. No-one in the village knows about his prison sentence. Except me, *bien sur*!'

'Well, I'm certainly glad that Sven went with you two.' Kelly said.

'Oh it was easy with Sven towering over him, Pascal suddenly a scared, whining little man. Of course, Sven and Leon were talking in French, so I only got the gist of it.'

'I don't understand 'gist' but I think you understood quite well, Robert. And your French is improving rapidly.' Leon said.

'Well, I was just repeating what you said, really. Not too sure of what it all meant!'

'Anyway, I am incredibly grateful to you both. It is very good to know he has left the village.' said Michelle

'Well, you should be grateful to Sven, too. Maybe you will have an opportunity to show your gratitude tomorrow night, Mich?' Kelly raised her eyebrows suggestively.

'Give over, Kelly. Will you stop trying to plan my love life.' Michelle laughed.

'What love life? Anyway, it's the sauce that makes the pasta, Mich!' Kelly replied and they all laughed and continued their meal.

Saturday passed by in a lazy way. After the week of work and problem solving they each enjoyed doing nothing. Leon and Kelly stayed in bed until nearly lunch time and Michelle and her father took Coco for a long walk through the vines. The sun was bright but the air had an autumnal chill. When they returned to sit on the terrace they sought the last of the day's sunshine.

'Only a week ago we would have been hurrying to sit in the shade,' said Robert.

'Yes, but I love the way the seasons change here. I wonder what winter will be like?' said Michelle.

'Damned cold if you don't get the heating sorted out.' laughed Robert.

'Well, Kelly has arranged a good advance of money from FGM films. Of course they want the Bastide to remain as it is, completely shabby! But I am getting an estimate from Sven's plumber to sort out the boiler. Kelly and I both think the ancient radiators should stay if possible.' Michelle smiled, remembering Kelly's sigh of desperation when Michelle had reported that she had been discussing plumbing on her romantic walk in the vines with Sven.

'Talking of which, I am going to be cunning and take my shower now while the water is hot.' said Robert, 'Anyway, we need to be ready in an hour or so for this party at Sven's place.'

'Hmm, don't think his Mama would like to hear you call the Château – Sven's place... *Maman* is well in command, I should say.'

'All the women round here are...' Robert laughed and went off to have his shower.
Michelle sat a moment longer, thinking back over the week and then forward to all the changes that were to be made. This weekend was the end of a wonderful time of discovery and new opportunities, but she had the feeling that now serious work had to commence. Michelle stood and looked across to the mountains and spoke to Coco who lay at her feet. 'And it won't just be plumbing that needs sorting. But now, I am going to dress up, up up and party, party, party!'

23 'the chandelier glinted with bright light'

Such a night... the moon hung like a bright, white globe high in the cloudless sky. Everything seemed touched with silver, the swaying treetops, the ridges of ploughed earth, the long stretches of vines and the ever present backdrop of Mont Ste.Victoire. Leon drove the old Citroen slowly along the winding lane. Kelly sat beside Leon and Michelle sat with her father in the back. There was silence in the car as though they were all struck by the magic of the night. As they rounded the bend to the gates to Château Gilbert, they all drew in their breath with surprise. Huge torches were flaming at each side of the open gates.

Kelly spoke first.'You know how just before you arrive at some parties, you have that moment of wondering whether you might be over-dressed... you know, that it might just be a casual night with friends...well, let's just say I'm truly glad I'm wearing my very best party frock!'

'Well, I thought a harvest party might be some sort of a barn dance.' said Robert. 'But I'm glad Michelle made me wear my best bib and tucker, too.'

'Leon said they would be inviting their local friends to dinner...' said Michelle, '... and anyway, I remember the last time I came here. Mme. Gilbert runs a very formal house indeed.'

'Am I wearing this correct bob and ticker too?' asked Leon, smoothing his immaculate white shirt.

'You are a prince among men, *mon cher* Leon, and this is not the time to worry about bibs or tuckers as we have arrived and it really does look as though a footman straight out of a film about Napoleon is waiting to open our car doors. I am going to enjoy every rich, aristocratic moment, *mes amis*!' said Kelly, looking quickly at the others before being first out of the car. She then stood demurely waiting to take Leon's arm before walking up the grand steps to the front doors. As soon as they arrived the doors were flung open and they were all ushered into the hall. A wide open space, similar to the hall at the Bastide but so completely restored that it glowed with wealth. The panelled walls were lightly edged with dark gold and the chandelier glinted with bright light. Michelle caught Kelly's glance and they both smiled and nodded. Each understanding the other's silent appreciation of the grand decor. Then Sven came into the hall, larger than life as ever, and welcoming them with open arms. He hurried them out of their coats, tossing them to the two maids waiting. The girls caught the coats and giggled, obviously smitten by their giant of a master.

'Welcome, *bienvenus*! Come into the warm, the hall always remains as cold as a mausoleum whatever my mother does to it!'

Michelle and Kelly exchanged another quick glance as they both thought of the icy draughts in the hall at the Bastide. Certainly, as they entered the next room, a warm blast of air met them. It was the long, formal room that Michelle had seen before but this time there seemed far more people.

Mme. Gilbert advanced across the room to meet them. Her slender, tall figure weaving elegantly between the groups of chatting people.

'Welcome, come close to the fire. The night is so cold,' She led them to the fireside and then Sven said,

'*Maman*, of course, you know Michelle and this is her father, Doctor Robert Phelps, and her best friend and work colleague, Kelly Atkinson and, last but not least, a compatriot of ours, Leon Batiste.'

The usual polite small talk was made and then Mme. Gilbert excused herself as more guests arrived.

'Now,' said Sven, 'I want you to meet my good friends, Calinda and Daniel. Remember, I told you about their pottery.' He ushered them over to a young couple who were standing near the window. The girl was extraordinarily tall and beautiful, her dark skin glinting in the candlelight. The young man was not quite her height but muscular and tanned.

'Is everyone here straight from a film set?' Kelly muttered quietly to Michelle as they approached.

'Good thing you have always practised being Marilyn Monroe then.' Michelle whispered back quickly.

'Okay, Audrey Hepburn, we can match all this!' Kelly replied back and then smiled sweetly as they reached the couple and exchanged handshakes.

'May I introduce Calinda and Daniel Rabin, my very good friends and very good potters.' Sven said, slipping his large arm around the delicate shoulders of the girl.

'Pleased to meet you.' the girl replied, flashing a stunning smile at them all. The young man held out his hand shyly, and muttered, 'Daniel, enchanté!'

'You won't be surprised to learn that Calinda was a London supermodel until she happened to be on a fashion shoot in the lavender fields of Provence and fell hopelessly in love with our local lad, Daniel.' Sven laughed, looking fondly at the young couple.

'Oh my God,' said Kelly, 'Of course, you are the Calinda... famous for disappearing off the catwalk and into nowhere!'

'Oh, the papers made a lot of fuss for a month or so and then forgot all about me!' Calinda gave another slow smile and rested her arm gently on Daniel. 'And it was the best thing I have ever done. I was studying art at Goldsmiths when I was led astray. Offered ridiculous sums of money to model. Well, I was a poor girl from Tunisia, struggling to make ends meet and modelling changed everything. I could even send money to my family in Tunis. So it went on and on... somehow I was caught in a honey trap but I began to hate waking every morning. Luckily I had a good friend in the PR world, Rosie... she's here tonight. Her life changed at the same time. Come and meet her and her husband, Jean-Michel, they're just over there.' Calinda waved a long elegant arm above her head and called out,

'Rosie, come and meet some of your fellow country men.' Calinda laughed and reached her long arm to run her dark hand through Sven's blonde hair. 'Really, Sven, you have no idea. You are always talking about your English friends. In fact, Rosie is the only one, Jean-Michel and Daniel are more French than you are, and I may have lived and worked in London but I am Tunisian. Or did you think I just had a good sun tan?'

The group moved together across the room, laughing and teasing Sven. Michelle wondered idly if she would ever ruffle Sven's hair herself and was surprised to find she no longer felt that sharp stab of desire. Before she could even laugh at herself and the idea, she realised she was being introduced to another young couple. More film star stand-ins, she thought.

'Hi, pleased to meet you.' The girl was about the same height as Michelle, pretty and vibrant with a mass of shining auburn hair that fell loose to her shoulders. 'My name is Rosie, Sven has told me all about you!'

'Well, I'm not sure that he knows all about me, but I hope he was kind.' Michelle replied, her voice slightly cold.

But Rosie giggled delightfully and said, 'Oh, Sven is always kind. Sorry, I know that's a dreadful opener. I hate it when anyone says that to me. Such pressure! Anyway, let me start again... how is it going back at the old Bastide? It must be a daunting challenge.'

Suddenly Michelle knew that she was going to really like this girl. So obviously from London and on her own wavelength. It was stupid to have started off on the wrong foot.

'No, I'm sorry. It's just that I have only just met Sven... but of course he knows all about my arrival out of the blue. The Gilberts have been incredibly kind.'

Rosie giggled again, 'Mme. Gilbert is the epitome of good manners which makes her super kind! There is only one person higher in my esteem and that is Jean-Michel's grandmother.' She turned to the young man standing beside her who was chatting to Kelly. 'Jean-Mi, meet Michelle de Rosefont, the latest English invader in your Provence. Beware! The English are taking over!'

The young man excused himself from his conversation with Kelly and turned to Michelle, his dark olive-skinned face alight with amusement.

'Enchanté, if all the invaders are as beautiful as you two London kids then we shall hand over Provence willingly.' He took Michelle's hand and lightly kissed it.

'Stop flirting, Jean-Mi, you are outrageous and making Michelle blush with embarrassment. I shall have to chastise you later.' Rosie gave Jean-Michel a light slap on his shoulder and giggled again.

'I look forward to that, my love.' Jean-Michel replied, nuzzling his face into her hair and getting another harder slap.

'Behave yourself, Jean-Mi. I shall tell your *Grandmère* how badly you are behaving. I am just going to introduce Michelle to her.'

'Now I really am scared! But you know, *Grandmaman* will never believe you. I am her golden boy. And she knows I am not often allowed out into society. It goes to my head!'

'And that is the dreadful truth.' Rosie smiled ruefully. 'You are always forgiven for your bad behaviour. Now you can return to flirting with the beautiful blonde that you were talking to before and...' Rosie ignored Jean-Michelle's attempts of outraged denial and took Michelle's hand. 'Anyway, Michelle, come with me and meet the real Mme. de Fleurenne... I am just a recent edition.'

Michelle followed Rosie through the crowded room, smiling shyly at the various greetings that they met on their way. She was surrounded by happy laughing people and suddenly felt a pang of loneliness. How she envied Rosie's full and obvious happiness, her complete trust in Jean-Michel, the easy teasing between them. She looked back across the room and saw Kelly, never having looked more beautiful, laughing with Jean-Michel but with her arm through Leon's. Kelly and Leon were so obviously in love, so obviously a couple. There was a definite air of confidence between them.

Then she caught sight of her father, standing tall and so English in his dark navy lounge suit, white shirt and old school tie. He was talking to Mme. Gilbert. Or rather she seemed to be talking to him, holding his arm and looking closely at his face, obviously absorbed in animated conversation. Her tall, Scandinavian beauty had come to life. Michelle smiled, had her father met his match? Then suddenly she found herself in front of a seated woman of great age and beauty.

'May I introduce you to Mme. de Fleurenne, Jean-Michel's grandmother, Mme. de Fleurenne may I present Michelle de Rosefont, our new neighbour at the Bastide de Rosefont.'

Michelle held out her hand and had the ridiculous idea that she should curtsey. Certainly, the elegant old lady seated in front of her had the air of royalty.

'*Enchantée*, my dear, what an adventure you have fallen into!'

'Exactly, Madame de Fleurenne, that is exactly how it feels. A huge adventure.'

Madame de Fleurenne gave a sweet smile and patted a chair beside hers. 'Won't you sit for a while and tell me a little about it? It is as exciting as Alice falling down a rabbit hole! Rosie, you go back to Jean-Michel and make sure he behaves himself. It is so rare that he takes a day off work he is likely to go wild.'

The three women laughed and Michelle took the seat offered. Soon she found herself relating all that had happened since Leon had come into her office. Mme. de Fleurenne was an attentive listener, her lined, beautiful face lighting up with interest when, finally, Michelle began to explain her ideas for an art inspired hotel.

'Why, of course, it is a quite brilliant idea and you may be able to fund it with the rental money from the film company. Imagine, vampires and zombies at Bastide de Rosefont!' Mme. de Fleurenne burst into laughter.

'Well, I must say I was rather shocked at the idea. When Kelly first told me I had imagined a period romp, maybe a knights in armour type film.' Michelle joined in the laughter.

'Oh goodness no, so much more money to be made with zombies, I'm sure. I have a live-in companion now and she has a little boy of ten years old. We often watch films together and one of his favourites... mine too... is all terrifying undead characters roaring around. We love it!' Michelle looked at Mme. de Fleurenne in surprise and admiration, as she continued, 'Oh yes, those period dramas can be very predictable, I find. Anyway, I was thinking that you may be interested in bringing your art lovers to Château de Fleurenne to our perfume museum. My clever daughter-in-law's brainwave. We were nearly bankrupt before she came into our world and changed it for us. Ah, *les jeunes anglaises*, you English girls, so clever!'

'Sven has told me a little about your perfume business. It sounds fascinating... and you have always been the perfume designer?'

'Yes, I am '*le nez*', the nose as it is charmingly called... I just have a natural talent for aromas, I suppose. Of course, I realised immediately you approached that you are wearing Givenchy's

'*L'Interdit*' ... so perfect for your gamine Audrey Hepburn look... and that little black dress, almost backless... it is a brilliant Breakfast at Tiffany's rip-off! I admired you the moment I saw you!' Mme. de Fleurenne laughed quietly and clapped her hands.

'Well, I notice you are wearing an original Otto Klinker... the softness of that pinkish grey velvet... superb!' Michelle nodded in quiet appreciation.

'Ah, you recognise the designer, I have always loved his work and now I work with him and Simon as they are friends of Rosie's. I design their perfumes but I am so very old... I am training Rosie now and she has great potential. You must come to Château de Fleurenne, I have a small collection of original Givenchy, vintage 60's. I think they would fit you and I am never going to wear them again. Rosie is too tall and a size bigger... and of course her style is her own.

'How amazing!' Michelle sighed at the thought of even trying on an original Givenchy dresses... but Mme. de Fleurenne was still talking.

'And your friend, so beautiful and of course perfect for the Marilyn Monroe look... and such a vibrant, exciting creature. The young man with her is captivated.'

Michelle looked across to where Kelly and Leon stood, close together. Kelly in the soft, clinging gold dress that made her hour-glass figure even more stunning that ever, still talking animatedly to Rosie.

'Yes, that's Kelly, we have been best friends since we met at school. We began the retro film star look in our teens. We used to pour for hours over Vogue and made all our own clothes from old dress patterns or found them in second hand clothes shops.'

'Ah, it must be wonderful to have such a friendship. Now she has her man and you are a little lonely perhaps?'

Michelle looked with surprise at Mme. de Fleurenne as she realised that the elderly woman had revealed a truth, a truth that Michelle herself had not quite accepted. She hesitated in her reply. 'Well, yes and no... I mean, we have both had men in our lives before, sometimes we have even liked the same man and worked out who would go out with him. We even fell out once, when we were teenagers, about just that... but it didn't last long. But, you are quite right, this is a new Kelly, and I have to get used to the idea. I knew at once that they were made for each other and I am so delighted for them both. But it is true I don't spend so much time with Kelly now... although of course we shall carry on working together.'

'And talking of work, which we business women always do... you must come with Kelly when you visit us as I think you will both be interested in our parfumerie. Your future hotel clients may want to visit...they can create their own personal perfume at our studio. It is very popular... coach-loads of visitors arrive practically every day from Spring to Autumn. Then... of course, we begin the lavender and flower harvesting. My darling Jean-Mi has the natural inclination to be a playboy but in fact he works so very hard... and Rosie, too. It is good to see them enjoying a night off.'

'They, too, seem wonderfully suited.' Michelle looked across the room again to where Rosie and Jean-Michelle were now talking with her father and Mme. Gilbert.

'Don't worry, my dear, you will find your own perfect partner soon, I am sure.' Michelle looked at Mme. de Fleurenne once again in surprise. Had she read her thoughts?

'Oh, I am not really looking at the moment!' Michelle said, blushing in embarrassment. 'I have the Bastide to keep me busy!'

'True enough! Work can be very absorbing but you will meet someone and then the work will become lighter. I must say, before I met you, I had thought you would be the perfect match for young Sven, especially when I heard his Californian beauty had run away... but, no...' Mme. de Fleurenne laid her hand gently on Michelle's arm. 'I am embarrassing you, I realise, but it is an old lady's privilege, you know. No, Sven will never do.'

'I'm afraid you are right, but how do you know? I have only just realised it myself.'

'Ah, it is easier for me. I can well understand on first meeting the handsome Sven you would fall under his spell. He is certainly the most perfect example of manhood! But for you, my dear, you need someone more cerebral.'

'Cerebral?' Michelle repeated, her eyes stretched wide with surprise.

'Oh that is not to say that dear Sven is stupid, far from it... his knowledge of vinology is encyclopaedic ... but there it mostly stops and I think you need a wider range of interests. Someone interested in the arts generally, someone with a sense of humour... well, I have just met you but I always rely on my intuition and, of course, my vast experience due to very old age.' Michelle nodded thoughtfully, but before she could reply, Mme. de Fleurenne was continuing. 'By the way, I see you are wearing the de Rosefont ruby pendant... I have never seen it look better. It positively glows on your young pale skin and a wonderful substitute to our little friend Audrey's Tiffany pearls! Now, before I embarrass you any further, would you be so kind as to ask your father over to meet me. I am sure you call him your father. It must be very difficult for you to accept the idea of Michel de Fleurenne as your birth father. If you take my advice, which of course you are not obliged to do, you will just enjoy your unexpected legacy and think no more about the man. I knew Michel from a child. He was good enough, a handsome devil, but not perfect, not perfect in many ways. He allowed his mother to arrange a marriage that was most unsuitable. I am sure he only found real love once, and that was with your mother... and so brief. The rest of his life he wasted away in regret and indecision... not to mention too much alcohol. No, if you take my advice, you will forget him and move on to the new future at the Bastide. Now, I really will stop advising you if you bring your father over... I can see Karen Gilbert is quite monopolising him and he looks as though he needs rescuing.'

'the water was as hot as a bath'

'Now THAT... that was what I call a party!' Kelly sat with her chin resting in her hands, still in her dressing gown, and sitting at the breakfast table.

'I have never known a finer evening.' Agreed Robert, sipping a small cup of black coffee.

'And that comes from the cruise-ship romeo doctor.' Laughed Kelly, 'My goodness, I thought Mme. Gilbert would never let you go.'

'Karen is a very gracious hostess.' Smiled Robert.

'Karen! So you are on first name terms with the grand Mme. Gilbert already. You are one fast smooth mover, Dr Phelps.' Kelly continued to tease him.

'You can't embarrass me young lady... but you are quite right, it was a grand dinner.' Robert smiled at Kelly fondly.

'The dinner was just the beginning,' said Leon, 'after that the *fêtes des vendanges* and the country dancing. I have never laughed so much ...seeing you two little girls being whirled around the barn by the local lads. *Oh, là là... c'était trop drôle...* too funny.' Leon began to heave with laughter at the memory.

'Whirled... that is definitely not the right word, Leon! Michelle and I were tossed around the barn like rag dolls... and you did not come to the rescue.' Kelly looked up indignantly and reached for a glass of orange juice.

'Admit... you enjoyed every moment... and one thing for sure, now the locals all think Michelle is the best thing ever to happen to the Bastide.' Leon struggled to reply through his helpless laughter.

Michelle, who had been sitting at the end of the table, quietly drinking her large cup of frothy coffee, joined in, 'Well, I am all for public relations that's for sure. My highlight of the evening was meeting Mme. de Fleurenne. An amazing woman!' Michelle thought back to their long conversation. Never, since her mother had died had any woman seemed to understand her so well. '... and she has invited us to Château de Fleurenne to visit her perfumery. Apart from that though... I thought the next best part of the whole evening was the swimming pool. Wow! The steam was rising up to the night sky, the water was as hot as a bath...wonderful!'

'And everything thought of... those packs of Monoprix black lycra swimsuits in the changing rooms...all sizes. Piles of towels and robes... oh my, Mme. Gilbert certainly knows how to throw a party.'

They all nodded in agreement and continued their breakfast in silence for a moment, each thinking back over the night before.

Then Michelle said, 'And now my friends, the work begins tomorrow. We have twenty-four days exactly before the film crew move on in. Twenty-four very busy days.'

'Well, we can divide the work.' said Leon eagerly, 'Let me know anything I can do.'

'Well, I can think of a thousand.' laughed Michelle.

'And I can think of another thousand,' added Kelly, 'But I was going to suggest that you begin recruiting staff from the village and round about here.'

'Exactly,' agreed Michelle, 'And to find a local builder to clean out the largest barn... the one joining the back of the kitchens. Kelly and I have drawn a first draft for turning it into a canteen... there's a huge stone fireplace that needs sand-blasting, beams to be cleaned off, walls to be lime-washed or rendered... but it will make a great self-service restaurant for the crew.'

Leon was making his usual neat notes in his little black notepad.

'If you could get a guy here for Wednesday... for a meeting that would be great. Mich and I are going to London tomorrow to begin sorting out things in Chelsea. But we'll be back Tuesday evening. I can't leave you longer than that, my sweet Leon.' Kelly leaned against Leon as she spoke and he put down his notepad and put his arm around her and said,

'I know just the man for the building work. He will be looking for some inside work at this time of the year. Then you'll want me to start recruiting cooking and cleaning staff?'

'Great!' Michelle and Kelly spoke as one. Then Robert said

'I shall go to England tomorrow, too, down to Sussex and see the estate agent. My plan is to sell my house and use the money to convert the attics into three flats. What do you think, Michelle?'

'I think I am just the luckiest daughter and girl in the world. I really am so grateful to you all.' She looked around the table at each of them.

'Rubbish, Mich, we are all doing exactly what we want to do... and you are just giving us the chance.' Kelly laughed and promptly sat on Leon's lap and hugged
him.

Michelle had counted the twenty-four days and, as always when more time is needed, they flew by. So, now it was the first of November and everything was completely ready for the arrival of the film crew. The French builders had worked long hours and transformed the barn into a rustic restaurant. Pale beams and white walls made the space seem even larger. Six long refectory tables and benches stretched from length to length, and each side of the newly restored stone fireplace were two large serving tables. The fire burned slowly and Michelle and Leon stood beside it surrounded by a group of people.

'First, I apologise for my French! By now you all know that I am trying to learn and that Leon is my translator and teacher.' The small group all laughed and some gave a gentle hand clap.

A young woman standing near to Michelle replied, laughing, 'I think we all want to speak better English. Perhaps before you speak French?'

'*Merci*, Monique. You may be right... and I suspect we will all be talking with an American accent soon. But now the first work is complete and I intend to study very hard. And work we have these last few weeks... and I want to thank every one of you for all you have done, and especially you, Leon.' Now there was a definite round of applause and calls of 'Bravo, bravo!' Michelle joined in clapping and just as she was about to continue her mobile phone rang. She glanced down and saw Seb Raven's name.

'Sorry, I have to take this... why don't we make use of the restaurant and all have a coffee?' Monique stepped forward and spoke rapidly in French and the group moved and sat at the tables.

Michelle phoned Seb back and he answered immediately. 'Hi Seb, sorry I just missed that...' Leon watched Michelle anxiously as she continued to talk. 'Don't worry, that is fine! Call me when you know for sure. Thanks, bye!' Michelle looked at Leon and laughed aloud.'They're running late at leaving LA. They won't arrive until next week!'

'I don't believe it!' Leon turned as Kelly joined them.

'Did I hear aright?' Kelly said, her eyes wide with surprise.

'Absolutely! He was very sorry to disappoint us and he made it clear they would start paying from today but the crew are not all back from Nevada, or somewhere or other where they have been filming, and so it will be at least another week. Let's tell the staff and relax!'

'I think this calls for a small celebration! Our first staff party!'

Two days later there was still no word from Seb Raven. Michelle carried her mobile in her jeans back pocket and even though she knew she would hear it ring she kept taking it out and looking at it. No missed calls and not even a text message. Kelly checked the bank account and money was rolling in, not just the first deposit but a month's rent in advance showed as a transfer from dollars.

'It's a bit spooky,' Kelly said, looking up from scrolling through the new Bastide bank account. 'I don't think we've ever been paid for doing nothing before. It should feel great but if feels sort of... I don't know, ominous.'

'I know, I don't think we've ever been paid so much before, let alone for doing nothing. It does feel like something is going wrong. Do you think I should call Seb?'

'Too soon, I think, not cool. I heard you ask him to let us know as soon as, sort of thing.'

The two girls looked thoughtfully out of the window above the desk.

'Hmm, I agree,' said Michelle, 'It's a bit frustrating as we could go back to London and sort out all the last hand-over to Jemima... there's so much to do there.'

'Exactly,' agreed Kelly, 'Does it occur to you that neither of us are very good at doing nothing, even when we are paid for it.'

'I bet the staff are making a better job of it. They seemed more than delighted at another paid day off. That's another thing, there is so much we could get them to do inside the Bastide but we can't touch it as it has to be zombie derelict.'

'Do you think we have just found a new designer look ... the zombie shabby Château look?' Kelly said.

'Or the distressed vampire look?' Their laughter was interrupted by Michelle's mobile buzzing. They froze for a second and then Michelle scrambled to take it from her pocket. As she stabbed to answer it, she nodded at Kelly.

'Hi Seb, how are things? Oh no... I see, well we will have to look into that. Let me think about it and I'll call you back.'

Michelle's eyes were wide as she cut the call and looked at Kelly.

'Tell me, tell me,' said Kelly, 'That didn't sound like a good call.'

'Sorry, I didn't have time to put it on speakerphone... the call was so short and I was so shocked. They think they have to cancel the whole film.'

Kelly sat back in her ivory leather chair and ran her fingers back through her long, blonde hair.

'Lets not panic, you handled it well, Mich. Very cool... telling him you would think about it.'

'Well, I didn't feel cool, more hot and cold. Then I began to think about the contract.'

'Exactly,' agreed Kelly, flipping open her laptop and scrolling hurriedly through a list of files.

'Actually, we printed out copies, didn't we? I'll look for the hard copy. I know our solicitor piled in lots of what-if clauses.' Kelly began to flip through a file she kept on her desk. 'Here it is, contract with FGM... blah blah blah... pages and pages... I know there's a delay and cancellation part somewhere.'

'Keep searching and I'll phone the solicitor... it's an hour earlier in England so I may catch her before she goes to lunch.'

'Hello, this is Michelle Phelps.' Michelle paused, hearing her own voice speak the name she was so accustomed to using and wondered for a split second how she had come to be Michelle de Rosefont. But the voice the other end was putting her through and, taking a deep breath to bring herself back to reality, Michelle began a calm explanation of the new situation with the film company.

An hour later they were sitting with Leon and Robert at lunch in the old kitchen. Bowls of soup in front of them and a long baguette ready to be pulled apart.

Robert was talking, for once he seemed to be speaking with the authority of age and experience.

'A contract is a contract, both parties have signed and that is that.'

'But it just seems too incredible that Seb's company did sign that cancellation clause.' said Kelly thoughtfully.

'Well, of course we do have a very good solicitor,' said Michelle. 'We've know her since school days and she was always meticulous to the point of boring about detail.'

'Quite,' nodded Kelly in agreement, 'She wasn't really my friend, she was such a goody-goody, you know, always handed her homework in on time, or rather, exactly on time. She was the sort of girl who wore her school uniform like it should be worn.'

'Rather than roll her skirt waist band over to make it a mini skirt, you mean?' Michelle laughed, 'But luckily we always stayed friends with her and stopped other kids bullying her. In fact, you introduced her to her first boyfriend at the end of school prom dance. Then she married him!'

'Exactly, first man she ever met. Oh my God, you mean she owes me, Mich?' Kelly laughed out loud. 'They were so well suited... I bet he's an accountant now!'

Robert spoke again, 'Well, it seems to me that your solicitor has now paid back any favour she might owe you two. The last clause re. cancellation makes it very clear that if the film company pull out within a month of the starting date then the entire rental term will be paid in full.'

'Six months rent for doing nothing!' Leon slapped the table in shock and delight.

'Actually we are entitled to eight months rent. She added in a clause... something about cancellation resulting in other lost bookings.' Said Kelly.

'Well, all I can say is that you may have thought your school friend boring but she has a good legal brain.' said Robert.

'Of course, we have to wait to see if Seb or his company make any appeals... but she says it is a watertight contract and they have to pay up or we sue.'

'Let's hope they do the decent thing and just transfer the dosh without any protest then.' said Kelly. 'We can start anyway on renovation now. Eight months rent will do very nicely!'

'Very nicely, indeed!' agreed Michelle, nodding. 'Four months rent for not having to fill the poor old Bastide with vampires and zombies.'

'C'est incroyable!' Said Leon.

'*Incroyable*! Incredible!' Michelle and Kelly repeated in perfect unison.

25   *'enthusiastic clapping and laughter'*

　　The next day Michelle called a staff meeting back in the newly decorated barn. Once again the fire was lit and coffee being brewed. Michelle stood beside Kelly and Leon, waiting for everyone to arrive and settle.
　　'This won't be easy, Mich, I mean they have all been looking forward to working with film stars and stuff...even though they would all have been zombies and vampires.' Said Kelly quietly.
　　'I know, but as they are all going to...' Michelle stopped speaking as her mobile rang. Once again she looked at Kelly and nodded, saying just the one word,
　　'Seb!' Kelly nodded back and stood close, pulling Leon beside her as Michelle switched to speakerphone. 'Hi Seb , how are you?' Michelle kept her voice light and friendly, hoping to avoid any argument.
　　'Hi Marquise, I guess I'm fine but it's hell on earth here right now. So many problems I can't begin to tell you, but I just wanted to ask you... what do you think about the idea of delaying the whole project until Spring next year? Give me a few months to pull things together over here?'
Michelle glanced at Kelly and they both shook their heads at once.
　　'No way!' whispered Kelly and Michelle nodded quickly in agreement.
　　'Well, I'd like to be able to help you out there, Seb, but I'm afraid we already have bookings for April. It would be impossible, I'm sorry.'
　　'Well, I just thought I'd reach out to you, Marquise, and give it a whirl, I didn't really think it would be a goer. We'll just have to call it quits and

pay up. No problem there. I'll make sure the funds are transferred by the end of the week. We've already had email from your fancy London solicitor... an email written like something out of Dickens. Gee, what style you English do have! Anyways, no need to recourse to legal intrusion, the eight months rent will be paid in full. No problem, Marquise... and it will go down as a tax loss this end.'

'Well, thank you for your honourable response, Seb.' Michelle smiled at Kelly and almost giggled.

'Wow, I'm not sure anyone's ever called me honourable before... but I like it, I like it a lot. My big regret over this whole issue is that I won't get to work with you, Marquise.'

'Well, I'll keep you up to date with all that we're planning to do here at the Bastide and perhaps you'll visit one day?'

'Now that I look forward to, Marquise. Shall...'

'Anyway, Seb, I have someone waiting on me now so I have to go. Speak soon, good-bye.' Michelle quickly closed the call and looked at Kelly and Leon and started to laugh. 'Oh my god, Kelly, I just had to cut him off... I couldn't hold up the Marquise act any longer... and he is sending the money without any dispute.'

'Holy Moly, Mich, how did you last that long. You sounded so haughty... I can't believe you thanked him for being honourable... honestly, Mich, honourable?'

'Well, he is honourable actually, it just slipped out as the right word... but I know it's not how I normally speak. Somehow the more American he became the more olde worlde English I sounded. Oh dear, it was dreadful.'

'Basically he just has the hots for you anywayzzz, it's kinda obvious Mar- queeeeze! Serve you right if he does come to visit here.'

'Yes, I realised I was going a bit too far at that point. Oh well, he'll never turn up really and if he does I shall hide in one of the attics whilst you say I've died or something.'

'Talking of attics... I can't wait to begin the conversion.' Kelly said.

'I know, me too, but first let's get this staff meeting over with... at least now we can tell them they can count on jobs for at least the next eight months.'

Michelle walked back the length of the barn and picked up a glass and lightly tapped it with a spoon. She stood between Kelly and Leon and broke the news. The group moved and muttered uneasily at first but Michelle continued confidently with Leon smoothly translating.

'So, to end up now, my father, whom you all know as Dr Phelps, brought me up to turn adversity to advantage. In fact, I don't really see this news as adversity but more an opportunity to move quickly on to our next project here at the Bastide. I want you all to know that you definitely have work for the next eight months at least... all through the winter and longer... but the work will be different. Anyone who does not like that idea can, of course, drop out at any time.'

Once again the group began to mumble between each other.

'Don't lose them now, Mich' muttered Kelly, 'You were going great guns.'

Michelle continued, her voice loud and clear. 'I suggest this... you all have talents... I have seen that already. Different talents and skills that I may not be aware of yet. I suggest I draw up a list of new work opportunities and you can apply. There will always be general duties, cooking, gardening and cleaning, of course. But if you feel you have an interest in any of the other offers I have, then let Leon know. He will spend the rest of the day with me and Kelly, drawing up a work schedule and outlining the new project. Then, of course he will have to translate it for me... which brings me to my last idea for today. You will soon find out that Kelly and I have at least one new idea every day... I suggest an evening, maybe two or three times a week, when we have a language school... English for you and French for me, Kelly and Dr Phelps. This will be voluntary and, of course, free for you all. Thank you for listening and, oh yes, this is your last paid day off... work begins again tomorrow at eight am. Thank you *et merci bien tout le monde!*'

Now there was enthusiastic clapping and laughter as Michelle smiled and moved away from the group.

Back sitting round the kitchen table, Kelly spoke first. 'That was great, Mich. Quite a speech! You had them all in the proverbial palm... don't even ask, Leon. No time for proverbs or idioms... Mich made a good speech and has set us up for a long day's work. I suggest we make sandwiches and retire to the upstairs office as fast as we can. We need a scaled down version of the hotel project, a detailed list of new work opportunities and general labour and, as if that is not enough... then Leon has to translate if all. Come on, let's get started.' Kelly bounced out of her chair and began to carve long slices through the day's delivery of baguettes.

Michelle stood up and began to lay out the plates and napkins.'Good idea, Kelly, this is just like old times when we used to eat at our desks.'

'Oh yeh, just like old times except we're in a 16th century Provençal Bastide that happens to belong to you, your Dad and your crazy dog will soon be back from walking your estate and vineyards and join us, along with my dark, handsome lover-boy Leon... what else is so like the good old times... oh yes, we have a staff of twenty to organise and, one last thing, the view of the mountain from our desk is a world heritage site. Yeh, as you said, just like old times!'

By the end of the first week of the new work programme there was a definite improvement in the Bastide. The response from Michelle's request to tap any skills of the workers had revealed hidden gold. Not just crafts-people - carpenters, stonemasons, painters and decorators but also computer specialists and artists.

'It just shows the problem of employment in these Provençal hill villages.' said Robert. 'Quite remarkable that people with these skills had applied to work as general cleaners and labourers.'

'Well, young people round here often have to move away to find work. They would have been delighted with the opportunity and now, even more so, if their skills can really be used to advantage.' said Leon.

'I spose they were a bit disappointed at first, I mean, quite exciting to be working with film stars, even zombied.' said Kelly, 'But now it really does seem to be going well.'

'I know, the work they have got through this week is phenomenal. But then, when you think about there being twenty people for an eight hour day... I guess it adds up.'

They were sitting in a small restaurant in Aix en Provence, celebrating the end of their first week of renovation works by eating out. The low coilingcd, candlclit rcstaurant was filled with other diners and a small band of Provençal musicians played quietly at the far end of the long room.

'Ah, it was a great idea, Robert, to come here.' Kelly said appreciatively as the waiter brought their first course. 'The new cook in our own barn kitchen is excellent... possibly better than this meal will be... but somehow, it's still linked with work. This is great.'

Leon put his arm around Kelly's shoulder. 'You have worked so hard this week, Kelly. I haven't seen you in action like that... impressive!' he said, kissing her lightly on the cheek. 'You, too, Michelle, both of you... *vous avez travaillé comme un boeuf*!'

'Did I understand that you just said Kelly and Michelle were like beef?' said Robert laughing.

'Careful, Leon, you may not live long enough to eat your dinner!'

Leon held up his hands in defence. 'Non, mais non, Robert... you are making big trouble for me... is a French idiom... it means they have been working so hard!'

Kelly and Michelle joined in the laughter.

'Well, I may forgive you,' said Michelle, 'at least until I have looked it up in my new French idiom book. Maybe, it's like our 'working like a dog'... anyway, I can forgive you anything after all the work you have done yourself this week, Leon. You haven't stopped.'

'*Alors, moi... je travaille comme un cheval de labour!* So how do you translate that old saying?'

'Well, that's easy... a work horse.' Kelly smiled brilliantly, 'You know, I think this French language stuff is going to be a cinch. I'm really looking forward to the lessons next week. That was a great idea, Mich.'

'Well, there was a perfect example of what I meant about the skills of our staff. I mean, finding we already have a French girl on the staff who has just finished a degree in teaching English... it's ideal. It will give her a chance to get some experience, too.' said Robert

'Yes, Louise... and did you know she's going out with the builder, the very tall one, Jacques, I think... he came to us from the Gilberts' recommendation.' said Michelle.

'Oh, yes, that reminds me, Karen called me today and...' Robert began but Kelly interrupted him,

'Really! Karen called you to ask you out for a hot date, Robert? Mmm?'

'Behave yourself, Kelly!' Robert continued, 'As I was trying to say, Karen Gilbert, Mme. Gilbert if you prefer, rang me to give me the website for the Fondation du France...'

Once again Kelly interrupted, 'Well, I have heard of some chat-up excuse lines but to give you a website address... Fond what?'

'Kelly, I warned you, behave! This is important... it involves money!' Robert said.

'Now you have my full attention, Robert, but do tell me what the Fond thing is about.'

'I think Robert is talking...or trying to...about the Fondation du France...it is a national heritage, maybe something like your National Trust, I think,' said Leon.

'Now you have my attention, too, carry on Dad.' said Michelle.

'Well, Karen,' Robert paused briefly and gave a warning glance at Kelly who smiled innocently, 'When we were talking at the party last week, she told me about the grant she had received from the Fondation du France. Apparently if you agree to open your property to the public for at least one day a year, then you can apply for grants to help restore a property of historic importance.'

'A grant! Why had we never thought of that? Of course, but it sounds too good to be true. And how can it work to be open only one day a year.'

'I'll find out first thing tomorrow.' said Leon. 'I am sorry not to think of it before. I do know of this a little... every year, on the third weekend in September, there are historic properties open all over France that are not usually open to the public. I will find all tomorrow. But I think to have a grant may be very slow... I don't know.'

'Well, Karen knows the head of the organisation here in Provence so she can be helpful.' said Robert.

'I'm sure she can... I think you should ask your Karen out for dinner tomorrow, Robert.' said Kelly

'She is not my Karen, now eat up young lady or I swear I shall tell the musician over there that you are a famous English singer and that you want to join them in a song.'

'That is a cruel threat, Dr Phelps, you know I can't sing a note.' Laughed Kelly, glancing over at the group of musicians. Suddenly she grabbed Michelle's arm, adding in a low voice, 'Mich, look over there in that alcove corner ... isn't that the lovely young man from the art gallery in Aix... the one you chatted up?' Michelle looked cautiously to where Kelly was looking.

'Yes, I think it is. Yes, it definitely is now I see him turned round. Oh my God, now he's seen me staring at him and he's coming over. Kelly, can you never shut up... first you try to set my Dad up with Mme. Gilbert and now you're having a go at me... you're like some demented version of a character from Jane Austen. What is it with you and match-making? And can I remind you that he was wearing a wedding ring and that young woman that he has now left sitting on her own is probably his wife. '

'Just want everyone to be as happy as little me!' said Kelly in her huskiest Marilyn Monroe voice.

Robert half rose from his chair as the young man approached and held out his hand. 'Good to see you again!' Robert looked around for an extra chair. 'We so much enjoyed our visit to your gallery. My name is Robert Phelps and this is my daughter, Michelle and her friends Kelly and Leon. Won't you and your friend join us?' The young man shook

Robert's hand and then all their hands in the traditional French manner. Michelle waited for a buzz of electricity as he held her hand in his but nothing happened... it was just a pleasant and warm handshake.

'My name is Marc Bernier, delighted to meet you all. That would be very nice... I am here with my sister. I'll ask her to come over.'

He walked back the length of the restaurant and Kelly immediately dug her elbow into Michelle's ribs.

'You see... his sister... not his wife. I knew it. He's really hot, Mich. I mean if I hadn't found perfection in Leon then...'

Before Michelle could begin to reply, Marc was making his way back toward them with a young girl following shyly after him. There was definitely a family likeness, Michelle decided, and suddenly the electric tingle that she had missed with his hand shake came back to hit her. Her stomach butterflied as Marc, sitting in a chair squashed between her and Leon, momentarily pressed his thigh against hers. Had Kelly said he was hot? The warmth of him flooded through Michelle and she felt her cheeks blush. She turned quickly to speak to Marc's sister, covering her embarrassment with polite conversation.

Then Kelly took over the conversation. Michelle briefly closed her eyes as she heard the first words and knew immediately where Kelly was heading.

'So, do you live in Aix, Marc?' Kelly asked, her face innocent and enquiring.

'Well, my family live here but I have an apartment in Paris as my work takes me there a good deal.'

'What about your wife? Does she go to Paris with you? Do you have children?' Kelly asked. Michelle closed her eyes again, awaiting the response. How could Kelly give the third degree to this man?

'Oh no, by family I meant my mother and father... and of course my sister, Marie. No, no wife or children, I'm sorry to say... not yet anyway.'

Before Kelly could continue with her interrogation... Michelle could well imagine her continuing to ask if he wanted a wife, how many children and if he liked dogs... she spoke hastily to Marc herself.

'You'll have to excuse my friend Kelly, she always wants to know everything about everybody she meets. It's just her way!'

'Not at all, it's charming and friendly... much better than our old-fashioned French ways of exchanging formal and banal greetings. I love the English for their direct openness. Maybe the Americans can go too far but, in my experience, the English always have it just so.'

Michelle looked at him in relief... and then realised she was looking closely into the darkest of brown eyes fringed with the blackest of lashes.

'leading up to asking her out'

'So, did he ask you out?' Kelly put her arm through Michelle's as they walked around the cobbled courtyard behind the barns.

'Kelly, you said you wanted to look at the barns together and go for a walk to discuss the renovation. Not to interrogate me about Marc Bernier.' Michelle sighed and took her arm away from Kelly's grasp and walked ahead quickly.

Kelly took a few little skips to catch up with her again and said, 'But Mich, you were talking together for ages. I mean, sitting so close together, you were practically in his lap... come on, what were you talking about. I bet he did ask you out.'

'We were talking about lots of stuff. I don't know... Aix en Provence, food, art... by the way, that's not his gallery... he works all over the place... often in Paris, sometimes New York, even Japan.'

'So... did you say... *ooh là*, I just love Paris in the winter and did he ...'

'No, no and no, Kelly... nothing like that... it was just a friendly chat.'

'Well, all I can say is that you are completely hopeless and I'm going back to the warm kitchen to have a large cup of coffee. We can discuss the renovation perfectly well there.' Kelly turned on her heel, her long leather boots smattered with mud, and stomped back in the direction of the Bastide.

'I suppose so,' said Michelle quietly to herself. She had to admit that Kelly was probably right. There had been several moments in the conversation when she had felt that Marc was leading up to asking her out but somehow... quite possibly through her own fault... she had fended him off. It was not exactly shyness, more some vague feeling that she wanted it to be exactly right. Of course, that was ridiculous and now she knew it. She had spent most of the night going over and over their conversation. Imagining how she could rewrite her side of it. But in the cold light of dawn, on the brink of finally falling asleep, she had felt nothing but regret. Michelle walked slowly after Kelly, watching her friend striding ahead. She gave a long yawn and then, calling to Coco, ran to catch up with her as they arrived at the back kitchen door. Kelly turned to look at her and gave a big smile.

'Coffee? Just like the old times? We'll heat a pot on the old range and sit at the end of the oak refectory table ... the only thing that I can actually think of that is just the same as our old times is the way we work together, Mich. No matter where! Now, you stop moping and I'll stop behaving like an old Pride and Prejudice aunt and we'll do what we do best... draw and plan.'

And so they did but somewhere in the back of Michelle's mind was the thought that Kelly could be right. Had she unconsciously given Marc the cold shoulder, somehow sending the wrong message? There was no doubt that she had hoped he would ask to see her again. Should she have asked him to visit the Bastide? As if reading her thoughts, Kelly threw down her pencil and said,

'Oh for crying out loud, Mich, why the hell don't you just take the afternoon off and drop in at his bloomin' art gallery?'

'Oh no, I couldn't... and I doubt he would be there and...anyway, I prefer to play it cool as... '
Kelly interrupted Michelle. 'And at least fifty other good excuses you can dream up. I know, you Mich, you will mope for a while and then throw yourself into work again.'

'Well, I'm not even going to mope for another five minutes... we have much too much to do. I am sure I shall see Marc again soon, somehow or other, and until then... work!'

'True enough. I am sure you will see him again very soon... actually if you look up from your desk for a moment you might notice that he is outside on the terrace, admiring the view of Mont Ste.Victoire and talking to Sven and your Dad. Oh my, just to complete the scene, there comes my Leon into the picture. Come on Michelle, we can work later. I think we need some fresh air.'

Michelle craned her neck and leaned forward over the desk, just in time to see the small group of men walk out of sight and round toward the front terrace.

'Quick, Kelly, I think he's going!' Michelle ran from the office.

Kelly followed, giggling as she said, 'Yeh, play it cool, Mich, very cool, just don't break your neck running down the stairs!'

The two girls landed in the hall just as the front door opened and Robert came in,

'Come in, Marc, there is always a pot of coffee in the old kitchen.' He said, spreading his arm wide to welcome Marc.

Michelle took a deep breath and then moved forward, with the help of a small push in the middle of her back from Kelly.

'There you are, Michelle,' her father said, smiling broadly. 'I told Marc you two were working upstairs in the office and he didn't want me to disturb you. I told him you wouldn't mind. Do we have any coffee on the go?'

'Yes, of course.' Michelle took another smaller breath and held out her hand, bracing herself for the electric shock treatment. And yes, this time as he held her hand in his she felt a jolt of something that could only be desire. Her knees weakened in a ridiculous way as she stood in front of him, so close and under his dark brown-eyed gaze. Marc held her hand for a long moment and then gently let it go and brushed his hair back from his forehead. Was he nervous... had he felt the same rush of heat? This French hand-shaking stuff was dangerous. Before Michelle could think further, she realised that Sven had followed Marc into the hall and was politely waiting for her to greet him. She wrenched herself away from looking at Marc and turned to Sven.

'Sven, lovely to see you. How are you?'

Sven bowed his huge body to kiss her on each cheek and then said, 'I was just passing and thought I'd drop by to see how it's all going. Of course it is all round the village that the film is cancelled. How is that going to work out?'

They all continued along the corridor, talking and chatting. Marc followed, rather on the outside of the group, as they explained about the film company's contract and the advanced work of the renovation.

As they sat round the table, Marc began to enter into the conversation, obviously interested in the history of the Bastide.

'How about a grand tour of the place, Marc, if you have time?' asked Robert.'

'I'd love to... I am catching the train to Paris later this afternoon but plenty of time.' He looked at his watch and Michelle caught a glimpse of a slim, gold watch on a leather strap around his tanned wrist. She took a small, inward breath, and subdued the sudden desire to take his hand in hers. Luckily Robert was speaking again and she realised it was to her.

'Michelle, are you with us or dreaming as usual?' her father was smiling fondly across the table at her.

'Of course, I'm listening, Dad.' she replied hastily, thinking that fortunately he didn't know all her dreams. 'Why don't we walk round the grounds first as the sun is so warm at mid-day, and then if everyone has time we can tour the dereliction of indoors later. Mind you, it's probably warmer out than in...'

Sven looked up and said, 'Did you ever get a quote from that heating engineer. I know our builders are here, I saw their lorry in the drive.'

'Yes, I have been meaning to thank you and your mother for the recommendations. It's great to have local knowledge.'

'Anything for you, Michelle!' Sven gave a charming smile and stood up, quickly moving to hold Michelle's chair as she, too, stood. Michelle noticed Marc give a quick glance at Sven and then to herself. Was he wondering if she and Sven were involved? There was nothing she could do about that and anyway, she thought wryly, she was probably being over-sensitive... especially as she seemed tuned in to every single body movement that Marc made. Now he was heading to the door and chatting to Leon in French. Kelly was talking to Robert and so as they reached the back door, she found herself next to Sven. Exhibiting his usual impeccable manners, he held the door as she passed through ahead of him and then they called to Coco at exactly the same moment. Michelle noticed Marc's head turn quickly to look back at her as she stood next to Sven, Coco circling round them, licking each of their hands in turn and jumping up excitedly. Michelle looked down at the dog in mock despair, did the dog really have to behave as if she and Sven were a married couple that took their dog for a walk every day? The small group walked along the terrace, admiring the spectacular view across the vines to Mont Ste. Victoire. Michelle strained her ears to hear what Marc was saying to Leon but she could only catch the odd word and guessed they were talking about Cezanne. But Sven was talking and she tried to concentrate...

was he really talking about plumbing again? Kelly was walking just ahead and turned round with a wide smile.

'Sven, I thought you always talked about wine but now I see you have other interests.'

Sven's handsome face was puzzled as he replied, 'True, Kelly, I think I do talk a lot about wine but it is the thing I know most about... and it is fascinating to me ... maybe boring to others... I don't know.'

Michelle felt a pang of sympathy with Sven and glared at Kelly. 'Don't worry, Sven, Kelly is just being Kelly. She is incredibly rude and nothing is more boring than that.' To prove her point she laid her hand lightly on Sven's arm and at that very moment Marc turned round again. Michelle could hardly snatch her hand away, so with a silent sigh, she just carried on. When they reached the square courtyard behind the barns they entered a scene of activity. Four men were busy unloading sacks of plaster, two others were erecting scaffolding against the rosy stone-walled corner tower and Monique was chatting to a group of six women. As they drew near she came over to them.

'Bonjour, Michelle, I am happy to see you... is just the good moment... we are planning how to begin on the next week's schedule of work inside La Bastide.'

Michelle joined the group and then noticed that Monique was staring at Sven, a blush tinting her olive-skinned cheeks as she said,

'Bonjour, Sven, comment ca va?'

Sven shook Monique's hand and then turned to Michelle.

'Can you excuse us a moment, Michelle. I knew Monique before she went to college... I'd like a word with her if you don't mind?'

'Of course not, go ahead. Monique and I will talk later. We really weren't going to work Saturday anyway. Everyone is working overtime.'

'*Merci*, Michelle, so many things to do, we all want to start but I will not talk long with Sven, thank you.'

Michelle watched as Sven and Michelle walked together across the courtyard. Suddenly, with her instincts that morning on red alert, she realised that Sven and Monique were in love, or they had been. There was something in the way he leaned over her as they talked and the way she looked back up at him. Of course, it could be her over-active imagination but Michelle made a mental note to find out more... or at least gossip to Kelly about it. Right now, she was determined to catch up with her father and Marc.

27   'he invited Sven as well'

'So finally, finally he asked you out? Do I have it right or not, Mich?' Kelly sighed heavily.

'Well, yes... well, sort of... there's a preview at the gallery next Saturday and he said he'd send tickets.'

'Did I hear you right, Mich, did you really say the word ticket with an s on the end? So your hot date is a family group outing?' Kelly swivelled round in her desk chair and glared at Michelle.   'Girl, you sure is gonna be the death of me. I know you're out of practice but even you should know that a bunch of freebie tickets to an art show is not the same as a romantic night out. Honestly, Michelle... hopeless again.'

'Well, Dad immediately told Marc that he would love to come but would be in England... and...'

Kelly interrupted, 'Ah ha...I see light at the end of the love tunnel...so it only needs for me and Leon to say we regrettably can't attend and you get to go on your own. Yes!' Kelly punched her hand in the air.

'Well, not quite alone.' Michelle said quietly, suddenly becoming very busy looking through files on her laptop screen.

'Not quite alone... now just what does that mean?'

'Well, he invited Sven as well. I mean he was there at the time and he just said he'd send us all tickets.'

'I totally despair. Are you trying to tell me that you are going on your hot date with Marc and Sven is tagging along too?'

Suddenly, Michelle swivelled her chair round to face Kelly. 'I quite forgot! I was going to tell you. I think there is something between Sven and our lovely Monique!'

'You're joking! How do you know?' Kelly bounced on her chair with excitement. 'Now here's another romance I can foster... hmm... the blonde Viking God and the dark Provençal beauty... oh yes!'

'Hold on, I don't really know anything for sure... it was just something in the way they were looking at each other... and Sven said something about he had know her some time ago.'

'Well, that's a big emotional statement coming from the stern Sven. And do you know what Monique studied at her uni in Marseilles, Mich?'

'No idea, some sort of natural science, I think. No, not sure, I can tell she has great organisational skills, she's a born leader.'

'I happened to be looking back at her c.v. the other day... and I agree ... she does have managerial skills... and everyone seems to like her. But, can you believe, her degree was in viticulture which is the posh word for growing vines.'

'Really? She actually studied vines... why, that's just perfect!'

'Oh yes, just imagine the romantic conversations they will have together!'

'Maybe she likes plumbing, too.' Michelle added in a quiet voice and both girls clapped a high five, span their chairs in a victory twirl and burst out laughing.

28   'in the afternoon dusk'

It was yet another perfect Provençal day. The low winter sun cast long shadows across the vines as Michelle took her afternoon walk with Coco. The red earth was hard underfoot and it was cold enough for her breath to steam the cold air in front of her. Michelle pulled up her collar and walked faster, Coco running ahead and then turning back to her, her tail constantly wagging. Michelle sighed as she considered the joy of the simple life of a dog. Her own life, although full of good fortune and friendship, was anything but simple. It was Friday and the end of a frantic week of planning, ordering materials and talking with workers. Her father had been over at the Gilberts all day and he was off to England tomorrow. Kelly had been in Chelsea managing the final stages of handing over their business to Melissa. Michelle frowned at the thought. Not that she had any regrets, but she should have been helping Kelly. She knew that Kelly didn't even want to be in London, even for a few days. Kelly and Leon were inseparable it seemed. Michelle thought back to her conversation with the elderly Mme. de Fleurenne. She had suggested that Michelle was finding it hard to adjust to losing the closeness of her friend. She supposed it to be true. Not that she wasn't delighted that Kelly had found her soulmate, but yes, in some ways there was a gap which Kelly's laughter and energy had always filled. A moment like now. Michelle walked on resolutely, determined not to wallow in self-pity when she had so much to be thankful for. She looked around for Coco and then saw her down the bottom of an avenue of vines, jumping up and greeting a man. A man who could only be Sven. Even at such a distance and in the afternoon dusk, his giant silhouette could be no other than the Viking god. As she looked he raised a long arm in greeting and began to walk uphill toward her.

'Be careful what you wish for... the Norseman cometh.' Michelle muttered to herself, now regretting that she couldn't continue in peaceful solitude. Squaring her shoulders, she raised a hand in return and added a quiet, 'Skol!' Coco reached her long before Sven had marched up the steep slope. Michelle leant down to pat the dog's head, 'Bravo, Coco. Did you think I was feeling a bit lonely?' Before she could waste any more sarcastic words on the dog, Sven was at her side. Huge and friendly and shy, yes, of course, he was shy, Michelle realised.

'Hi Sven! Isn't it a wonderful afternoon. Cold, but the sky so unbelievably blue!'

Michelle turned her cheeks for the obligatory kisses of greeting. How could she once have thought she was in love with this man? Well, that was obvious, Michelle almost laughed aloud at her own question as she had a quick close-up of his smooth tanned skin stretched over high cheekbones and then, with the second kiss, a fleeting touch of his slightly bristly square chin. He was too handsome to be real.

'Good to see you, Michelle. I always mean to ask you how you are getting on with Coco? I can have her back at the Château any time if she's too much of a handful.'

Michelle looked at him in horror, 'Oh, God no! I love her. I couldn't bear it if you took her back.' Michelle rested her hand on the dog's collar as if to maintain possession.

Sven's stern face creased into unusual laughter as he replied hastily. 'Don't look so scared, Michelle. I was only checking. I'm delighted you like her. I'll bring over her pedigree details and you can be the real named owner on her paperwork. You know the

French, several copies in different colours for everything.'

'You talk about the French as though you are not one of them yourself.' laughed Michelle, relieved at his answer. 'I was just going to turn heel and go back to the Bastide when I saw Coco had found you. Will you come back for a cup of English tea?'

'I'd love to. It has made so much difference to me having you living here nearby.' Sven put his arm gently around Michelle's shoulders as they walked together back up the hill.

Michelle felt sure this was a companionable arm around her shoulder. Well, almost sure. Like any beautiful woman she was always aware of a man's approach and closeness. Had she been completely wrong in her interpretation of Sven's feelings for Monique? In one way it was good to feel the friendliness of being held in his strong arm and almost propelled up the hill... but, and a big but... did it mean more than friendship? Coco circled around them enjoying the simplicity of her life.

When they arrived at the Bastide they went straight to the kitchen door and over to the warmth of the range. Coco slumped down in her usual place under the table and Michelle hurried to rinse her hands and put the kettle on the range. 'Take a seat, do... I've some cake in a tin somewhere. I expect someone else will be along for tea soon. We always seem to end up here round the table, endless coffees and cups of tea.' Michelle found herself talking nervously to fill the silence. Never had the kitchen seemed so quiet and empty. She busied around Sven, finding cups and saucers and the cake tin. He sat uneasily at the table, his wide shoulders hunched and his head forward as though he was deep in thought. When the kettle finally boiled and Michelle poured the boiling water into the teapot he suddenly stood up, as though concerned he had neglected his usual impeccable manners.

'Sorry, can I help you, Michelle?' he stood uneasily, hovering over her as she stood at the range.

'No, no of course not! It's all ready at last. The kettle takes forever to boil on this old range.' Michelle took the teapot and hurriedly moved away from Sven and sat at the table opposite to where he had been sitting. She poured the tea and Sven returned to his place. Again there was an awkward silence between them as they both sipped the hot tea and then Sven spoke,

'Michelle, I know we haven't known each other very long but I feel we have become good friends.'

Michelle's heart sank, was this an awkward opening to a declaration of love. True, they had not know each other that long but didn't he realise that some of that time she had longed for him to make a move and the rest of the time he had been engaged to Melissa... and now, most important of all, she knew she was falling in love with Marc Bernier. Before Michelle could answer, Sven continued to speak,

'There is something I really want to talk to you about...well, to ask your advice, really.'

Advice, that was a new one, Michelle thought although she answered, 'Go ahead, Sven. I should be happy to give advice but not sure it would be worth taking. I mean, is it something I would know about?'

'Oh yes, you see it's... well, I suppose you would say... a girl thing?' Sven raised his head and gave her the benefit of one of his best wide toothpaste ad smiles.

Oh my lord, thought Michelle, you're about to tell me you are gay. The Viking god! Why, oh why, did nobody come into the kitchen. It was now teatime for goodness sake, where was everybody... anybody?

But Sven was continuing, his blonde head dropped low as it seemed he was studying the grain of the old oak table,

'I think you may have guessed the truth anyway?'

Michelle shook her head vigorously and answered hurriedly, 'No, really, Sven. I have no idea what you want to ask me about but go ahead. I'm listening.'

'Well, it's about Monique...' Sven looked up again at Michelle as she struggled to smother a huge sigh of relief.

'Monique!' Michelle's voice was squeaky high with the relief. 'Are you trying to tell me that you are in love with Monique?'

It was as though the sun had come out in Sven's troubled face and he began to talk as though he had never talked before.

'I knew you had noticed, Michelle. You have such a sympathetic nature. I told you that I had known Monique before she went off to university. Well, that was less than the whole truth. Monique and I first met when we were four years old at our first day at school. I loved her then and asked her to marry me! Well, I think we were both about eight years old when I got round to proposing and she accepted. I even bought her a ring. Then, I was sent away to school in England, I was absolutely wretched and miserable. I begged to be able to go to the lycée in Aix, where Monique went... but my mother refused. I lived for the long summers when I came back home and could be with Michelle. Then, the last summer before we were both going to university... I remember, such a hot summer... when I came home I went straight to her house and her mother told me Monique had gone out with her boyfriend. Well, you can imagine my misery. At first, I just couldn't believe it, but after a week or so and a few rows, I even threatened her boyfriend... it was hopeless. Well, I just went to work in the grape vines and tried to forget her. Then, four years at university, then a final year studying and working in a large winery in California... and there...well, finally I met Melissa.'

Sven came to a halt and sat back in his chair as though exhausted at his long speech. Michelle continued for him,

'Finally, there in California you met and became engaged to Melissa?'

'Exactly so,' Sven took a deep breath, his wide forehead creased with the effort and the memory. 'Melissa was so beautiful, irresistible and she even seemed to like me. Her parents own this vast wine empire in the hills above LA. It seemed meant to be... and of course my dear mother was ecstatic. Well, at first, anyway...'

'What went wrong?' Michelle asked, leaning across the table toward Sven who seemed to be struggling with an inner demon.

'Well, two things at once, I suppose. I had a huge argument with Melissa... not long after you came on the scene... well, I suppose that was it really, you arrived out of the blue and into the middle of our lives.'

'But, but how could I change everything?' Michelle quickly leant back again in her chair. Was this long and awkward conversation going to end up where she had thought it started?

'Melissa was jealous of any woman that came near me. I know she asked you to go riding as she wanted to find out if you had a man in your life.'

Michelle gasped in surprise, 'I thought she was just being friendly!'

'Yeh, well, that's because you're a nice person. I'm afraid Melissa was not as nice as she looked. I know she had the excuse of a miserable childhood. Her parents are ridiculously rich but totally uncaring.

They bought her everything her heart could desire but never showed her any love or attention. She was very insecure and I was sorry for that but she could be hell to be with sometimes. She said I was cold... and I think she was right. Especially once you came along.' Sven ended miserably.

'But how did I change things?' Michelle asked.

'Well, you were so sweet and so beautiful. Delicate as a flower but strong, too. I loved being with you. Something began to change in me... if Melissa was right that I was cold, then I began to melt. It suddenly seemed possible to be with a woman and not feel worried about every word I said. Then, I so nearly kissed you that evening when we were caught in the rain. Oh my God, you were so lovely, drenched in rain... well, no red-blooded man would not have longed to kiss you. And then suddenly, I realised. I was about to go down the same sort of path I had taken with Melissa... but this time you were a special and wonderful girl and would end up hurting... because in the end... the only girl I can ever truly love is Monique.'

'And then, of course, you saw her in the courtyard here.' Michelle said, still reeling from all the sweet things that Sven had said about herself.

'I was so shocked, I nearly fell to my knees in front of her there and then, pole-axed! You see, I had heard she had gone to live in Paris after she finished her degree. And, suddenly, there she was... working for you. I can't begin to tell you how I felt when I saw her again...'

'So it's all ending happily ever after for you, Sven?' Michelle said hastily, wondering if the normally taciturn Sven was going to struggle through another long speech.

'Hmm, well, it's not so easy. My mother is set against it, of course.'

'But why? Anyway, you can't let your mother organise your life... does she think you should go back to Melissa or... what?'

'Since you came to dinner that first night at our place, my dear *Maman* is quite determined I should marry you, Michelle de Rosefont.'

'Holy Moly, your mother is worse than Kelly... trying to arrange marriages.'

Sven looked at her bewildered and Michelle waved her hand and shook her head to dismiss her last words. It would be impossible to explain the ridiculous Jane Austen syndrome that seemed to be revolving around her life.

'You may have guessed that my dear mother is an outrageous snob! At first she thought you would be a commoner from London, possibly a money-grabbing impostor...well, her imagination ran wild. Then I met you and went home to tell her how lovely you were and she was straight off on another track. Then, of course, when she met you herself, she could suddenly see a new dynasty shining ahead. The Rosefont lands joined with ours... your charming and erudite father was a bonus!'

'But it's unbelievable, this is the 21st century not mediaeval France... and anyway, isn't your mother Swedish? How does that work out?'

'Yes, *Maman* was born in Sweden, as high born as one can be in such a democratic country...she even has a family shield and a coronet. She left all that to marry my father. I think it really was a love match and her family disapproved at the time...'

Michelle interrupted angrily, 'So she married for love but wants to arrange a marriage for you? Doesn't add up, Sven. You have to stand up to her and just tell her you are going to marry Monique.'

'I know, I know. It should be simple. But I don't want a battle, I want her to love Monique and to understand why I love her so much. I love them both and want them to love each other. My sister's marriage to Pierre seems to be perfect and I know my mother wants the same for me...but she is prejudiced. Sadly her marriage to my father did not end well. In fact, it was disastrous. He was a handsome, foolish man and had endless affairs, gambled and drank himself into an early grave. *Maman* had to take over running the Château and keep it all going. My father was a drinking friend of Michel de Rosefont. My mother had a soft spot for Michel even though he was like my father in some ways... obviously he had a love affair with your mother and I know he drank too much and neglected the work of running the Bastide. My mother made the lease of his vineyards... she took over everything, really, until I was old enough to help. That's why I do admire her. But she respected your father, sorry, your birth father, for his intellect. Something else I'm afraid my own father lacked. Michel de Rosefont was a very cultured man, always in his library reading and studying his collection of art work... even if he did have a glass of good wine in his hand at the same time!'

Michelle smiled and listened with interest. These small nuggets of information about Michel de Rosefont began to build an image of the man her mother had loved before she met Robert.

'I wish I could tell you more about him but I really hardly knew him.' Sven added. Michelle sat still for a moment, thinking how she had misjudged Sven. Maybe it was his outward appearance, his physicality made it hard to believe there was a shy but real thinking man inside the perfect body.

'Thanks, Sven. You're right, I do want to find out more about this unknown father of mine. Of course, it has been wonderful inheriting the Bastide and jumping into this crazy new life but it has all happened so quickly I have hardly had time to take a breath, let alone think.'

'You should talk to my mother some time. I know she doesn't seem particularly approachable...' Sven gave a small laugh, 'well, that's an understatement. I know she is an appalling snob but on the other hand, she's a very clever woman and I know she likes you. That's the problem, she likes you a lot and thinks you would be my ideal life partner. Not to mention she wouldn't have to buy your land.' Sven laughed aloud and put his head into hands. 'I know she's impossible really!'

'Does she want to buy my land then?' Michelle asked in surprise.

Sven looked up, running his hands back through his blonde curls and switched on the usual smile. No matter how many times Michelle was subjected to the flash of impossibly perfect white teeth in the handsome face, no matter that she was definitely not in love with this man sitting the other side of the table... still that smile could not fail to make her sit back in pure admiration. But he was answering her question.

'Why, of course, she has been hell bent on buying that land for as long as I can remember. I think she led a long term campaign with Michel, trying to persuade him. She hates having to lease them from the Bastide. Now, as you said, like something out of mediaeval times, she sees me marrying and getting the vineyards that way. She is one very determined woman!'

'Don't worry, Sven, so am I!' They both laughed now and, at the same time, reached for another slice of cake.

'You know, from the moment I first met you, Michelle, I have felt this amazing bond. We think and act alike even though in such different ways. I can talk to you like I should be able to talk to my sister.

Yes...' he said thoughtfully, 'that's it, I really feel a sort of brotherly fondness for you.'

'Wow, Sven, I have always longed for a brother. That's one of the nicest things anyone has ever said to me. And, now I can boss you around and take care of you!'

They both laughed and, again at the same time, held out a hand to the other across the table. Michelle felt the warmth of his hand enclosing hers and then his other hand folded on top. There was no sharp jab of electricity, just a warm and very nice comforting glow.

They were lost in their thoughts for a moment and both jumped as the door flung open, bringing a gust of cold air into the warmth of the kitchen. Coco jumped up and enthusiastically welcomed Robert. Ever the Harley Street doctor, he immediately sensed the atmosphere in the room.

'Not disturbing anything, am I?' he asked cheerily.

'Hi Dad, in case your caring doctor and father antenna is reading the wrong signals, Sven has just been telling me that he is in love with Monique.' Michelle spoke hastily and stood up to pour her father a cup of tea. Sven stood up too, with his usual good manners, and shook Robert's hand.

'Well, I'd be a very poor doctor if I hadn't already noticed that.' Robert smiled and patted Sven on the back. 'Good for you lad, Monique's a beautiful and clever woman.'

Michelle and Sven both looked at him in surprise.

'How on earth did you know, Dad?'

'Well, I do have eyes in my head and apart from that ... I have spent most of the afternoon listening to your mother bemoaning the fact.'

'Oh no, did she tell you all about the row we had... and that she thinks I should marry

Michelle.' Sven asked anxiously as he sat back at the table.

'Oh yes, she did begin going down that path but I soon dissuaded her.' Robert took a large slice of cake and bit into it.

'Dissuaded her? That just doesn't sound like a word to use when talking about my dear mother.' Sven shook his head.

'But what did you say to her?' Michelle demanded.

Robert shook his head and pointed to his full mouth. Michelle poured him another cup of tea and went round to sit beside Sven as they both waited impatiently for him to finish eating.

'Never talk with your mouth full. You know that Michelle.' Robert smiled as he swallowed and picked up his tea cup. 'Sound advice actually, breathing in through the mouth whilst eating could cause unwanted obstruction...'

'Dad, stop teasing us! Tell us what you discussed with Mme. Gilbert.' Michelle whipped her father's plate out of his reach before he could take another bite.

'Hungry work, this family relationship chat. Your mother is another very clever woman, Sven. In fact, we are surrounded by them and don't have much chance... but I did manage to talk her through to the fact that Sven was in love and aways had been with his Monique. There was no way I would stand by and see him marry my daughter... a way that could only load to miscry. Not to mention that Michelle is now falling in love with Marc Bernier. By the way, Michelle, you ought to be getting ready to go to Aix. Now, please give me back my cake.'

29   *'his strong throat and his dark hair'*

The gallery was packed with people talking and drinking champagne when she arrived. Michelle walked in, head held high and smiling brightly as though she knew everybody there. It wasn't as though she wasn't used to this sort of event in London. Chelsea evenings were full of gallery openings, one-man art shows and general occasions from the weird to the wonderful... but this was so different... he would be here. Somewhere in the crowded room Marc Bernier would be waiting for her. She scanned the room and accepted a glass of champagne from a waiter. She couldn't see Marc anywhere... was he behind the scenes, organising sales or... then there was a soft tap on her shoulder, her bare shoulder, and a voice behind her.

'Michelle, I have been waiting for you to arrive. *Bonsoir.*' The last word, '*bonsoir*', was whispered into her ear, and she felt his hot breath on her neck. Michelle turned slowly, relishing the moment of seeing Marc again... and so close. She felt a shiver of what could only be shameless desire rush through her body, her stomach clenched, her heart beat faster... and finally she managed to speak,

'Good evening, Marc, thank you for inviting me, the gallery looks wonderful ... and what a crowd!' she spoke softly and the noise of raised voices all around them made him lean even closer to hear what she was saying and to reply,

'You look beautiful, Michelle. Very beautiful... I wish we were not in the midst of this load of baying clients. Well, I hope they are clients anyway.' He laughed and as his head tilted back she was swamped with another wave of longing as she saw his strong throat and his dark hair falling away from his forehead. She looked and liked every thing about him... could she say she already loved everything about him? Of course, it was ridiculous. Pulling herself together she said,

'I don't know anyone here. Are they mostly people from Aix or...'

'Actually, you do know a few people here, I think.' He took a sip from his glass looked at her over the rim. His eyes were the darkest brown eyes Michelle had ever seen, and yet, now she was so close, she could see they were flecked with golden amber light. Beautiful eyes that conveyed more meaning than words as he continued.

'Not that I want to share you with anyone in the world.' He clinked his glass lightly against hers and pushed his shoulders back resolutely. 'Follow me and I will introduce you to people you don't yet know and find some that you already do.'

He took her hand and led her through the crowd, weaving in and out, introducing her here and there, stopping to chat with some groups and then moving on. It was obvious to Michelle that although it was a business event, the guests greeted him like a good friend, all wanting him to stay and talk longer. Finally, reaching the far end of the room, she found herself in a familiar group. The first person she recognised was Sven, his height alone making him stand out from the crowd. Then she saw, Monique, close by Sven's side and holding his arm. Next she recognised Sven's sister, Gertrud and her husband, Pierre... and finally, seated in an elegant gilded armchair, she saw the elderly Mme. de Fleurenne. Amongst the general greetings and chat, it was Mme. de Fleurenne who held the floor.

'How good to meet you again, Michelle. Come and talk to me for a minute.' Mme. de Fleurenne raised her hand toward Michelle in a regal gesture.

Michelle was delighted to see her and leant forward to kiss her on both cheeks.

'Ah yes, the Audrey Hepburn look continues, a charming little powder pink dress, my dear, it shows of your tiny waist so well... and still wearing '*L'Interdit*'.

'Yes, you're quite right. I love this perfume for special occasions.'

'Hmm...' Mme. de Fleurenne shrugged and gave a disparaging smile, 'Of course, it is a quite good combination of floral aroma... and a clever touch of powdery delicacy. Hubert de Givenchy had talent not just for fashion design but also for finding the right people. It was Francis Fabron who created '*L'Interdit*', way back in 1957. Hepburn wore it exclusively until it was released to the eager general public some time in the 60's. I can't remember exactly. My memory is so awful... but I never forget a perfume!'

Michelle looked at her in admiration, 'What amazing times you have lived through, Madame. It's fascinating.'

'Well, I have been fortunate, and yes, we had good times and some very dreadful. If you are interested in an ancient woman's gossip, perhaps you will make that visit we talked about before. Why don't you come over for lunch tomorrow. I'm afraid my son, Jean-Michel and Rosie won't be there. They are in Nice this weekend. But if you wouldn't be too bored...then... perhaps tomorrow?'

'I should love to,' Michelle said, not sure how to explain that there was nothing less boring that she could think of, especially as Marc had already said he was leaving for Paris after the gallery event. Mme. Fleurenne smiled with pleasure.

'*Entendu*! I shall look forward to it, and, of course, bring your business partner or friends if you wish. I love to be amongst young people. By the way,'

Mme. de Fleurenne took Michelle's hand and pulled her closer as she said very quietly,

'I see I am right about one or two things we talked about last time, The handsome Sven Gilbert has found his true love. I knew he was not for you.' Mme. de Fleurenne gave a wicked little laugh, 'And already I know where your heart lies. Hmm, very suitable, I would think!'

Before Michelle had a chance to reply, Mme. de Fleurenne had deftly turned to Gertrud Gilbert and begun to talk to her about a painting they were thinking of buying. Michelle smiled and raised her glass to Mme. de Fleurenne who quickly called out.

'*À demain*, Michelle, about noon.' Then turning back to Gertrud she carried on talking animatedly.

Michelle stood for a moment, laughing to herself about the old lady's shrewd guesswork and then turned to make her own tour of the paintings. After all, she thought, this is why she was supposed to be here. She walked very slowly from one painting to the next and then stopped abruptly. A small painting, glowing with rich colours and texture in the spotlight, a landscape... Michelle did not need to read the small card with the title. It was her own view, her vineyards leading to the magnificent back drop of Mont Ste Victoire. She stood transfixed, looking at it closely. The artist had caught the light and feeling of every moment of every day that she had looked out of her office window at the Bastide. She leant closer to examine it, wary of not getting too close and setting off the alarm system. Close to she was surprised to find the effect lost. Now it was a blur of smudged colours, brush strokes and thick sweeps of paint. Then once again, she heard Marc talking to her... was it her imagination or had she sensed he was there even before he spoke?

'It's a gem, isn't it! I knew you would love it. Your very own view. If it wasn't an original Cezanne, I'd buy it for you!'

Michelle drew back from the painting and turned toward Marc.'It has taken my breath away.' she said, 'So beautiful, small and absolutely perfect.'

'My thoughts exactly but then I wasn't looking at the painting. I've seen that before.' Marc smiled and then laughed at Michelle's obvious embarrassment. 'I know, I know, I am shamelessly flirting with you. I am sorry but... no, actually, I am not sorry at all. I have never behaved so badly before and it feels great!'

Michelle joined in his laughter, a sense of pure joy and exhilaration filling her from the heel-tip of her five inch Manolo Blahnik's right to the very silky end of the longest hair on her head.

'some crazy Cinderella stunt'

'Are you sure she invited me, too?' Kelly was sitting at the breakfast table, idly pushing a spoon around in a bowl of muesli. 'You know, I can't think why anyone bothers to eat this stuff, Mich, it's horrid. I mean, cereal to me means, sugar-coated something or other... or little chocolate puffy things. I mean what is this exactly?' She pushed the bowl away from her. Coco stood up from under the table and looked at Kelly hopefully. 'My dear Lord, this dog understands everything I say. He's scrounging for a bowl of soggy muesli now. Don't you ever feed her, Mich?' Michelle turned back from the range and looked at Kelly fondly. 'Which question do you want me to answer first? Invite, content of muesli or Coco's diet rules? Kelly, I know you in these moods. You're a bit bored and wondering what to do with your Sunday.'

'True enough,' Kelly agreed readily, sneaking a crust of toast to Coco under the table. 'Well, Leon is pleased to be off helping your Dad begin his moving. It's great they get on like best friends... your Dad is taking him to some rugby match in Bath. They probably won't even begin packing... no way I wanted to go.... brrr… a rugby match... imagine. Anyway, Leon will be back Wednesday. He can't take more than three days off... he's always worrying that there is more he should be doing. How I can end up loving a workaholic, I shall never know.'

'That could be because you are a workaholic yourself, but in self-denial... which is exactly why you are fidgety on Sundays. Anyway, I'm not going to psychobabble on because...to answer your first and most important question... yes, Mme. de Fleurenne definitely invited you and any of my friends, in fact...'

Kelly interrupted, 'So I can go to the ball, Mich? Anyway, you don't have any other friends...'

'Well, that's where you're very wrong, Kelly dear, I may just phone up Sven and ask him if he'd like to bring Monique... or...'

'Ok, ok, I know, that cool guy from the gallery, what's his name...'

'Could be?' Michelle smiled angelically, 'Anyway, I happen to know that Sven and Monique are having Sunday lunch with her family, Marc is in Paris, my Dad and your Leon in Sussex... so it will just have to be you and me, won't it? And, you'd better get a move on as we are invited for twelve noon and goodness knows how long it could take us to find the place.'

'Yeh, much as I love your retro Citroen I think I may buy you a sat nav next time I'm anywhere near civilisation. Twelve noon, are you joking me, Mich?' Kelly ran her fingers through her long curly blonde hair and looked dismayed. 'and, dear Lord, whatever does one wear to lunch with the queen of perfume?'

'Well, I'm guessing not pyjamas, so get going. Mme. de Fleurenne is a hard fashion act to compete with. If ever I should get to her age I would want to look just like her. She looked amazing last night... I think she was wearing Valentino. But in a way, it's not just the wonderful clothes, it's her whole attitude.'

'Yes, I know what you mean... we hardly spoke but she was right on the ball... you know, sassed my Marilyn Monroe look straight away. What a laugh! I'm really looking forward to today now... and on the way there you can update me on your snail pace romance... I mean, what did you talk about with Marc, plumbing? Hurry up, Mich! Don't hang around!'

Less than an hour later the girls were in the old car, rolling and bouncing along the small country lanes. They passed though sleepy hill villages and small Provençal towns, far-stretching vineyards, olive groves and winding mountain passes. They had managed to leave early enough to take the scenic route to Château de Fleurenne. It was yet another day of impossible blue sky without a cloud in sight, but the air was cold.

'How do you think I can crank up the heating in this jalopy, Mich?' Kelly peered at the car's long walnut fascia and began to turn the small cream knobs. 'This car is like a lot of retro stuff we deal with... beautiful and totally impractical. My feet are turning to ice.'

'That last knob, try that again, I thought I felt a whiff of heat just then but you turned it off again.' said Michelle, resolutely keeping her eyes on the road as it dipped and twisted in front of her. 'Yes, that's it! Leave it where it is .... I can definitely feel hot air filtering through.'

'Mmm, that is a lot better, should be almost cosy by the time we get there. Anyway, talking of hot, you haven't told me a word about last night.'

'Well, not really a lot to tell, except it was a lovely evening and ...'

'Michelle, I think I can guess that but what about Marc Bernier, I mean, he presumably was there?'

'Oh yes!' Michelle answered dreamily, 'He was definitely there.'

'So... what happened. Mich you can be so exasperating, you know what I mean...'

'Well, we talked about painting...'

'An improvement on sorting out your plumbing, I suppose.' Kelly interrupted, sighing heavily.

'Ok, if you must know, he flirted so outrageously he even apologised.'

'Flirted outrageously, is that retro speak because we're in this car or am I talking to the Marquise? Cut to the chase, then, how did the evening end, kiss, more than a kiss, promises of eternal love? Tell, Mich!'

'Ok, well, Marc was really busy. There were two gallery assistants putting little red sold stickers on quite a few paintings and, of course, Marc was talking to buyers. Finally, a few people began to leave and he was still surrounded by a group of French people and so... and so, I slipped away quietly without saying good-bye.'

'You're teasing me, right? You're just joking, having a laugh... I mean, there's no way you could pull some crazy Cinderella stunt. Right?' Kelly turned to look at Michelle, examining her profile for some sign of a smile.

'Well, I did, I really did. But unlike Cinderella I kept both my Manolas on my feet.' Michelle said as she kept looking straight ahead.

'Ok, I resign, I give up completely on organising your love life. That's it, Mich, you are a hopeless case.'

'I don't actually remember appointing you to be my official romantic date organiser, anyway. Now take another look at that old map, it's no good trying to get a signal on your phone in these hills. I think we must be nearly there now.'

'You know I feel car sick if I read maps. Especially this car, the springs make it more like being on a yacht at sea. I thought Leon told me that Citroens had amazing suspension... I practically have to hold on to stay in my seat!' Kelly grumbled, 'And if I look at the map I shall only see that we were mad to take the scenic route and should have gone straight along the motorway toward Grasse. Still, I have to admit, it is the most scenic scenic route I have ever been on. The colour of earth... it really is dark red... and against the deep blue sky. It's amazing. I just love it here.'

'I was just thinking the same about the colours, and the silvery green of the olive trees... maybe we can use something of that in the Bastide colour scheme?'

'Exactly, I'll do some research into historical decor, too.'

Both girls were silent for a minute, each thinking of plans for the restoration of the Bastide and the huge amount of work ahead.

'I guess this should be our last day off for a while, Mich. There is a mountain of work to get through if we are to open the Bastide as a hotel in the Spring.'

'Exactly what I was thinking.' Agreed Michelle, 'So let's really enjoy it. We must be nearly there, surely?'

Just at that moment, Kelly bounced up from the depths of the deep leather seat and pointed, tapping the windscreen with force.

'Land ahoy! There, a huge sign saying *'Château de Fleurenne, Visitez la Parfumerie, 5 kilometres à gauche.'*

Michelle pulled the car into a grassy siding and they both slowly read the large sign.

'Hmm, elegantly done but very eye-catching. This Fleurenne lot must be quite commercial.' Kelly said thoughtfully.

'Just what I was thinking.' said Michelle as she took a quick photo on her phone. 'It's the way to go, don't you think? Mme. de Fleurenne said that Rosie, her grandson's wife was in PR in London. It shows, doesn't it.'

'Yeh, I talked with her for a while at the Gilbert's party... and him. He could be a bit of a playboy, certainly looked it... and she was fun and bubbly but had a steely sort of determination, I thought. Anyway, very professional so far...important to look classy but still effective in catching passing trade. They have a boutique shop, tours of the lavender fields and even a perfume laboratory.'

'Yes, Mme. de Fleurenne told me they are always fully booked from Easter through to October with coach-loads of people who take the tour and then design their own perfume. She said it had all been Rosie's inspiration and that they were nearly bankrupt before she came on the scene. I think we may find the elderly Mme. de Fleurenne has a keen business side to her too.' Michelle started up the car. 'Anyway, it's five to twelve, our usual perfect timing... let's go!'

The lunch had been perfect. Mme. de Fleurenne sat between the two girls and asked all the right questions and listened carefully to the answers. She seemed genuinely interested in how their lives had been before Michelle inherited the Bastide. The coffee was brought to the table by a woman almost as elderly as Mme. de Fleurenne herself.

'You know, Adelaide, I think it would be lovely to take coffee in the *orangerie*.
Perhaps, you will join us?' The old lady nodded and looked pleased. She began to walk slowly away with the tray.

'Oh, please let me take the tray, I haven't done a thing all morning, if you'll lead the way.' Kelly jumped up and went to take the tray but the woman clung on to it, looking anxiously at Mme. de Fleurenne.

'*Bien sur*, Adelaide.' Mme. de Fleurenne nodded and smiled and Kelly succeeded in taking the heavy tray.

'Adelaide and I are both so ancient, we are grateful to graciously accept any help. Will you take my arm, Michelle, if I sit down for more than five minutes it seems I am permanently bent in two. But how lucky I am to even be here! Adelaide, too, she is about my age and has been with me for years. Now her grand-daughter and little son, the one I told you about, the one who loves zombie movies, now she looks after me so well. Yes, I am a lucky woman! The winter sun is very pleasant in the *orangerie*... we'll take coffee there. *Si la personne est agée, son coeur n'est pas lá!*'

'Young at heart.' Michelle quickly translated and was rewarded with one of Mme. de Fleurenne's sweetest smiles.

The conversation continued but Michelle and Kelly were both experienced enough in business meetings to notice that Mme. de Fleurenne was skilfully leading from talk of the past to the future.

'Your idea for an art hotel is most interesting. When do you hope to open now that the film company are not moving in?' Mme. de Fleurenne asked.

'Well, my father has a provisional booking from the cruise company he works for... the first guests would arrive in April. There is so much to do that it doesn't seem possible. And of course the renovation work is so costly.' Michelle said with a worried frown.

'We are used to working together under pressure and to a deadline but this is certainly a huge challenge,' added Kelly.

'Certainly, I can see that. Do you think the film company money will cover the costs?' Mme. de Fleurenne suddenly sat up straight and put a hand to her mouth, 'I must apologise, I should not ask these questions, really, none of my business.'

'Not at all.' Michelle answered quickly, 'Actually it is a relief to have someone to talk with ... I have begun to worry about money. The builders are very good and we have a large team of great people... but the materials are so expensive...'

'And we are determined not to skimp on quality,' added Kelly, 'We both have high standards and anyway, a place like the Bastide merits the best possible quality materials.'

'Exactly, it's as Kelly says, only the finest will do... I am beginning to wonder if I shall have to accept Karen Gilbert's long-standing offer to buy my land.'

Both Mme. de Fleurenne and Kelly turned to Michelle in surprise.

'Non, non, non, mais non... this you must resist at all costs. A grand Château or Bastide depends on its lands...it would be like a ship without the sea. No, always better to sell off a few paintings. I have heard that this what your father, sorry, I mean Michel, your birth father Michel did on occasions. You know, you could ask the charming Marc Bernier's advice... ask him to go through your art works.'

'Now that is a great idea!' said Kelly, with a wicked smile.

'*Exactement!*' Mme. de Fleurenne's usual sweet smile was now almost as wicked as Kelly's, and her eyes were alight with silent laughter as she gave a little clap of approval. The sleeping Adelaide stirred in her sleep. Mme. de Fleurenne raised a finger to her lips and added, 'I mustn't wake my dear Adelaide, she always has a long siesta. I think I have worn her out working for me over the years. I am a very tiring person! Oh, but the energy I had in my youth... mostly wasted on having a very good time. I came to work only after my husband died and even then it was only my nose that was any good at it! No, Rosie is the one to talk to about business concerns. Next time you come, I hope Rosie and Jean-Michel will be here. They will have more energy to show you around. Rosie is particularly involved with the perfume boutique and the tours. You three will get on very well, I am sure. Some of your young London energy is needed in these sleepy backwaters of

France. We had relied too much on the past... you understand the world of today and what it wants.'

'Well, you may be right, but in some strange way, the style and life of your world is what many people are searching for... probably why so many young people like dressing in retro fashions and we buy retro Scandinavian furniture.' said Michelle.

'True, which reminds me, I wonder if you would like to see my collection of vintage fashions?' Kelly sat forward eagerly, 'That would be wonderful. I am simply mad about clothes, particularly vintage.'

'Good, now help yourselves to another chocolate and we'll go to my apartment. Dear Adelaide has fallen fast asleep so we'll creep away.'

Michelle and Kelly turned to look over to the corner of the *orangerie* where Adelaide was comfortable asleep on a wicker chaise-longue under a huge orange tree.

'This glass area is superb.' said Michelle, 'We've designed the interiors of a few orangeries in London and around... but nothing on this scale... or style. Then there is the way the southern winter sun warms it so perfectly. The orange and lemon trees are all in blossom, and the orchids... the perfume is amazing!' Michelle breathed in and sighed with pleasure.

Mme. de Fleurenne passed the silver bowl of chocolates. 'My daughter organised the renovation of this place not long before she died.' A shadow of sadness passed swiftly over Mme. de Fleurenne's face but she continued talking brightly. 'Then Jean-Michel had it redecorated for his marriage to Rosie. Ah, that was a day! He completely filled our little chapel and this place with flowers. Of course the perfume of real flowers is as pleasurable as created scents. Now, come on girls, have a last little chocolate and finish your coffee as we have so much to do.'

Kelly took another chocolate and said, 'I have never tasted a more wonderful chocolate... and I am a self-confessed chocaholic!'

'Chocaholic... now that's a new word for me! I like it very much.' Mme. de Fleurenne laughed,

'Workaholic... chocaholic... yes, I understand.'

'Michelle accused me of being a workaholic earlier today... although she can talk... so now I am summed up in two words... chocaholic workaholic! Talking of perfume... I've just realised, there is a delicate perfume to these chocolates... not violet but ...' said Kelly.

'Lavender!' Mme. de Fleurenne clapped her hands with pleasure. 'We are surrounded by fields of lavender here. These scented chocolates sell very well in Rosie's boutique. That is something else you must see... but another time, this afternoon we shall enjoy looking at clothes and begin designing a perfume. Now help me up Kelly. I may be young at heart but I have such very old bones.'

31 *'an original Givenchy wool suit'*

'That was one incredible day!' Kelly was sitting curled up on an old sofa near the roaring fire in the salon. 'Coco, come and sit by me... keep me warm! How I miss Leon!' She patted the seat beside her and Coco obliging jumped up and settled beside Kelly, resting her big head on Kelly's shoulder. 'Ah, you're so sweet, Coco popsy.'

'You're only making a fuss of her as Leon's not here and you're a bit cold. I am not sure if that is more insulting to Leon or Coco. Really, Kelly, you have no conscience.'

'I know.' replied Kelly, smiling happily, 'I have never needed any moral fibre because you have more than enough for both of us put together. These huge log fires are all very well on one side but the entire other side of my body is turning to ice, literally, Mich.'

'Well, actually, not literally Kelly... and anyway you could always put on another sweater. Here, there's a rug on this sofa.'

'I know, but after a day at Château de Fleurenne it's a reminder of how much we have to do here. Heating, does comes to mind.'

'Do you want to talk about plumbing, then?'

'No, shut up, Mich, you're being so, so annoying. I want to talk about the amazing wardrobe of la grande femme fatale, Mme. d'amazing Fleurenne. I just can't believe she gave me that gold lamé dress... I mean, it's not just amazing but on top of that, it must be so valuable. Pure and glorious fifties glamour.'

'Well, she was so right... you did look simply fantastic in it... every inch Marilyn. But my present was even better... an original Givenchy wool suit...

such a wonderful duck egg blue. I've never seen or worn anything the remotest bit so fantastic. I can't believe Rosie wouldn't want them.'

'I know, we just struck lucky with our vintage look. Did you hear when Mme. de Fleurenne said that Rosie only wears jeans or her designer friends' clothes. Imagine being friends with Otto and Simon.'

'Yes, I heard... it's all amazing. Come to think of it though, that sort of dark bronze dress with the beading that she wore to the Gilberts' party... that looked like one from their Russian collection. Superb... and on top of that, what about the perfume library.'

'I know, truly fantastic. It really will make an ideal outing for guests here at the Bastide. And to design one's own perfume... how great is that. Do you think Mme. de Fleurenne will remember that next time we go over there she is going to create perfumes for us?'

'Absolutely! She doesn't seem to be the sort of person to forget a thing. Quite a woman.'

'Exactly, she said your *L'Interdit* is based on woodland flowers and that she would work on that. I wonder what she will think of for me. I don't think she approved of my Issey Miyake... she made me laugh, the way she screwed up her famous and aristocratic nose and muttered something about chemicals.'

'I know, she's so sort of out there... anyway, let's talk about the Bastide while we have a chance...' But just then, Michelle's mobile phone rang and interrupted the conversation. 'Hi, Marc, how are you?' Michelle said as calmly as she could manage. Not helped by Kelly and Coco sitting side by side, bolt upright on the sofa, the rug now thrown to the floor. Michelle glared at Kelly and stood up and walked to the far corner of the room to hold the conversation in comparative privacy, yet worried that she might lose the signal. After a brief exchange of words she rang off and turned round to find that Kelly and Coco had crept across the large room and were standing right behind her.

'So, did I hear you say something about tomorrow?' Kelly demanded, 'Where are you meeting, what time, what else did he say?'

'Kelly, stop, stop... you were trying to eavesdrop on my private conversation, you're so rude!'

'I know, I know I am... and, as you just said, I have not a shred of conscience. Anyway, I couldn't quite hear what art-lover-boy Marc was saying...tell me, Mich or I swear I shall have to strangle you.'

'Well, then, as Leon told you, you'd never find out. Anyway, don't be so melodramatic. Yes, Marc has asked me out to dinner, tomorrow at seven o'clock in that restaurant in Aix, the one we met him in the other evening.'

Kelly gave a whoop of delight and raced round the room chased by Coco, the firelight casting their dancing shadows around the walls.

'Mich and Marc, Marc and Mich!' Kelly chanted, as she bounced around the room, jumping over sofas and chairs and followed closely by an excited barking Coco.

'For goodness sakes, Kelly, it's only a dinner date.' Michelle said quietly. But, in the firelight, her face glowed with excitement and anticipation.

32 'fell together onto the bed'

Dinner was over and Marc leaned toward her across the table. 'Will you come back to my place for coffee?'

Then, they were hardly through the door of his house before he took her in his arms and began to kiss her. Her lips parted, his tongue met hers. Michelle felt the thrill of desire as her thighs pressed against his. His hands ran down her body, her thin silk dress rising up as he pulled her even closer. She threw her head back as his mouth left hers and moved to kiss her throat and then down to her breasts. Then she was undoing his shirt and pulling it off him. His breath was fast and warm on her body as he pulled her dress over her head and began to kiss her stomach. His tongue ran over her skin and she gasped with pleasure as he lifted her up and quickly she encircled him with her legs as he carried her into the bedroom. They fell together onto the bed, pulling at each others clothes... but somewhere, a bell was ringing, strident and familiar...

Michelle awoke, panting and hot. She reached out and turned off her alarm and then almost cried with the feeling of loss that enveloped her. She lay still for a moment, recalling the dream and then it began to fade. She tried to cling onto the detail but it was gone. She sat up in bed impatiently. Was she so frustrated and lonely that she had to dream about love? And then she remembered. It was Monday, but not a boring any old Monday, because tonight she was meeting Marc, the real life Marc. A wave of energy rushed through her and she threw back the covers and jumped out of bed. Coco pushed her nose through the door and looked at her anxiously.

'*Bonjour, Coco, ca va?*' The large dog bounced into the room, sensing an air of excitement. 'I know, it's a lovely day and I haven't even opened the curtains yet! You don't have to say anything because I just know you agree!' Michelle pulled on her dressing gown and went over to the window. She pulled the long heavy curtain aside and peered out. To her surprise there was a man in blue overalls standing in the middle of the derelict fountain. It was Leon. Michelle tapped on the glass but he was too far off and much too busy to notice her.

'Hurry up, Coco, we'd better have quick showers and get down there... it seems like work at the old Bastide has already begun. The dog looked at her as though she understood the word shower and made for the door. Michelle laughed aloud and waited, watching Leon as he shovelled mud and slime from the basin of the fountain. Sure enough, a moment later he was joined by Coco. The dog jumped up to look into the fountain and Leon stretched over to pat her and then looked up to Michelle's window and saw her. He waved and shook his spade in the air. Michelle waved back and smiled... another week at the Bastide de Rosefont had begun.

Half an hour later, after a snatched breakfast, Michelle went out into the winter sunshine to talk with Leon.'Whatever are you up to, Leon?' she asked, staring with amazement at the mound of green slime and wet leaves that Leon was piling up on the ground beside the fountain edge. 'I thought you were staying in Sussex with my Dad.'

Leon rested on his spade and rubbed his back, '*Alors*, that was the idea but, you know, he had everything very planned, very organised and I thought of all the work here... and Kelly!' Leon flashed a smile and carried on shovelling.

'But why the sudden attack on the fountain?'

'Well, I want it for my special *projet*. It is so beautiful and I am sure I can make it work again. Also manual work helps me think about problems.'

'Well, it would certainly be wonderful to see it sparkling with water. I suppose, now I look at it closely, the stonework is in quite good condition. I love the cherubs with their sweet faces and round bottoms.'

'Very charming but when I have finished they will each *fait pipi*!'

'Do I hear aright?' Kelly came out and joined them. 'Are you seriously clearing all this muck away so that the sweet little cherubs can pee in the water? Really, Leon, you French have no idea of decorum. Our fountains spout water from their lips at worst.'

'Well, I shall leave you two to argue that out. I'm going to find Monique and go through the new week's schedule.' said Michelle, beating a retreat before Kelly could get into full flow.

'Don't work too hard today, Mich, don't forget you need to be fresh as a daisy for this evening.' Kelly called after her.

'This evening, what is happening this evening?' asked Leon, stopping shovelling again.

'I am sure Kelly will tell you, Leon. I'm off... lots to do, come on Coco.'

Michelle spent the rest of the day working with Monique and other members of the staff. Although she was busy, the day seemed to last forever. Finally, at five o'clock, she decided she could reasonably stop work and get ready for the evening ahead. After a long, hot bath and a wasted half hour trying on different clothes and shoes, she was ready. She looked around her bedroom, strewn with clothes... but suddenly she seemed to be running late and there was no time to tidy up. She ran down to the kitchen to find Kelly and Leon.

'I'm off now. Keep an eye on Coco.' she said, popping her head through the door.

'Oh no you're not... come in and show me what you decided to wear then!' said Kelly, who was stirring a saucepan on the range.

Michelle went into the kitchen and twirled around, the fine pleats of her pale, grey silk dress flying in a circle.

'Perfect, hmm, good choice, Mich, demure and sexy.'

Leon looked up from the table where he was sitting reading. 'Do you have your phone? Is it charged ... do you have enough petrol?'

'Yes, yes and yes... you sound like my Dad, Leon.' Michelle laughed, unable to suppress the high spirits that made her feel as though she could fly.

'Off you go then, Marquise. Don't do anything I wouldn't do!' said Kelly.

'I shan't bother to make the obvious answer to that. Bye then!'

33 *'in grand disorder with clothes all over the bed'*

Michelle parked almost outside the restaurant. She had been lucky to find a place as the old Citroen was awkwardly long. After the final manoeuvre, she turned off the engine and sat for a moment, wondering whether to change her flat pumps for high heels and hoping her heart would stop beating so hard and fast. She was about to check her make-up in the driving mirror when she realised there was a man standing beside the car door. And, of course, it was Marc. She glanced up through the window and her heart beat even faster. He was hot, he was cool, he was even more of everything than Michelle had thought. She smiled, he smiled... not a wide, toothpaste ad smile but a slow and gentle movement of his perfect lips... her whole stomach butterflied as she looked at his lips. Then, he was opening her door. No time to change shoes, so when she stood beside him, he seemed taller and larger. In fact, he towered over her until, until... he bent to kiss her on both cheeks. Michelle felt her beating heart would actually give up the race and stop. She had a mad desire to throw her arms around him, reach up and stroke his silky, dark hair. But this was real life, so, she turned each cheek for a fleeting kiss and then, swallowing hard, managed to say,

'*Bonsoir, Marc, comment ça va*? Have you just arrived, too?'

'Good evening, Michelle... no, I have been here well over half an hour, waiting for you... but then, I have been waiting for you all my life.' Suddenly he burst out laughing, his face radiant with happiness. 'Sorry about that last line. I don't know what has happened to me... when I am with you I seem to talk like the hero in a romantic novel. You have bewitched me, Michelle.' He put his arm lightly around her shoulders as they made their way into the restaurant. Michelle laughed, too, but could think of no reply that would not sound equally melodramatic.

The restaurant owner greeted Marc like a long lost friend and then ushered them to a table for two, set in a quiet corner of the crowded restaurant. Marc stopped to greet a few of the diners and briefly introduced Michelle. Several offers were made for them to join a table. Marc politely refused and received some joking replies that were in such rapid French that Michelle could not understand. Finally, they were seated and Marc leant toward her over the table.

'I hope you don't mind, I refused several offers for us to join friends at their tables. I just wanted to keep you to myself.' Marc suddenly smiled and, in a strong American accent continued, 'I wanned quality time with you alone...' then resuming his normal voice, low with a slight French accent, 'I thought perhaps if I spoke in American I might sound less like a hopeless, romantic fool. Did it work?'

Michelle had a flash memory of Seb Raven and his ardent voice calling her Marquise. 'Well, your American accent is appalling and I'm sure Americans can be more lovey-dovey than the English or even the French.'

'Lovey-dovey... I have never heard that expression... it's so good. And your dress... such a beautiful dove grey. Love and doves...yes, very descriptive. Dove, the symbol of love and peace.'

'I suppose so,' Michelle answered thoughtfully, 'I've never really thought about it.'

'Well, it struck me because I have been looking at images of doves all day, drawings by Picasso.'

'How amazing, you are very fortunate in your work. I can't imagine anything more wonderful that to be paid to look at fine art works.'

'Well, yes and no. A great deal of my work is research in laboratories. I work with several colleagues to establish whether a work of art is genuine or not. This weekend we had to work all day Sunday as an important auction is coming up in New York. There is a great deal of doubt about the authentification of this drawing by Picasso... or not!'

'Still, fascinating stuff. And did you discover the truth?'

'Oh yes, about an hour or so into the dating of the paper and other factors we knew it was a fake. Quite sad really, it was still, in its way, a beautiful drawing of a face, an olive branch and a dove. Cleverly done!'

'But a copy is always just that, surely? Of no real value?'

'Sadly, I agree with you in principle. But some of the art work that I have to reject is actually of high quality. What I don't understand is why on earth an artist with the ability to create such accurate copies would not paint his own works.'

'Well, lack of inspiration or imagination, I suppose. Surely, it's one thing to have the skill and quite another to have an original thought.'

'Hmm,' Marc answered slowly, 'I get where you are coming from, I shall have to give that idea more thought. But I don't want to bore you with talk of my work. How is it going at the Bastide?'

'You're not boring me at all, in fact, I wanted to ask your advice about art works.' Michelle looked at him shyly, 'I thought it might be rude to talk shop over dinner!'

'Talk shop? Another fine expression. It says so much in two little words. I love the English language, it is so expressive. Anyway, I could watch your lips move for hours on end. Oh dear, Cupid has shot me with an arrow again... please, my lovey-dovey, talk shop quickly while we order our food.'

Michelle realised the waiter was hovering and quickly picked up the menu.

'Last time we were here I saw they do something called Bourride, but I wasn't sure what it is! Is it good?'

'Aha, now we are in the language of food, yes, very good, fantastic! It's a fish soup recipe from Marseilles, the owner here is a Marseillais and he makes it to perfection. It is served with a garlic mayonnaise...quite strong... so, perhaps we should both eat it?' Marc raised his dark eyebrows and his eyes were smiling as he turned the last part of his explanation into a question.

'Well, I never eat very much so perhaps we could share.' Michelle looked back at him with wide-eyed innocence. 'But now, should we talk shop again?'

'I think we had better as I was just thinking of skipping the food and ordering coffee... so, what is your question, my beautiful little Marquise de Rosefont... is it about your art collection?'

'Well, I'm not sure it's an art collection exactly...' Michelle began.

'But it's common knowledge that your birth father, Michel de Rosefont, had a fine collection of art. The Rosefont family were renowned in the second world war. They worked against the Vichy and hid many Jewish refugees at the Bastide... at great risk to their own lives. Your grandparents were the bravest people in the entire area. I haven't worked down here for long but I have heard the stories.' Michelle looked at him in amazement. Why had she never known this? Suddenly her family history was coming to life. But Marc was still talking. 'One of the refugees, a rich Jew from Hanover, gave your grandfather an important work of modern art. It is thought that the rest of the collection was lost in a bomb raid in Hanover but I only know from local rumour as Michel de Rosefont was practically a recluse... I never met him. One never knows with rumour, of course.'

Now Michelle interrupted him. 'Yes, but my so-called father managed to drink his way to poverty and I think, every so often, he sold a painting or two to keep the Bastide from completely falling down. I certainly haven't seen anything like a modern piece of artwork anywhere. If my blood grandparents were heroic then I think Michel de Rosefont was the opposite.'

'Ah, I see, yes... maybe calling him a recluse is being polite. It must be very hard for you finding out piece by piece about your birth father. I could tell from the short meeting I had with Dr Phelps that he is your real father and always will be. Maybe Michel de Rosefont was a weak man but then, one never knows about another man's hidden demons. To be fair, I must say it quite often happens that art work is sold off to keep one of these crumbling piles from falling down. Of course, the upkeep must be horrendous.'

'I'm certainly finding that out right now. Everything you say is very true.' Michelle looked at him and saw he was looking at her with such sympathy that she felt tears spring to her eyes. It seemed so long now that she had been struggling to accept this new birthright. Marc reached out and quickly took her hand and held it gently in his.

'Local gossip also tells me you are doing a great job with the restoration, Michelle, and giving local people employment. There is plenty of talk about new life at the Bastide de Rosefont. You should be proud.'

'Oh, I've been so lucky... you see I have my friend, Kelly, working with me and her boyfriend, Leon... and my father... as you rightly say, my real father... and then we had the luck of the money from the American film company's broken contract... that was really amazing because another friend of mine, my solicitor had tied that up brilliantly... but...' Michelle's words ran out and she smiled ruefully. 'Our plans for a luxury hotel are ambitious and I can begin to see the bottom of the money pot. I have an offer to buy my land... I may have to... unless you can find a priceless work of art ... then I could follow in the downhill footsteps of Michel de Rosefont.'

Marc raised her hand to his lips and Michelle felt the soft touch of a kiss. Her stomach muscles tightened sharply and suddenly the money worries back at the Bastide seemed a million miles away. But Marc was still talking and looking at her hand. 'Such a ring! It must be an heirloom, *un objet de famille, quel héritage*!' He laid her hand down gently on the table. Michelle felt the warmth of his hand fade from her skin. What was happening? Marc's face was shadowed with something she could not understand.

'What is it, Marc, what are you thinking?' Michelle reached across the table and touched his shoulder.

'What am I thinking? Indeed, what am I thinking.' He sat back in his chair, moving out of her reach. 'If you really want to know, I am thinking how ridiculous I am being. I was dreaming that one day you might let me put a ring on your finger but you are a woman out of my reach.'

Michelle angrily pulled the ancient ring off her finger and dropped it into her glass of water. Her eyes flashed as she replied,

'As far as I am concerned, if inheritance can change who I am, then I would walk away from it all tonight. The waiter can take the ring away and...' But before she could end her sentence, Marc had stood up and was leaning over her, kissing her.

She reached up and put her arms around his neck as their lips met. The kiss was brief but passionate and for a second the world was lost to them. The next moment they realised that a ripple of applause was passing round the restaurant. And cheers of 'Bravo, encore!' Marc kissed her once more, very lightly on her forehead and then gave a small bow to the amused diners.

'*Merci, tout le monde, continuez a manger, maintenant! Bon appétit!*' There was general laughter as Marc sat back in his seat.

'Now, I have pronounced my love in front of the good people of Aix en Provence... well, I am sorry, Marquise or not, you will have to take me on.'

'Then that is sorted!' Michelle laughed, her face still flushed pink from the attention of the whole restaurant, his words, her own anger and, she realised suddenly, excitement and happiness.

At that moment, the waiter arrived with a large tureen. He placed it carefully on the table between them and then picked up a fork and deftly hooked the ring out of the glass of water and placed it on the table. Michelle and Marc both looked at it for a moment as it lay sparkling richly on the plain, white cloth.

Marc picked it up and examined it closely. 'It's very beautiful indeed, not my field of knowledge, but I would think it must be more than four hundred years old. I shall never be able to buy a ring to match it, but one day, I hope to find a very modern ring, something that flashes with fire... a ring to reflect yourself, Michelle.' He passed the ring to Michelle and she placed it back on her finger.

'Yes, it is beautiful and very old... but it only fits my first finger. It is really too big for me.' She answered slowly, not sure how to respond to what was almost a proposal. She closed her eyes briefly, imagining a future life ahead with Marc. Of course, it was ridiculous that they should be talking like this... they had only just met. Michelle smiled to herself as she imagined telling Kelly how out of hand the whole thing had gone. Yes, even Kelly would be more sensible, she must pull herself together, right now. Luckily the waiter returned, bringing a fresh water glass.

'*Voilà, mademoiselle, et bon appétit!*' He lifted the lid away from the soup tureen and a wonderful aroma of fresh herbs and fish filled the air between them. Suddenly she realised she was very hungry.

'I hadn't realised how hungry I am!' Marc's words could have been her own.

He carefully ladled some soup into Michelle's bowl and the rest of the meal passed in happy and easy companionship.

They had been sitting over their coffee for so long, talking avidly to each other, that they hadn't realised they were the last diners left in the restaurant. Marc hastily paid the bill and apologised for keeping them open. The waiter held the door open for them as they left, smiling and wishing them *bonne soirée*. They emerged into the cold night air and Marc put his arm around Michelle to shelter her from the cold wind that was blowing from the East. They stood for a moment, neither wanting the evening to end.

'My car's right here.' Michelle said, unnecessarily as they were standing right beside it.

'Would you like to come back to my place? I mean, my family's home? Maybe a coffee, they would love to meet you? Never before have I wished my own apartment was not in Paris.' They both laughed and Michelle took out her car keys and opened the car.

'Why not come back to the Bastide?' She looked at him across the top of the car roof and suddenly they both laughed again.

'Isn't their some English joke about 'come up and see my etchings'? asked Marc as he quickly jumped into the passenger seat.

'Exactly!' said Michelle, 'But I think you are supposed to be shocked and to refuse.'

'Hmm, well, that's definitely not going to happen. Now, how does this car heater work?'

Soon they were bouncing down the pot-holed drive to the Bastide. Michelle had concentrated on driving and trying to avoid the warmth of Marc's hand resting lightly on her thigh. As the huge bulk of the building loomed into sight, Marc removed his hand from her thigh and stroked the back of her neck.

'Thank you for inviting me back to your little place, *ma chère marquise*!'

As she turned off the engine, he ducked his head and kissed her. Not with the swift passion of the kiss in the restaurant but a deep searching kiss that demanded more. Michelle responded, one hand holding the back of his head as though she could never be close enough. Then, they pulled apart and Marc jumped out of the car and came round to open Michelle's door. She almost fell into his arms as he pulled her toward him. Oblivious to the cold, night air, they kissed again and Marc's hands were inside her coat, running over her body in the thin silk of her dress. Slowly they began to walk toward the Château, arms around each other and stopping to kiss again every few steps. The old lanterns glimmered each side of the steps but the rest of the Bastide was in complete darkness. Michelle laughing with excitement, pushed Marc gently away from her, as she struggled to push open the heavy door. As it swung open they heard the distant barking of a dog and then Coco was there, jumping around Michelle to welcome her.

'Ah, your beautiful dog, she's a Braque Francais Gascogne, isn't she, a very special dog!

Marc caught Coco by the collar and stroked her head and ruffled her ears. Coco, delighted by his attention, rolled onto her back as Marc continued to make a fuss of her.

'Hmm, as you can tell, she's my guard dog!' Michelle laughed. 'Anyway, she approves of you, obviously.'

'What's her name?'

'Coco, she's called Coco, not sure why, but it suits her.'

'Coco Chanel, obviously, she is so elegant!'

'Why yes, I hadn't really thought of that. I'm sure you're right. She used to belong to Sven Gilbert but apparently she was gun shy so...'

'Well, she has found a good home.'

'Sorry it's so cold in the hall. Come through to the kitchen and I'll make some coffee or hot chocolate...which would you prefer?'

'I'm not sure I want either... my sweet lovey-dovey.' Marc went behind her to take her coat off her shoulders but then his hands moved over her breasts and he cupped them in his hands as he whispered in her ear.

'Not coffee, not chocolate and I am not at all cold.' Michelle leaned back into him as he gently caressed her breasts and his fingers circled her nipples as they pressed hard against her silk dress. She tried to turn round to face him but he held her close, kissing the back of her neck and pushing one leg between hers. Finally when she felt she could no longer bear the force of passion running through her, he spun her round and was holding her completely enfolded in his arms. Then she began to kiss him, opening the buttons of his shirt and kissing and biting his neck. She ran her hands down his back and felt him shudder with desire.

'Follow me!' Michelle suddenly broke away from his embrace and ran up the stairs, closely followed by Coco. Marc laughed and ran after them. Before he could catch her, Michelle ran along the long corridor and into her bedroom. Marc was close behind her as she switched on the bedside lamp and saw the room as she lad left it, in grand disorder with clothes all over the bed and thrown across chairs. She turned to Marc, laughing, delighted to find that she couldn't care less. She gently led Coco to her usual place on the rug outside her bedroom door and then closed the door on her. Marc was waiting for her by the bed, standing in the soft light of the lamp, his face alive with desire and love. Michelle went to him and, slowly now, they kissed. Pulling slightly away from him she said quietly.'Marc, will you pinch me?'

Marc drew away from her in shock.'Certainly not! You're not into that sort of thing, are you?'

Michelle began to laugh helplessly,'No, no, nothing like that ... I just wanted to make sure I'm not dreaming!' she fell back on the bed, 'It's just I've been having these wild dreams...' Michelle could not speak for laughing.

'OK, one day you can tell me all about your dreams but I have a better way to prove that you are not dreaming, much better than pinching!' He fell on top of her and began to kiss her again and again. 'But if you want to be quite sure, maybe a little pinch here and here...' His fingers closed tight on each of her nipples in turn as he spoke. Michelle let out a small cry of intense pleasure as she felt him around her and inside her. She lay still for a moment, feeling the weight of his body on hers. And then their night of love began. No doubt now in her mind that this was the real thing.

'I just cannot believe it! Michelle Phelps, first date, brings home man to see her etchings. No, if I hadn't seen him here at the breakfast table I would never, ever have believed it.' Kelly shook her head in disbelief.

'I know, I can hardly believe it myself... but it's true, beautifully true!' Michelle stretched luxuriously, every bone and muscle in her body remembering the love-making. 'And this morning, before breakfast, we did actually go round the Bastide looking at the paintings. We used your inventory, Leon.'

The three friends were seated, side by side, at the long desk in the office. The winter sun shone brightly outside but the earth had a light layering of frost. Leon had lit a fire in the office and Coco was sprawled happily in front of it.

'Oh my god, you don't think he's after your paintings, do you? I mean he is an art expert.' Kelly swivelled her chair ,first toward Michelle and then spun round toward Leon, her eyes wide with shock.

'I really don't think so.' Michelle smiled confidently, 'I really think I'd know. Anyway, we didn't find anything of great interest. One or two family portraits are apparently of some age... but not painted by anyone famous. Marc ...' Michelle paused for a moment, just to enjoy the sound of his name on her lips, '... Marc did say there was local rumour that my family had been leaders in the resistance in World War II and that a grateful and rich Jewish refugee had given my grandfather a modern art-work. But, if you remember, Kelly, Mme. de Fleurenne hinted at the same and that my feckless birth father had sold the lot to keep the old Bastide from falling down. Mind you, I can see his problem.'

'Yes, with you right there... I've just been on Excel. The FGM money is vanishing fast. The wages are nothing compared to the building material costs.'
'I think the building guys are good... very skilful, and the hourly rate is average... but the materials have to be of such high quality, not to mention vast in quantity.' Michelle flicked through the pages on her screen and sighed. 'I know it's a last resort but I could always sell the land to Karen Gilbert. Her offer has gone up since the last time I turned it down... and she seems to have accepted the fact she's not going to marry me off to Sven.'

'I think you and Sven have to thank Robert for this. He is telling me about it on our journey to England.' Leon rolled his office chair to sit between the girls as he continued. 'When he spent the day at Château Gilbert, I think your father is very good at the psychology... well, he is a doctor, bien sur!'

'Good old Dad, he is great at sorting out problems. I hope he gets back soon.' Michelle said and Kelly and Leon nodded quickly in agreement.

'I have been researching the Fondation grant for ancient buildings. It is very possible but, unless Mme. Gilbert can, how do you say, 'pull ropes', then it could take up to a year to receive the funds and they insist many regulations.'

'Pull strings, my love, pull strings,' Kelly smiled and reached over to smooth Leon's hair back from his forehead. 'You look so worried, but we can try...never say never!'

'Well, in French we say "*Fontaine, je ne boirai pas de ton eau*", replied Leon, catching Kelly's hand and kissing it. 'And talking of fountains... this afternoon I want to carry on with my grand effort to restore the fountain in front of the Bastide. But right now, I have another idea... Michelle, do you have that letter from Michel de Rosefont?'

'Letter?' Both girls looked at him in puzzlement, then Michelle added, 'Oh yes, the letter he wrote to my mother. Yes, well, the original is in a bank safe with the title deeds of the Bastide... but I scanned it. Yes, I have it on file.'

'I think we should read it again.' Leon said.

'Ok, I can find it easily,' Michelle turned back to her screen, 'yes, here it is.' She opened the file and her screen filled with the hand-written letter. 'It's a good copy. Do you want to read it again?'

Leon rolled his chair nearer to Michelle and studied the screen. Then slapped the desk with his hand. Coco jumped up and came over to see what the excitement was about, pushing her large head onto Michelle's lap.

'Coco wants to read it, too.' laughed Kelly, 'What is it, Leon?'

'*Voilá*, I knew there was something stayed in my head... there, at the end 'if this letter should find you then read again the book we both loved so much, and, here is another promise, you will find something of great interest." Leon turned to look at Michelle and then Kelly, his face alight with excitement.

'It's true, I never really thought any more about the letter. I suppose it was too sad.' said Michelle.

But there's something more, reading the original letter in French, the last word 'interest' has been translated into English from the French word *'intérêt'* ... I think the better translation may be 'advantage'.'

'Advantage... as in value?' Kelly raised her eyebrows and stood up 'Michelle, I am going to make a pot of coffee and Leon, could you light another fire in the library? I think we should shut up shop here and look for this book... and where else to begin than the library. I'll bring the coffee and see you there.' Kelly ran from the room, closely followed by Coco. Leon looked at Michelle and said,

'It may be nothing, Michelle, maybe just an old photo in a book, I may be wrong about the value part... maybe my imagination.'

'I know, Leon, I know. Kelly is always keen and optimistic... but you know, it is worth a try... except there are a great number of books in the library. It could take days!'

'I'll light a big fire and you print out the letter in English and French so we can all read it again.' Leon went quickly from the room and Michel stood for a moment, looking across to the mountain she was beginning to think of as her own. It rose, chalky and white against the pale, blue sky, a few clouds around the summit, as if hooked to the peak. The vineyards stretched away downhill, bare and touched with frost. No sign of Sven or any workers today. Winter had really arrived. She yawned as tiredness began to creep over her. She closed her eyes briefly, remembering the feel of Marc's hands on her body, the warmth of him. Her eyes flicked open as her mobile rang. She snatched it up from the desk and looked at it eagerly, yes, it was Marc, a text message. 'words are not enough... even the 3 words i love you are not enough... i return tomorrow from paris... when can i see you?'

Michelle tapped back quickly.'i love you too - call me as soon as - come to the Bastide any time - i am waiting longing for you x'

'tomorrow then - hope late afternoon xxxx'

Michelle sighed and closed the line. Just when she had been thinking of him. Then she smiled at herself. Not surprising, really, as she had been thinking of Marc constantly. But now, she must get back to work and try to save the Bastide finances. She looked out the window for one brief moment longer, just time enough to think again how lucky she was to have such friends to help her ... and now, to have found love.

35   *'a dark red volume with gold lettering'*

'I have to admit, this is a bit harder than I thought.' Kelly was standing on the library ladder, carefully going from book to book. 'And the dust, clouds of it!'

'Well, it's past lunch time and I work out we are about one-fifth through the whole.' Leon was sitting on the floor, searching through books on the bottom shelf.

'One-fifth of the whole... trust you to work it out like that, Leon,' said Kelly, impatiently, 'I suppose you have worked out how long it will take to go through the whole library and find nothing, too?'

Before Michelle could intervene from her place on another library ladder, the door opened and Robert Phelps walked in. Coco jumped up from her place by the fire and wagged her tail.

'What are you all doing in here? Lovely fire and everything... but is spring-cleaning the library a priority suddenly?' Robert asked.

Michelle and Kelly came down their ladders and Leon stood up, they gathered round Robert, pleased to see him back.

'You're back early, Dad, we were all saying how we missed you, the Bastide is not the same without you here.' said Michelle, and Kelly and Leon nodded in agreement.

'And I think we need your advice and help, we're in quite a state!' said Kelly. Robert listened carefully to her explanation of the letter, then nodded thoughtfully as he sat at the table and read through it carefully.

'So, it's this last line, then... well, it seems to me we have to try and imagine what type of book it might be. Of course, this may be easier for me than for you three, even you, Michelle. I mean, it's a little difficult for me to imagine my very own Anne with this Frenchman... but I hope I am grown-up enough to cope with that... of course.' A shadowy frown passed across Robert's face and Michelle rested her hand on his shoulder as he continued, 'But, as I am sure your psychology degree will have taught you, Leon, people don't change so much in another relationship. Your mother and I, Michelle, always read a lot. We liked to read the same novels so that we could discuss them, but Anne's real delight was in looking at atlases of the world. Yes, I think you should see if there are any large map books or atlases... yes, that's where I would start. Now, you carry on with the hard work and I'll make some sandwiches. I've brought a whole ham from Sussex to show Leon that the English know how to cook.' He left the room, closely followed by Coco.

'It looks like Coco understood the word ham!' Kelly brushed the dust from her jeans and shook her hair. 'Isn't it great to have your Dad back again, Mich. I knew he'd have a good idea. So, anyone seen any huge old map books?'

'Yes, there's a whole shelf of them!' Michelle groaned, 'But I think Dad might be right, shall we leave off searching book by book and give it a go?'

'Definitely,' said Leon, 'Make sure you leave a space in the shelves so you know where you were and let's restart with le collection d'atlas.'

'At last, two words that are the same in French as in English... collection and atlas. Now, that has to be a lucky sign!' Kelly ran over to the long shelf of atlases and eagerly pulled out the first one. Leon and Michelle exchanged glances of amusement at Kelly's new enthusiasm.

'Wait a moment, attends Kelly, first let us look at the whole shelf and see if there is one book more ... I don't know... more used looking?'

Kelly stood up, holding the first heavy atlas in her hand and took a pace back. They all looked at the long shelf and then all three gasped. There was one book, a dark red volume with gold lettering, it stood out from the rest as it was not quite pushed to the back of the shelf.

'Et *voilá*! Perhaps it is that ... you try Michelle, you open the book,' said Leon. Michelle took a deep breath, and helped by one of Kelly's usual small pushes in her back, she stepped forward and heaved the large book from the shelf.

'It's so heavy, I'll take it over to the table to open it.' Michelle carried it ceremoniously across the room and laid it flat on a small, leather reading table and switched on the old brass reading lamp. She knew she was delaying the moment of discovery. Would she find another letter to her mother, a photo or...

'Holy Moly, Mich, will you just open it?' Kelly insisted, her voice high with tension.
So, very slowly, Michelle opened the cover and began to turn the pages. It was a beautiful book, each page interspersed with a thin page of transparent paper. She carefully turned page by page, smoothing the tissue each time, and looking briefly at the coloured maps of Europe. The only sound in the room was the slight whisper of the turning pages and the crackling of the fire. Then, nearing the end of the book, a thin edge of paper slid into sight.

'There is something ... there is... it's right at the back of the book, I think, just in the back cover!' Kelly squeaked with excitement, Leon remained silent and Michelle continued to turn page by page. Finally, as she turned the last map and reached the index, the piece of paper slid diagonally into her hand. Very carefully, Michelle took it from the book and rested it on the table. It was a very large and thin, brown folder. Gently Michelle opened it and there was a small, dark painting.

'A painting, but it's rather horrible! So dark and such strange black brush strokes!' Michelle drew back from it in dismay.

Kelly and Leon drew nearer and peered at it.

'Well, it certainly doesn't look much to me.' said Kelly her voice betraying her disappointment. 'But I guess it is what we have been looking for... I mean, maybe it's valuable?' Now her voice was doubtful and disappointed.

'Well, no signature or date... but one never knows...' said Leon.

'Don't start with that never say never stuff and start talking fountains again, I'm starving. Ah, our saviour, Robert, just in time. Well, come and look...what do you think?'
Robert put down the tray of food and came over to the reading table. He looked closely at the painting.

'Hmm, very dark indeed, especially for a water-colour! I have no idea... but it may be worth showing it to an expert...'

Suddenly they all turned to Michelle.

'Yes, it's worth a try. I'll take a photo and send it and then let's eat.' Michelle pulled out her phone, snapped a quick photo of the painting and sent it to Marc. They all pulled chairs close to the fire and began to eat.

'You're right, Robert, your English ham is superb!' said Leon, eating happily. 'Especially in some good French bread. It will give me the energy to go out in the cold and carry on my grand work with *ma belle fontaine*'.

'I'll give you a hand, I need...' before Robert could finish his sentence, Michelle's phone bleeped. She snatched it up and read the text aloud.

'very exciting, send better photo by email... love you my dove'

Michelle had read the last words aloud before realising. Her father looked at her sharply. 'I go away for a long weekend and what have you been up to, my girl?'

'Never mind for now what your surprisingly mad daughter has been doing in your absence... how about that Marc said 'exciting'. I don't even know how he could see anything but black on a phone image. Last word I would use to describe it. Maybe he wasn't talking about the drawing?' said Kelly, surreptitiously giving Coco a piece of ham and glancing across at Michelle.

'Don't think I can't see you every time you give Coco titbits, Kelly. You'll make her fat. Anyway, Marc wants a better photo so the painting must at least be interesting.' Said Michelle, glaring at Kelly.

'I'll go and get my camera.' Said Leon, 'we can send a high resolution photo, won't be a moment.'

There was silence for a moment and then Robert said, 'So, you like this Marc chap then, Michelle?'

'I do, Dad, I really do... I know it's all very sudden but it feels like I have known him all my life. I don't know how to explain it... it just seems right.'

'Well, he seemed a very nice guy to me, although, of course I only met him briefly. Anyway, you're a big girl and quite able to make your own decisions. As long as you are happy... then I'm happy.'

Leon came back in the room and began to set up the painting in a good light. He took several shots and then dashed off again to download them and send them to Marc.

Kelly sighed with annoyance, 'Now we shall have to wait to hear back, I hate waiting, I'm going to check on the work outside. Come on, Coco, come for a walk, don't want you to get fat.'

Michelle sat with her father by the dying fire. 'We've never had a fire in here before, it's a beautiful room, isn't it? I do so hope I am going to be able to keep it all going here, Dad.'
'Well, the money from the sale of our place in Sussex will be through soon... that will boost the funds.'

'That would be great, but you know, I worry about all the money being poured in here.'

'Well, you're the business head, Michelle, but I should think it a good investment. I mean, if all goes very wrong and you do have to sell, I am sure you will see all the money back and more.'

'I suppose so, or I could always sell the land to Karen Gilbert.' said Michelle sadly, 'Even that would be better than giving up the whole place.'

'Well, I know nothing about it really... but history tells that to sell land is near the end of a family history in a place like this...even your birth father seems to have held out against that solution. You get good rents from Karen. Although I know she wants to buy... she had a go at me... asking me to persuade you. And she is a very persuasive business woman herself.' Robert laughed and sipped his glass of wine thoughtfully.

'I know Kelly teases you about Karen, but really, Dad...what do you make of her?'

'Well, there's no doubt she's a beautiful woman and very clever, too. Good company and she flatters me...which powder puffs my old ego... but you know, there was and still is only one woman for me, Michelle and that was your lovely mother.'

'I thought so, but you know, Dad, maybe it is time to move on... or whatever they say...closure or something?' Michelle drew to a halt, in her heart she knew Robert Phelps, the man she had always loved as her father, would stay faithful to the memory of her mother. But she continued, 'I would understand, Dad, you know I would.'

'Well, thank you for kind words, Michelle, but isn't it me that should be advising you about your love life. Anyway, you may not exactly be my daughter but, maybe by nurture, you have inherited my nature. Faithful is our strong suit. Whoever you eventually marry will be a lucky man. As for Karen Gilbert, let's just say she makes a very nice girl-next-door!'

They both burst out laughing at the idea of the haughty Mme. Gilbert in her Château being so described. Then Michelle's phone bleeped. She read the message and then stared at the father with wide eyes.

'Marc says the drawing is more than interesting and could be very valuable. Quick, Dad, let's find Kelly and Leon.'

An hour later they were all four seated at the desk in the office. Four screens glinted as the room darkened in the winter twilight.

'When can Marc get here?' asked Kelly, turning a moment from her screen and rubbing her eyes as she looked at Michelle.

'Tomorrow afternoon earliest. He's finding out all he can about any works of art that Michel had sold in the past. That may give a clue to the whole collection belonging to the Jewish refugee. Of course a lot of reference would have been lost... but he's going back through archives of auctions and sales.'

'Well, there's endless reference on the web but I have no idea how relevant.' said Robert. 'I think I'm wasting my time now... going round in smaller or maybe bigger circles.'

'Research does that often.' Agreed Leon, 'but from what Marc said and from what we have found in other works, it certainly looks like it could be a Cezanne study for his painting of the old Bibémus Quarries, near Mont Ste.Victoire. It could be worth a fortune.'

'I can't believe such a dreary little painting could be by Cezanne. From what I know of his work, not much agreed, but I've seen his stuff at Courtauld's... all so bright and full of Provençal colour. So...well, different.' Kelly shook her blonde curls doubtfully. 'I don't get the connection.'

'Anyway, it could be a clever fake... I mean, there's no signature or anything.' added Michelle. 'I guess we shouldn't get too hopeful.'

'Well, if it is genuine, at least it's so gloomy you won't mind selling it.' Kelly peered at the image on her screen. 'I have to say, I think it's just horrid.'

'Exactly, almost sinister. I had no idea there even was a quarry near the mountain.'

'Oh yes, I could take you to it. It is a strange place... there are all sorts of local stories about it... even murder!' said Leon. 'Anyway, we had better try and be patient until tomorrow when Marc arrives.'
'Yes,' said Kelly, 'We'll all await the arrival of Michelle's expert art lover!'

'for you, that and much more'

So, wait they did. With so much work to do at the Bastide the time passed quickly enough, although Michelle found herself constantly checking her phone. At last, just before three in the afternoon, it bleeped. She was talking with Monique in the kitchen barn and quickly excused herself to read the text.

'arrive at best 3.30 with luck and love-dove x' Michelle called back to Monique,

'Sorry, have to continue discussion about the oven later, must go!'

Monique waved a hand and Michelle dashed out to the fountain where Leon and Robert were working, closely watched by Coco.

'Marc's on his way... be here soon!' Before they had time to reply she ran into the Bastide and up the stairs to the office, followed by Coco.'Kelly, Marc will be here very soon!'

Kelly turned from her work and looked at Michelle. 'Go brush your beautiful hair, girl, you look a scruff!'

Michelle laughed and ran to her bedroom. Here, she had restored normal order and the room looked tidy and shabbily elegant. Michelle ran into the bathroom and quickly washed her face and hands and brushed her hair. Kelly had been right, she did look scruffy. She looked in the mirror at her over-sized sweater and torn jeans. Should she change, did she even have time? Suddenly she realised that it really didn't matter. Marc loved her and she knew it. He would love her in whatever she wore. She smiled at her reflection. Hmm, there was a definite Audrey Hepburn look to the smile but she doubted if Audrey had ever been quite so dishevelled. Then, she heard Coco barking and jumping up at the window sill. She went back into the bedroom and looked down at the terrace. There stood Marc, surrounded by her father, Kelly and Leon. She smiled at the picture. All the people she loved most in the world.

'It has all the right obvious qualities.' Marc said seriously, looking at the drawing through a strong magnifying glass. They were all back in the library, all staring mesmerised at the dark painting.

'Of course it will need forensic testing in a laboratory... but my instinct tells me...or rather hints that it could be the real thing. Could be the lost watercolour from the series of Cezanne's studies of the quarry. And the evidence I found that several works, including a watercolour by Cezanne, had last been recorded in a collection in Hanover... well, it could lead to your grandfather having been given one as a gift from a German Jew fleeing from the Nazi regime. All I could find out about works that Michel de Rosefont had sold in his lifetime were not very interesting. A few minor oil paintings, Flemish school, nothing of great value.'

'Forensic evidence... does it tell everything?' asked Leon, 'I mean, definite proof? Fascinating!'

'Well, the paper is easy to test for age and comparison with other works in the series, and the paint... then other experts will work with me on the actual style and technique of the brush strokes. I have already worked on an oil painting by Cezanne, titled 'Corner of the Quarry'. I can honestly say that is very possibly a study for that work... the bold, overlapping brush strokes, three main planes... quarry wall, trees and mountain...well the suggestion of the mountain in the background...very convincing. But nothing is definite. I'm sorry, I can't say more. There are some very clever people in the fake world. But having found it in the library here, well... but no, I don't want to say more. You will have to take the painting to Paris.' Marc carefully closed the folder and they all looked at the plain brown cover, spellbound by his words.

'But, if it should turn out to be genuine,' said Kelly slowly, 'I mean, it must be valuable... wouldn't it be a bit risky trotting off to Paris with it. Michelle might lose it on the Metro or be mugged or something!'

'True, in fact it is a very delicate work, obviously I can seal it in a better folder but, in my opinion, it would be better to keep it in the library at the Bastide, where, by the way, it has been very well conserved, flat and away from light and humidity in this big folio... and ask the experts to come here.'

'Well, we already have you, how many would we need?' asked Kelly, always straight to the point, 'And what would their fee be?'

'Oh, don't worry about that, I can call in a few favours and anyway, they will be excited when I tell them about it. If you could offer lunch, that would be fine, I'm sure.'

'Really?' said Michelle, 'Could you do that for me?'

'Oh yes, for you, that and much more!' Marc replied softly, looking across to Michelle where she sat on the sofa close by the fire.

Robert stood up quickly, 'Well, it's all very exciting, and all very well for you youngsters, but I've had a long day... digging fountains and researching art... I've had enough and I'm off to bed.'
Kelly jumped up, too. 'Come on, Leon, it's our turn to wash up and then I'm ready for bed, too.'

'Not sure about the wash upping but I am always ready for bed!' Leon replied, standing up and putting his arm around Kelly, 'Come on, you too, Coco, I'll race you round my fountain.'
Suddenly Michelle and Marc were alone together. Marc poured two glasses of wine and came over to sit next to Michelle.

'You have very good friends and a wonderful real father, Michelle. They look out for you. I think Kelly had the idea I might run off with the drawing and never be seen again.'

'Oh, you have to get used to Kelly, she has a vivid imagination. One minute she's imagining me being mugged on the metro and the next you are a wicked art thief. Don't worry, she relaxed as soon as you said that you would bring the experts here. Are you sure you can arrange that?'

'No problem at all. I would bring you Mont Ste. Victoire if you needed it. And the most precious thing in the Bastide is sitting right next to me.' Marc placed his wine on a side table and then took Michelle's glass from her hand and placed it next to it. And then they kissed, softly and sweetly at first, and then hungrily. Marc groaned with pleasure as Michelle ran her fingers through his hair and then down his back, her fingernails lightly pressing into his skin as their kisses deepened. Marc's hand opened the front of Michelle's jeans and slipped inside. She shuddered with desire and then, locked in each other's arms they slipped from the sofa and onto the thick Persian rug in front of the fire. Marc pulled Michelle on top of him and she arched her back as he pulled her sweater and t-shirt off and began to kiss her breasts, gently sucking her nipples. Frantically, now, she pulled at his clothes baring his chest and soon they were both naked, skin touching skin, moving together in the firelight.

37   'the rug in the firelight'

Michelle struggled all the next day to concentrate on anything other than her need to be close to Marc. She forced herself back into working mode, checking on the progress of the building work, running again and again over the Excel pages of dwindling money, anything to try and keep her mind and body from remembering every moment of the night before. How she wanted Marc... but Marc was in Paris.

'So, are you going to tell me, or not?' Kelly asked as they sat, as usual, side by side at their long desk. The day was cold and the sky unusually grey. A low mist hung over the vineyards, completely obscuring the familiar backdrop of Mont Ste Victoire.

'Not.' Michelle answered, staring dreamily out the window. 'Isn't it strange, not being able to see our mountain. This is the first time we've ever had such a heavy mist. It's hard to believe the mountain is actually there.'

'Yeh, well, before you go all metaphysical on me, Mich, can we talk about the physical. I mean, last night in the library, it was obvious you and Marc wanted to be alone. I thought it was hilarious when your Dad jumped up like he'd been shot and said he was off to bed. Then he glared at me and Leon! Oh, he's great your Dad, Mich. I just love him!'

'I know, he really is so aware and tactful. I think it means it must approve of Marc, too. I'm so glad.'

'Is that a clue to say you are serious about your art expert lover, then? Wait a minute... is he an art expert lover or an expert lover of art or...?'

'OK, Kelly, give over! Yep, I'm serious, he's serious and that's all you're going to get, Kelly. I'm sure you don't want a kiss by kiss account of how we rolled around on the rug in the firelight?'

'Holy Moly, Marquise! Say no more... get back to work. I do wish Marc would ring with some news about that painting though!' Kelly laughed and Michelle dragged her mind away from sweet memories and returned to jiggling with the bills to be paid. They worked on for an hour or more, almost in silence, the fire crackling in the hearth but not keeping the office warm. Kelly looked down at her fingers.

'Do you think it's possible to get frostbite indoors, Mich?'

'Probably not, especially as we do have a fire in the room and you are wearing cashmere gloves.'

'Fingerless cashmere gloves, Mich, fingerless... the ends of my fingers are turning blue, I swear.'

'This is the coldest day we've had so far... shall we give it a break...' Michelle's words were interrupted by her mobile bleeping. Both girls looked at each other for an instant and then Michelle said,

'It's a text from Marc!'

'What does he say?'

Michelle blushed and then read aloud, 'la la la and then ... can bring guy from New York lunch time today, by luck he is in Aix right now. Is that OK? la, la , la.'

Kelly rolled her chair away from the desk and stood up.'Well, never mind your la la-ing, I can well guess... but today, that's great! Certainly a fast worker, your art expert lover-boy, very fast indeed!'

Michelle was tapping her mobile rapidly, 'I've asked him what time today.' Before she could say another word, a second message bleeped in.

'now not possible lunch but 4 in afternoon if OK? Also cezanne museum boss and others ... OK?'

Michelle tapped quickly into her mobile and then turned to Kelly,'Oh my god, Kelly, this is getting serious.'

'It seems so, certainly Marc must have some clout in the art world, and he must have a strong idea that it is genuine. Unless his head is in the clouds right now, just like our old mountain. I mean, you're floating about a foot off the ground today, Mich, I've never ever seen you quite so distracted from work.'

'Well, they're firmly on the ground now, Kelly and freezing cold. There's no time to waste... this is an important meeting and we need to set the scene.'

'Isn't it a bit late to renovate the entire Bastide to create the impression you don't need the money, Mich?'

Michelle laughed and began to rub some feeling back into her hands. 'True, but we can show them how the English take tea, I'm going to bake a Victoria sponge and you can wash up that Royal Doulton tea service we found in the pantry. Let's set the scene of English nobility at least... oh, and we must relight the fire in the library.'

'I'm surprised it's not still burning hot... and we'd better smooth out the fireside rug, too.' Kelly laughed and ran from the room, followed by a giggling Michelle and a barking Coco.

By half past three, the scene was set. Leon had lit such a huge fire that the heat was slowly spreading across the room. Robert had found boxes of candles and placed them in each of the wall sconces. The light shimmered, reflecting on the glass doors of the bookcases and shelves of leather bound books. Four of the staff had been called in for emergency cleaning work and the long room smelled sweetly of lavender and beeswax polish. The rugs had been taken outside and beaten and now the rich wool colours glowed in the half light of the afternoon. One lamp was burning, a bright pool of light directly onto the brown folder lying on the leather-topped reading table. Their work was done.

'It's quite a transformation, girls!' said Robert, standing with his back to the fire and nodding with approval.

'Should I leave the file with the painting on the table like that?' Leon asked.

'No, I don't think so.' Michelle and Kelly spoke together and then laughed.

'What were you going to say, Mich?'

'I think put the folder back in the atlas, on the shelf between the others, just as it was when we found it.' replied Michelle.

'Exactly what I was thinking!' Kelly agreed and Leon went over to the table and carefully replaced the folder into the large book. He carried it ceremoniously back to the shelf and as he leant to fit it into the gap, he suddenly stopped,

'Un moment, there's an envelope at the back of the shelf.' Kelly dashed over and looked to where Leon was trying to point as he still held the heavy book.

'Attention, careful Kelly, take it out carefully and then I'll put the book back.'

Kelly knelt on the floor by the low shelf and reached in. Slowly she pulled out a small envelope and looked at it for a moment then, stood up and carried it over to Michelle.

They all grouped around the bright light, watching Michelle as she carefully opened the envelope and pulled out a single sheet of paper.

'It's a letter to Michel de Rosefont. It's all in French... I think it's about art or something. Leon, you had better read it.' Michelle passed it to Leon who took it gingerly by the very edge as he read it through quietly to himself.

So, come on Leon, what does it say! Leon, come on!' Kelly bounced up and down impatiently.

Leon replied slowly, 'It is a letter from an Artur Rosenwald. I think, as it is dated *juin* 1944, that the letter is addressed to your grandfather, another Michel, I mean, not your biological father.' Leon gave a quick glance at Robert and then to Michelle.

'But what does it say?' asked Kelly, 'Translate it, Leon!'

'It says... well, it is a letter of gratitude. Sincere thanks for saving his life and all his family. That he will write when he gets to New York... and... here it is smidged, the ink has... how do you say?'

'Leon, this is no time for an English lesson, for God's sake just give us the gist.' Kelly moved closer to Leon, trying to see the letter.

'Gist... what is gist? *Alors, je continue*,' Leon said hurriedly after a warning glare from Kelly, 'from there, after the smidge it is about... little he can do to repay except to leave a gift ... not gist, Kelly, a gift of a little painting. *Voilá!*'

Leon looked up at them with a triumphant smile. Michelle had been standing, slightly apart from the others, standing still and quiet as once again her history closed around her. Robert moved and put his arm around her shoulders.

'Sounds like some good evidence, Michelle! What do you think?'

At that moment the front door bell rang and Coco rushed barking into the hall. Michelle smiled and looked at them all, and said,

'I think so... and I think that is probably Marc and our guests.'

'hide their excitement'

'Jesus Christ! Christie's in Paris!' Kelly was staring into her coffee cup as though seeing the future. 'This is getting very serious, Mich. I mean, all the expert guys were nearly choking with excitement. I was beginning to worry that fat guy with the deep, red face was going to have a heart attack.'

Michelle and Kelly were sitting alone in the old kitchen, huddled at the end of the table near the heat of the cooking range.

'I know, they certainly didn't try to hide their excitement and then, the letter seemed to mean so much to them. That will go with the painting in the security van to Paris.'

'Strange, isn't it, Mich? Ever since the war that little painting has been in that dusty old book and the letter just jammed at the back of the shelf... then suddenly it has to be guarded all the way to Christie's showrooms.'

The kitchen door flew open and Robert and Leon came in, followed by a muddy Coco.

'Have you girls left any coffee?' asked Robert, flinging his tweed cap on a hook at the back of the door. 'Sitting around by the old range... you should be out in the winter sunshine.'

'Too damn cold!' Kelly poured two coffees and topped up her own, 'Anyway, Michelle is in shock and has to be kept warm and I am her dear carer. More coffee, Mich?'

'No, I think I've had enough caffeine to whizz me through the next week or so. But, you're right about the shock, allowing for your usual dollop of exaggeration, Kelly.'

'Certainly, an exciting afternoon yesterday.' agreed Robert as he sat warming his hands around the coffee cup. 'When is the Securicor van arriving?'

'They said before twelve, so should be any time now. I thought that was surprising... the way they arranged everything so quickly... the painting has to be an important find. They all were very... dans un état de grande agitation... particularly reading that letter.' said Leon.

'Well, you must have understood every word, Leon. They were all talking so quickly there was no way I could keep up... what did they talk about between each other?' Robert asked.

'Marc will be able to tell you correctly but, basically, everything made them think it was a genuine watercolour by Cezanne. A late work, a preparatory study for an oil painting of the quarry... most important was that there is record of the studies in a series and this one has been missing, thought to have been destroyed in a bombing in Hanover. Tomorrow they have booked a series of tests in the Paris laboratory. They are working so fast because Marc... how do you say... *laisséz entendre*? They all stared at him blankly and so Leon continued, '*Alors*, Marc was very clever, he told them that Michelle wanted to sell and that she had interest from a private buyer, an American.'

'Did he? Do I?' Michelle looked at Leon in surprise.

'No, no... it was a good way to make the mec... the guy from Christie's take notice. He was the one with the little black beard. The one always shaking his head and stroking his beard... you know, looking like he did not believe it to be a genuine Cezanne. But, *mon dieu*, when Mark casually...err ... *laisséz entendre*…'

'Oh, I get it,' said Kelly, 'you mean that Marc hinted!'

'*Exactement! Oui, oui oui*, he hintered the interest of another person.'

'Hmm, good psychology!' Robert smiled, 'I noticed a sudden change in attitude in the bearded man. Marc saw he was playing a game. Very clever and certainly that was when the ball really started rolling.'

' I did not see a ball... was there a ball?' Leon asked. The others all sighed and drank their coffee.

'Ah, I see, one of your ridiculous idioms. I refuse to learn any more. *C'est ridicule!*'

'*Ridicule!*' both girls chorused loudly.

'Ridiculous doesn't even come near.' added Robert. 'Come on, Leon, let's go back to the straightforward work at the fountain and leave these two girls to dream of future fortune.'

'Good idea, Robert, and we can watch out for the security van coming up the drive.'

39 *'everything is so dreamlike'*

Their was an air of excitement as people settled into their seats or stood around the sides of the room. Michelle sat between her father and Kelly, Leon beside Kelly. Marc was near the front standing in a line of men and women with telephones. This was Christie's auction house in New York and today was an important sale of modern art. Lot number 13 was simply listed as 'Bibemus Quarry', by Paul Cezanne 1904, aquarelle. The extraordinary part was the estimated sale price of six to nine million dollars. In fact, Michelle sat clasping a hand-written note from a man, a man she had never even met, offering ten million dollars if she would withdraw from the auction and sell to him privately. Michelle sat nervously, twisting the paper in her hand, her head buzzing with the loud voices all around. Then, Kelly was digging her elbow into her ribs. Michelle came back to reality. This was no erotic,surreal dream, this was reality and happening right now.

'Mich, you look as white as a sheet. You're not going to faint on us, are you?' Kelly gave Michelle's arm a gentle shake. 'Have a sip from this water bottle, it's still ice cold. Let me know if you want me to throw it over your head.'

Michelle smiled gratefully and obediently sipped the water. The cold revived her and cleared her head. 'Thanks, Kelly. Certainly what I needed... everything is so dream-like.'

Leon leaned forward from where he was sitting the other side of Kelly, 'A fast-moving dream, too. It's not much more than a month since we found the painting. And you have been in quite a storm of media interest ever since.'

'Well, Michelle and I are quite aware that the story had to be told to build interest for the sale but... well, we had never guessed how it would get so out of hand.' Kelly took back the bottle of water and added, 'But just in case, Mich, if you want a piece of paper to screw up would you use my auction catalogue and I'll look after that letter offering you ten million dollars. Oh my God, I can't believe I just said that...ten mil... I'm not even sure I can count the zeros.'

Michelle smoothed out the piece of paper and looked at it. 'I know, it just seems ridiculous. A piece of ageing paper with a few brush strokes... to be worth so much.'

'I think finding that letter made all the difference. From there the proof, the provenance was easily found. Marc made an excellent work of it. The day I spent with him in the Paris forensic *laboratoire* was fantastic.' said Leon, and leaning further forward, he added, 'Robert, that was a good time in Paris, non?'

Robert gave a start, hearing his name and replied, 'Oh yes, great day and then the rugby at the Stade Jean Bouin... yes, indeed... memorable. Sorry, I wasn't really listening. I am not normally a nervous man but I find myself sitting here like a zombie.'

'Just think, Mich,' said Kelly, 'instead of sitting here in New York in our glad rags, by the way the Givenchy suit looks amazing on you, what was I saying? Oh yeh, imagine we could be chasing zombies round the derelict Bastide right now.'

Before Michelle could reply there was a silence across the room. The auctioneer took his place in the centre of the rostrum and began his welcoming speech into the microphone. Michelle looked across the room to where Marc was standing amongst all the other dealers handling telephone bids. He was looking straight at her and he smiled and raised his phone in the air. He silently mouthed a few words to her and Michelle gave a wide smile and relaxed. She knew the words were 'I love you my dove,' small words that meant nothing to anyone in the crowded room but her. Here, amidst all these rich buyers, the nervous tension of other sellers and dealers, the atmosphere of suspense ... even here... they were connected. There was an invisible line of emotion that held them together. Suddenly, her nervousness completely vanished as she knew that whatever sky high price the dark little painting achieved, it meant nothing compared to her love for Marc. And then the bidding began.

40   *'at the end of the day'*

They were all once again back in the library at the Bastide de Rosefont, sitting close to the fire. As usual, it was Kelly who broke the companionable silence.

'You know, Mich, I was thinking, now you're so mega rich and all that, do you think you could fix the heating?'

'I know, I know,' Michelle laughed and snuggled closer to Marc, 'Even with Leon's huge fire it really is not warm in here.'

'You're not going to be like one of those infuriating lottery winners, you know, I've just won twenty million pounds but I'm not going to change a thing!' Kelly groaned, 'Oh, and I'm going to go back to work at the supermarket because all my friends are there. God, that makes me so mad when they talk rubbish like that.'

'Well, before you go any further on that track, Kelly, if the Bastide could be a metaphor for the supermarket then yes, I am a bit like that, I suppose. I mean, I have thought about everything a lot, of course, but actually, at the end of the day, as they say at this point... really, I can't think of anything I'd rather do than live here, surrounded by you lot and working on our project to make the Bastide an art-lover's hotel.'

'Are you really sure, Mich? I mean Leon and I can eff off and leave you to enjoy your riches. Don't worry, we would still visit!'

'Absolutely!' Leon added quickly, 'You are rich enough to restore the Bastide and live here in comfort now.'

'And don't worry about your old Dad, either.' Robert smiled at Michelle across the room, 'I am flexible... maybe find an apartment in Aix and leave you in peace. Of course, I'd be dropping in for cake and coffee!Anyway, you must make your own life and I'm guessing you have plans?'

Well, that's all very thoughtful and generous and all that ... but it sounds horrid. I can't imagine for a moment being here on my own.'

Marc squeezed Michelle tight and spoke for the first time. 'Well, that's never going to happen. My rich little Marquise, I intend to be your devoted servant for the rest of your life. In fact, I realise it is slightly unconventional... in front of your father and friends... but Michelle, I have something to ask you. Will you marry me?'

Everyone gasped and then burst out laughing.

'Well, if that's the way to do it... and while I think of it... will you marry me, Kelly?' Leon dropped down onto his knee in front of Kelly and looked up at her beseechingly.

'Holy Moly, this is getting out of hand, guys!' Kelly laughed and tried to pull Leon up from the floor and Coco joined in the battle, barking with excitement. 'What about you, Robert, why don't you slip out and ask the girl next door for her hand in marriage? Then it would all be so neat and tidy.And what about you, Coco, are you going to remain single?'

Coco looked from one to the other, and then went to stand next to Robert, her tail wagging as she looked up at him adoringly.

'Well, it's no good looking at me, Coco, but I'll take you for a walk,' said Robert, shaking his head in despair, 'Let's get out of this madhouse. Come on, Coco, let's escape!'

Leon stood up and put his arm round Kelly and said, 'Actually, I want you all to come outside!'

'Are you asking for a fight, now, or what? 'Kelly said, smoothing her dress and shaking back her curls. 'What now?'

'There is a surprise for you all, well, Robert already knows it. *Allez-y!*'

They all left the warmth of the log fire and went through the hall. Leon was ahead of them and he flung the front door wide open and stood back. Michelle went through first, out into the stark cold night. Then, stood stock still, blocking the doorway. 'So beautiful, so very beautiful!' she gasped with pleasure.

'What, what, shove out the way, Mich!' said Kelly, pushing Michelle in the back, and then, she too was suddenly silent.

In front of the Bastide, the fountain was spouting water, clear and sparkling in the bright moonlight. They stood in a row at the top of the steps, all dazzled by the tall arcs of water splashing and rippling down into the dark waters of the stone pool.

'Wow, so beautiful! Leon, it's amazing! And you, Robert, great work!' Kelly broke the silence of the night, 'So is this the fairytale ending, Mich, are we all going to live happily ever after?' she laughed and slipped her arm through Michelle's.

'That would be another story, Kelly. This is not the end, never say *fini!*'

I do hope you have enjoyed reading

'Provence Love Legacy'

Have you read my other Provence title

Perfume of Provence

if so, you may recognise some of the de Fleurenne family.
Calinda and Daniel are also to be met again in my next book,
provisionally titled 'Provence Fire'.

My other published title is

Dreams of Tuscany

and Zoe will also take time off from Sienna to visit Provence very soon.
As you may have guessed, I thoroughly enjoy writing my books and I hope,
as I began by saying at the top of this page, you enjoy reading them.

'a good book is the best of friends'

Printed in Great Britain
by Amazon

'words are the voice of the heart'

Confucius